MURDER AT THE U

A.M. HOLLOWAY

Your Book Company

eBook ISBN: 9781956648379

Paper ISBN: 9781956648386

Library of Congress Control Number: 2025909717

Printed in the United States of America.

Prologue

Leaves scooted across the rooftop gathering place as the wind pushed them to their next resting place. This was the setting for a meeting of several professors who voiced concerns about the university's finances.

The group spoke low amongst themselves, like anyone could hear them twelve stories in the air. Their current state had them afraid for their jobs and constantly looking over their shoulders.

They stood on top of the university's administrative building, which was the tallest building on campus. This university seemed to grow money, and no one had an explanation for it. Others knew something was wrong, but no one could find it. This university was new to the scene, having only been open for a few years. The grounds and building still had a fresh smell. Every year, attendance grew by double digits. So, why was the group discussing the issues if everything was going in the right direction?

A professor asked, "Professor Gregory, what are your thoughts?" Most of the professors looked up to Professor Gregory for his wisdom. But the professor had no idea why. He had been here the shortest time, but the group looked to him for guidance.

The group listened intently as Professor Gregory described his findings until the rain came. Then everyone scattered, leaving Professor Gregory alone on the rooftop.

He felt a presence as the professor walked closer to the roof's edge. When he turned, his mouth formed into an O. It only took a small amount of pressure on his shoulder for Professor Gregory to sail from the roof. But as he did, his fingers scraped the roof as he tried to save himself.

The assailant didn't bother looking over the edge. There's only one expected outcome. Relief and nerves ran together at the thought of Professor Gregory lying splattered on the concrete for someone to find.

Chapter 1

Mac and Nathan entered I^2 shortly after Myles, Mac's dad. They watched him enter, shared a glance, then proceeded through the doors of the next chapter in their lives. Neither knew what to expect after leaving their careers as FBI agents. But the time was right, so they jumped at the offer from Mac's dad, who owned I^2.

Since Mac was familiar with the office, she didn't gawk as they headed to Myles' office. But Nathan did. Mac chuckled as she witnessed Nathan's head on a swivel. When he slowed, he said, "We made the right decision. Never doubt that."

It surprised Mac to hear Nathan speak his thoughts aloud. Especially something this serious. "Really? You're not sorry you left your FBI agent status behind?"

"Mac, this is perfect. I get to work side by side with you every day and hopefully go home with you soon."

Another surprise for Mac that caused her to stop in mid stride. "You are full of surprises today."

Now, her mind swirled with ideas of moving in with Nathan or the possibility of marriage. Were they ready for that? It's too early to say, now that they are starting a new career, one that will last forever, if that's what they want.

Myles stood behind his mammoth desk as his newbies entered his office. He walked around his desk with his hand outstretched for Nathan, then he turned to Mac and waited for a hug. "Good morning. I hope you have no regrets about joining us."

Mac looked at Nathan and he let her answer. "Not yet." Then she grinned.

"We're starting you off running. A new case came in this weekend that I'd like you two to review and see if it's something you'd like to accept."

"Wait, sir. We get to decide if we want a case. That's odd." Nathan muttered.

"Nathan, this isn't the FBI. Everything I do is because I've agreed to do it. If I don't like it or if I have a bad feeling about a case, then I decline. This is your business now. You decide."

Mac's mouth hung open as the enormity of their new careers unfolded before her eyes. Once her stomach settled, she asked, "Do you have coffee in this place?"

Myles laughed. He should have expected Mac asking for coffee. "Right this way."

He led them down the hall to the break room. Nathan couldn't believe his eyes. The break room was nicer than his apartment. Myles stopped in front of the coffee bar, and they watched George finish with his coffee.

"Ah, here they are. Welcome, you two. Let me know if I can help." George reached over and hugged Mac. "I've waited a long time for this."

"Thanks, George." Mac stammered as she recalled the event where she found out about her dad and his expertise in martial arts. Myles was a hostage at a bank where he subdued three guys in five seconds.

When Mac turned around, she saw Nathan staring at the coffee. "Where are the coffee pods?"

Then George and Myles laughed. George explained, "We have no use for pods. Place your cup under here. Choose your size and press the button. It's automated, so the coffee stops on cue."

"Oh my. Mac will be in heaven." Nathan said.

"I heard that." Mac countered.

Once their cups were full, they joined Myles and George in the conference room. George had their case up on the big screen. Someone laid pens and paper on the table. Mac and Nathan slid into the chairs, grabbed a pen, sipped their coffee, then settled for the meeting.

George and Myles explained the details of the case over the next forty-five minutes, while Mac and Nathan jotted notes and questions. At the end of the presentation, Mac confirmed that their role was simply to confirm Professor Gregory had committed suicide.

Myles nodded his head.

Then Nathan asked, "What happens if we can't do that? Suppose Professor Gregory didn't take his own life?"

George glanced at Myles. "Then the case takes a different turn. We still get paid for our investigation, but if you determine something other than suicide, we'll turn it over to the police."

Mac and Nathan nodded and in unison asked, "Can we discuss this between us?"

Myles replied, "I'd be worried if you didn't." George and Myles left the duo to decide on whether to take their first case.

Nathan initiated their conversation by bringing up the autopsy, as it was not included in the file. He felt it odd that the university would hire outside investigators. Then Mac added she felt something was amiss with this case, but it didn't stop her from wanting to dig into it.

Twenty minutes later, the duo stood in Myles' office agreeing to take the case. "Sounds good to me. Let me show you to your offices."

Mac and Nathan followed Myles down the hall a few steps, then he stopped. Their offices were next to George's. Neither Mac nor Nathan had ever had an office of this size. Deep mahogany desks and credenzas outfitted them. Brand new laptops sat in the middle of each desk. Lying beside those were the latest cellphones.

"Dad, you didn't have to do this," Mac said as she stared at her new office.

"Yes, I did. You two are important to this operation. You'll have everything I have. Your new cars are in the parking lot. I hope you're okay with black Suburbans."

"Whoa, Mr. Morris, this is too much. I can't take this," Nathan stammered as George joined them.

"Get used to it, Nathan. This is the way we do business. We take care of those that take care of us. Trust me when I say you'll earn it." George patted Nathan on the back as he entered his office.

Then Myles said, "Please call me Myles. Everyone does."

Everything that had happened so far today astonished Nathan, and it wasn't even noon yet. No one had treated him like this in his lifetime. He worked for everything he had, so he knew he had to produce results and he was ready for the challenge.

Myles turned to leave the duo, then said, "We have loaded our software onto your computers." Everything is encrypted, including the phone."

He left Mac and Nathan staring at each other. Nathan shrugged and said, "Let's write our plan of attack before we get started."

They sat side by side and hashed out their plan. The autopsy was first. Neither could explain why they didn't include it in the file. Then they would visit the investigating officer and head over to the university to visit the crime scene. They agreed the case might be completed today between the autopsy and the crime scene inspection.

Nathan and Mac sat back in their leather chairs, reviewing the case notes provided by Myles. Something niggled at Mac, but she couldn't determine the reason. So, she watched Nathan's eyes rove over the page he held. He seemed to search for something. "What's troubling you, Nathan?"

"I can't place it, but I'm definitely getting a niggle."

Mac grinned when Nathan mentioned a niggle. They've been on the same page since they met. She had no reason to be apprehensive about a relationship with Nathan, but she was. When she joined the FBI, she was Spencer's partner. They grew close, and she thought they would marry, especially since he'd comment about it. She figured it was just a matter of time. But then her world turned upside down when FBI Agent Spencer Lawrence was assigned to the FBI SWAT team his mentor had left vacant after his murder. Spencer never discussed it with Mac, instead he moved to Quantico, leaving Mac in Atlanta.

But things changed for her too. She recalled the day there was a shift in her feelings for the FBI. Nathan was there by her side, letting her talk through her feelings and aspirations. He never told her she was wrong. Nathan listened to her until she finished and then she asked him for his thoughts.

Nathan unburdened himself of his feelings for Mac. Then he shared that if Mac moved to her father's company, he wanted a chance to work with her. That left Mac speechless. No one had ever agreed to follow her, but Nathan did.

Nathan asked, "Mac, are you okay? You seem a thousand miles away."

"I was because I remembered how we got here, and I'm glad you're with me." Tears started welling up in Mac's eyes and she worked to stop them. She is not one to cry.

"I'm glad I'm here too. This is an unbelievable opportunity. I never thought I'd get the chance at something like this." He reached over and pecked Mac on the cheek.

"Ok. Back to work. Let's find the autopsy." Mac tapped her new laptop, and it popped into life. The home screen had only one app on it. She clicked it and then she sat back. "Look at all of this. We need a month to learn the system."

"Let's find what we need. When this case is over, we'll take time to dig into the system." Nathan suggested.

Mac found what they were looking for. She entered the query for the professor's autopsy and waited. It took several minutes for the report to load. She clicked print, and they heard a machine come to life, but the location was a mystery.

Nathan walked to the credenza and slid open the bottom right section. "Here it is." He reached into the cabinet, fetching the papers. "That's a neat idea. It keeps it off the desk." Nathan nodded as he made his way back to his chair.

They each had a copy of the report, so they took time to review it. After several minutes, Mac asked, "What do you think?"

"The victim's fingers show scrape marks along with broken fingernails. That makes me wonder if he tried to save himself before he left the roof."

Mac agreed. She lifted her pad and showed Nathan she had the same thought. Then she added, "There was no alcohol in his bloodstream. His family and friends say he would never take his own life. So maybe the school hired us to prove it suicide. But I wonder why?"

"Let's go find out." Nathan stood and Mac followed him to their new Chevrolet Suburban. They stared at them. "Who drives first?" Nathan grinned.

"You can." Mac gave in because she knows Nathan loves to drive. He drove them across many states during their last FBI investigation.

They jumped in and took a deep breath. There's nothing like a new car smell. Mac buckled her belt, then thumbed through her folder. She jotted notes as Nathan drove north on I75. Once they reached I575, she glanced around the mountains. "I'm thinking about moving closer to the office."

"Whoa. Where did that come from? You haven't mentioned that before. Would you move to Marietta?"

"Yes. There's no reason to live in the city now. Would you consider it?"

"Absolutely. What about sharing? I know you're not ready for a relationship and I respect that. I'm here for you whenever you decide. But what if we got two or three bedrooms? One bedroom could be our office. We'd split everything down the middle." Nathan suggested with a longing in his eyes.

Mac didn't know what to say. If they lived together and worked together, would that be too much togetherness? "I had thought it would be next door because of my lack of commitment." She stopped, then added, "But that would be nice. Wonder how long it would take before you tire of me?"

Nathan's head snapped around. "Why would you say that?"

"Forget I said it," Mac's phone blared, giving her a reprieve. She answered the phone in her business tone. "Oh, hey, dad. I didn't recognize the number. I'll save it. Yes, we are on our way to the university. We pulled the autopsy already, and we found an inconsistency we'd like to check out. I'll call later."

As Mac ended her call, Nathan's phone sounded. He answered and chuckled. "Hey, Travis. Yes, I miss you. How are things without us?" Then Nathan went silent as he listened to Travis. He kept his eyes on the road, but his ears turned red. Mac knew something had happened.

When his call ended, Nathan glanced at Mac. He shared that Travis and Margot miss them terribly and they want to get together. Then he stopped talking. Mac waited, but when he didn't continue, she asked, "What else did he say?"

Nathan didn't want to tell Mac, but she wouldn't leave it alone until he did. "Drake made an appearance. He stopped Margot on the sidewalk outside the coffee shop. Drake asked her where you were? He says he needs to speak with you, and only you."

"I can't believe the nerve of this guy. It's been years. He's had ample opportunity to meet with the FBI to solve his issues. There's nothing I can do for him." Mac turned her face to the window. Her insides flipped at the mention of Drake's name. She still looked over her shoulder every time she walked

14

the downtown streets. Drake was always there, watching. She could feel it.

Shortly after Travis' call, Nathan turned into the police department parking lot. They had an appointment with Detective Chinni. Mac's face told Nathan everything he needed to know. She was angry.

"Sit still a minute. You can't go in there with bottled up frustration. The detective won't be obliged to share anything. Take some deep breaths." Nathan leaned his head back and closed his eyes.

Five minutes passed before Mac said, "Ok. Let's do this. We still need to run by the university, too."

They emerged from the vehicle and headed inside. A patrol deputy sat behind a partition, and once Nathan gave him their names, he ushered them to a meeting room. Some moments later, a young man entered the room. He sported light brown, close cropped hair, and tattoo behind his right ear.

Mac tried to read it, but it was impossible from her vantage point. The duo shook hands with Detective Chinni, then they peppered him with questions. He stammered several times, but recovered enough to answer their questions. Mac had questions about Chinni but would hold those until they left.

Upon hearing Nathan's mention of heading to the crime scene, Detective Chinni agreed to escort them without hesitation. They accepted with apprehension because there's something about Chinni that didn't fit.

Chinni pulled his unmarked car from the back lot and Nathan followed him out of the lot. Twenty minutes later, they entered the university grounds. It was spectacular. The buildings were tall, with glass from top to bottom. Every window provided a view of the splendor of the mountains, and during this time of year, the bursting colors were visible.

With the administrative building standing the tallest amongst the others, Mac craned her neck to see the roof, then she cringed. How could anyone jump to their death by choice? That's between 120-150 feet of reaching the ground.

Chinni entered the building by swiping his badge. Now the duo was glad he came along. It made reaching the scene easy. They rode the elevator to the top floor, then took stairs to the roof. When they stepped out onto the roof, Mac paused. This was more than a roof.

"People used the roof as a meeting place. There was no mention of that in your report." Mac stated.

"Yes, they do. Professors use the roof to meet or unwind. Students may not use this space. They have a similar set up on two educational buildings." Chinni explained, skipping his lack of including the information in his report.

Mac and Nathan walked to the edge of the roof where the yellow crime scene tape hung . "Has anyone been here other than the CSI team?"

"Not to my knowledge." Chinni offered.

Nathan went to the right, searching the edge of the roof for evidence while Mac went left. Mac took two steps, saying, "Nathan, here." She pointed to dried blood on the roof's edge.

He walked to her location and leaned down for a closer look. Then he surveyed the ground below. "I don't see how this blood got here, if his body landed in that marked area."

Mac tried following his reasoning, so she glanced over the edge of the building. The trajectory seemed off. It appeared Professor Gregory left the building roof at an angle, and that didn't bode well for a suicide.

"You're right, Nathan. Why would Professor Gregory jump from the roof at an angle? I don't think I've ever heard that from a suicide." Mac glanced back at the dried blood.

"Detective Chinni, did anyone test this blood against the victim?" Nathan asked.

"I'm unsure. Once CSI arrived, I started looking for witnesses. Of which, I found none." He replied, but his eyes showed skepticism, like he was unsure how to answer.

Mac spoke to Nathan. "I'll go get our evidence bag. We'll test it ourselves." He nodded.

Chinni stopped Mac. "Where are you going? You'll need a badge to reenter the building."

"Then you better come with me." Mac started toward the door when she heard Nathan tell Chinni he better hurry if he wanted to catch up.

Mac grinned. Chinni knows something or at least suspects something is up with this case. But can they trust him with their thoughts? On the elevator ride to the first floor, Mac probed Chinni about his relationship with the faculty. She discovered one tidbit that might explain Chinni's behavior. The captain of the police department is friends with the university president.

After grabbing her bag, they loaded onto the elevator for the return trip. Neither spoke. Mac worked through the scenario with the police captain and the university president. She couldn't figure how that played into the investigation of the professor's death. But it was still interesting.

Nathan stood at the spot where Mac found the blood. He didn't want to lose it. Mac walked over to him, placing their evidence kit on the ground. She donned gloves before grabbing a swab and a vial. As she swabbed the area, she explained her conversation with Chinni to Nathan.

He nodded because they heard footsteps getting closer. "How much longer do you think you'll be?"

"You can leave. We do not need to reenter the building. If we do, we'll make an appointment with you. Thanks, Detective Chinni." Nathan said as he reached out to shake his hand.

With that, Chinni turned and headed to the door. When the door closed behind him, Mac and Nathan spoke freely. They worked through scenarios of the professor's death, and they struggled with the location of the blood and where he landed.

Mac stood near the roof's edge, while Nathan stood at an angle of Mac's right side. They stared at each other, working through their ideas. Mac came to her conclusion first. "Someone was on this roof with Professor Gregory. Either he slipped, fell off the roof, or he had help. Why else would I find blood and skin stuck to the edge of the roof?"

Nathan muttered. "He tried to save himself." Then he added, "Just because they found him where he lay, doesn't mean he fell from the roof directly above the body. The CSI and the detectives didn't look for anything else."

They searched the roof from one side to the other, looking for anything the crime scene investigators missed. Red solo cups and a few empty cracker sleeves sat in the bottom of the trash can. It frustrated Mac when things were left behind at crime scenes that might hold viable leads. She reached inside and lifted the black trash bag from the can.

Nathan glanced at her. "They left that." Then he nodded as he stopped walking. Stooping down, he glanced at the ground. Is this a cigarette? Maybe someone ground it into the roof. "I might have a cigarette, but I'm unsure of its usefulness."

Mac joined him and sighed. "We'll take it and see what we can get off it. It looks like it's been here a while." Mac used another pair of gloves to retrieve the cigarette. She had to use tweezers to pull it away from the gravel.

They continued scouring the roof but found nothing else useful. Once they loaded their kit, Nathan took the kit while Mac carried the trash bag. Mac felt strange about this case and she wondered how it would play out when they told their client they didn't feel Professor Gregory's death was suicide. But the more evidence they have, the easier the sale.

Once they made it to the parking lot, they loaded the vehicle, then they sat in the front seat, staring at the building they had just left. Neither understood the death, but the evidence they collected might help them explain it.

Nathan eventually started the truck and drove them from the lot. Mac surveyed the area on the way out. Nothing stood out as unusual as she watched folks walk to their cars or head into the buildings. She pondered reasons for the professor's death, but she ended up not knowing why he fell from the roof.

As they passed through town, Nathan asked, "Have you figured out why the professor jumped? Or do you think he had help?"

"It looks like he had help. I want to process the solo cups for prints and DNA. That will give us people to question, and maybe even some people that were with Gregory that night. What are your thoughts?"

"The same. Should we stop at the medical examiner's office? Wonder if they've released the body yet."

"That's a great idea." Mac plucked her phone from her pocket and entered a query for the medical examiner's address. It just so happened they were ten minutes away. So Nathan changed course, driving them to the next stop.

The medical examiner sat at her desk when the duo arrived. She stammered when they introduced themselves and explained their visit. "I'm Doctor Rowe. Join me in the back."

Mac led with Nathan following. He glanced around the area, noticing the doctor worked alone. She opened the door for the duo and the temperature dropped twenty degrees. Mac shivered as she rubbed her upper arms.

Dr. Rowe led them to the back wall with drawers stacked on top of another. The second drawer from the wall, in the middle line, opened to find a man covered with a sheet. Mac inhaled as the doctor unfolded the sheet down to the man's chest. The face appeared completely broken.

Nathan asked about injuries to the victim's hands. So, the doctor slipped each hand from under the sheet, showing the damage. Both hands, especially the fingertips, showed signs of scrapings. The evidence collected today would prove Professor Gregory tried to save himself.

Doctor Rowe pointed out another anomaly on the right side of Gregory's chest. "This bruise here didn't form until days after the autopsy. I've photographed it and sent it over to Detective Chinni, but I've heard nothing from him."

Mac leaned in for a closer look. "It appears to be fingertips. Or I am imagining things."

"No, you're not imagining anything. That's why I sent it over to the police. They asked me to conclude suicide, but now I'm uncertain my classification was correct." Doctor Rowe stated.

"If you don't mind me asking, who specifically asked you to say Gregory died from suicide?" Nathan asked.

"Paul Drummond. He's the university president. Paul claimed the board of trustees wanted this matter handled quickly, so it didn't tarnish the school." Doctor Rowe's eyes told the duo something else. She questioned Paul's reasons but to him personally.

"Are you comfortable leaving the reason for death as suicide?" Mac questioned.

"Until I have more evidence, I have no reason to change it. But if the police had completed a thorough investigation, I think that would have already happened."

"I think you're right, Dr. Rowe. We gathered evidence this morning and will process it ourselves. We'll share our findings with you." Mac offered.

Nathan snapped a photo of the bruising on Professor Gregory's chest before they left Dr. Rowe. Once alone, Nathan said, "Something is definitely going on here."

"Let's get back to the office. I'd like to start on this evidence."

On the way to the office, Mac called Myles to report in on their first day. When she explained what they found, Myles couldn't believe it. He exclaimed, "I offered this case to you and Nathan because it sounded like a slam dunk. It would have been great for you two to solve your first case on your first day."

"That will not happen. If anything, we're getting ready to open a big can of coverup when we tell the board of trustees that Professor Gregory did not commit suicide. Instead, someone murdered Professor Gregory. We don't have a clue why he died, but it's apparent he didn't jump of his own volition."

Chapter 2

Myles waited for the duo at the office. He and George wanted to see what evidence their two newest investigators had found. If only he'd suspected this case might not be what it seemed, he would have passed on it. But he didn't and now they're into it too deeply to abandon it.

George watched emotions play across Myles' face as the men stood in the break room. "Myles, let me be the first to say it. You're not responsible for the kids in this place. They're smart. They know when something doesn't add up. That's why you wanted Mac here."

"I agree, but it's different when your child."

Nodding, George replied with a chuckle. "She's smarter than anyone of us." The elevator dinged moments later.

Nathan carried their evidence bag while Mac toted a black trash bag. Myles and George looked at each other. Then he said, "You weren't kidding when you said you collected evidence."

Myles walked to Mac and instructed them to drop their things in the lab. "I'll process this before going home. We want a head start in the morning."

"Ionna is waiting for you. She's one of your lab techs. We'll introduce you." Myles stated.

Nathan and Mac entered the lab. It still fascinated Mac to see all the machinery and tech gadgets. Her dad has a small lab set up at his house and Mac was familiar with that one, but this lab was massive. It boasts every machine known to the CSI world. After a closer look, Mac says, "This lab resembles the FBI lab."

"It should. Our equipment comes from the same place. But we're fortunate because we get the upgrades first because we don't wait for government funding." Myles explained. Then Myles looked to Ionna, who stood from her stool.

She was a beautiful girl with flawless skin. Mac envied her skin. After the introductions, Mac and Nathan described their findings. Ionna separated the evidence into sections. "This helps with the speed of processing. We can test each section together, which helps with the speed of processing.

Nathan asked, "How long do you think it will take?"

"The DNA from the blood will be the fastest results because we know who we are comparing them to, but the cups will take a little while longer. I'll process the outside for fingerprints first, then move to the inside for DNA."

"That's great, Ionna. Anything we can do to help?" Nathan asked.

Ionna glanced around the room. "Nothing that I can think of right now. I'll call you when I have something."

Mac and Nathan passed Ionna their new business cards, then she followed with hers. The foursome turned, leaving Ionna with hours of work.

When the group returned to the break room, Mac headed straight for the coffee. As she waited for the machine, Myles suggested everyone eat supper tomorrow night at home. Mary was cooking. Nathan grinned, rubbing circles around his belly.

Everyone laughed. Then Mac offered, "Who are we supposed to contact at the university with our findings?"

"The Board of Trustees hired us. So, we'll go back to the guy that sent me the request. Joe Rogers. Don't worry about contacting him tonight. Wait until morning. The outcome won't change in ten hours."

Mac agreed. "I know. I was just curious. We want to speak with Professor Gregory's wife before finalizing our investigation."

Myles and George nodded. They knew Mac was thorough, but this proved it. The duo had enough evidence to say the death wasn't by suicide, but yet, they are going one step further. Nathan added, "We'd like to hear about Professor Gregory's activities over the last month or so. Maybe she'll tell us about his mental state, too."

"I like it. You two are the perfect fit. Now, go rest." Myles said, as he turned to leave. Over his shoulder he said, "George, that includes you." Then he left. George chuckled as he crossed the threshold.

Mac and Nathan stood at the coffee machine, savoring the warm liquid. Nathan leaned over, kissing Mac on the cheek. "We've had a great first day. Busy, but great. Thank you."

Placing her cup on the counter, Mac turned to Nathan and kissed him, drawing him closer. "Thank you for being here with me. I could never have done this without you."

Mac's comments floored Nathan. He stood there with his mouth shaped into an O. Mac placed her fingers under his chin and lifted his mouth. He chuckled.

"It sounds like we need each other." He winked, then finished his coffee.

Nathan fell asleep quickly when he got home, but Mac couldn't turn her mind off. So, she spent an hour preparing her notecards. There were no reasons to do this since they completed their case requirements, but she felt the Board of Trustees may ask them to solve the murder. In that case, they would need the cards. And they would be ready.

The following morning, the duo received a call from Ionna. She had the test results. It shocked Mac at Ionna's speed. Instead of going to their offices, they went to the lab. Ionna stood at her desk, ending a call when the duo entered. She waved them over to her desk.

They greeted each other, then Ionna gave them the news. The blood evidence gathered from the roof matched Professor Gregory. Ionna confirmed it with the medical examiner.

Next, she lifted six sets of fingerprints from the solo cups and swabbed the insides for DNA. There were no matches in the database for any of the prints, which wasn't a surprise.

Mac and Nathan jotted notes as Ionna spoke. When she stopped, the duo glanced up. Then Mac said, "If other teachers were on that roof with Gregory, we should be able to get the prints from the university or the state, since they have a license."

Nathan concurred with Mac, asking Ionna to forward those prints to their email. They would track down the fingerprint owners.

As they left, they thanked Ionna for her hard work and looked forward to working with her again.

When the duo entered the elevator, Mac said, "I'd like to speak with Gregory's wife before we spend time tracking down the fingerprint owners. If the

Board of Trustees doesn't want us to find his killer, then we've wasted time."

"I agree. No sense spinning wheels if there's no need." Nathan paused, then added, "Do you want to meet the wife in person? I like watching their expressions when I interview someone."

"Me too. Let's call her and see when she can meet us," Mac suggested. Nathan let Mac call her, thinking she would be more apt to open up to a female.

Mac spoke with Mrs. Gregory for a few minutes, setting a time for the interview. They had two hours to get there. Mrs. Gregory was visiting a funeral home this afternoon, and they didn't want to wait until tomorrow.

After sharing their plans with Myles, the duo raced to the parking lot for Nathan's truck. Mac chuckled. She'd only driven her vehicle to her apartment and back.

They discussed questions for Mrs. Gregory on the drive, arriving with only a few minutes to spare. She greeted them at the door before they knocked. Mac and Nathan introduced themselves first, then she invited them inside. The house was small but well taken care of. Mrs. Gregory dabbed her eyes with a tissue as she sat in a leather chair facing the fireplace.

"Thanks for coming so quickly. I'm waiting for the medical examiner to release him. Is that why you're here?"

Mac nodded, uncertain where to start. Her first statement set the tone. "Mrs. Gregory, We don't feel your husband took his own life." Then she braced for backlash.

"Well, finally. Someone is listening. I told the police that from the first moment they gave me the horrible news. James had so much going for him. He was brilliant. We wanted to start a family now that he joined a faculty. The money was there for me to stop working for a while and raise our kids. Now, I'll never get that chance." The tears poured down her face.

Mac exhaled and looked down for fear of crying, too. Nathan realized the struggle, so he asked, "Has James had anyone upset with him? Or have you noticed any changes to his behavior?"

Mrs. Gregory paused, then replied, "He had trouble sleeping lately, but brushed it off when I questioned him. He blamed work. Then I noticed he carried a black notebook everywhere he went. That started about six months ago."

"Any idea what was in the notebook?"

"No, I don't Investigator Morris. I never pressed him. But now I realize I should have. Did you find the notebook?"

"Please call me Mac. And no, we didn't find it, but we didn't know about it then either. We'll look into it."

Mrs. Gregory ended the interview by saying again she knew in her heart that James didn't jump off that roof. Someone pushed him. As Mac and Nathan left, she asked them to find out who killed her husband.

Mac left first with Nathan in her wake. Nathan noticed Mrs. Gregory twisted Mac's emotions, and he wanted to give her space. But she surprised him when she turned and said, "Nathan, I'm going to find out who killed the professor."

While he felt the same, he was unsure how Myles would react. This was their first case, and he couldn't imagine Myles handling cases for free. "Maybe we run this by your dad. If the university is satisfied, and their funds cease, then maybe Mrs. Gregory would pick up the remainder."

Mac nodded as she thought it through. "It shouldn't have to stop now. It's obvious that someone killed Professor Gregory. But who and why?"

They drove in silence for a while until Mac's cell phone blared, then it connected to the vehicle. "Hi Dad."

"Well, what's your consensus on the case?"

Mac glanced at Nathan, then answered. "Someone helped Professor Gregory over the roof. But we don't know why or who?" She paused, waiting for Myles to respond.

"I'll discuss your conclusion with Joe Rogers, the Board of Trustees' leader. He may ask us to continue, but he may not. Are you prepared to walk away if he doesn't want us to continue?"

"No, I'm not. I want to know who killed Professor Gregory and why. It seems so senseless." Mac explained.

"Does Nathan agree?"

"Yes, sir. I agree. You should have seen Mrs. Gregory. She was the epitome of a schoolteacher. They were trying for a family now that he was on faculty at a university."

"Sounds like a heartbreaker all the way around. I'll touch base once I speak with Joe. Don't bother coming back here. See you at home for supper."

Mac grinned. She had forgotten about them joining her parents for supper. "I need a shower before supper. Want me to pick you up?"

Nathan grinned, "I'm ready to go, so I wait for you while you dress."

"Perfect." He pulled into Mac's apartment complex tons of emergency vehicles. "Uh, Mac. Your apartment building is on fire."

"Oh no. Wonder if I can salvage anything?" She raked her hands through her hair, then she pointed. "That's Tyrone. What's he doing here?"

Mac jumped from the truck and raced to meet Tyrone. When he heard his name, he held his arms open for a hug. "Hey Mac. When I heard the address, I came flying. What's going on?"

In all the changes, Tyrone didn't know about her career change. So, she unloaded by introducing Nathan and explaining that she now works with her dad. "I figured that would come in time. Good for you. If you ever need the best fire investigator on the planet, you know who to call."

"What can you tell me about this one?"

Tyrone leaned into Nathan and Mac and said, "We've had multiple reports throughout the city about apartments being torched. Everything appears random, but today we have a witness that saw a white pickup pass just before the flames appeared."

"I'm glad you're here, Tyrone. We're heading up to see Dad and Mom tonight. I'll share with him that I saw you. Any chance I can reach my apartment?" Mac asked with a head tilt.

"Not today. The embers are too hot. You'll need to report this to your insurance company and stay at your parents' or bunk with Nathan. I'm sure he'll make room." Tyrone winked at Nathan as his ears turned red.

Someone called for Tyrone, and he left them, promising to call Mac later. Mac watched as the fire department dumped gallons of water on her apartment building. She didn't know what to feel. Material things didn't bother her, it was the pictures. It's always about the pictures.

Nathan tried consoling Mac, but nothing he said seemed to resonate with her. "Do you want me to call your parents?"

"No, there's nothing they can do. Mom would just worry. I guess we need to go to the office and get my car. I'll have to go to the store for clothes."

"Get in. I'll take you shopping. We've not experienced that yet," Nathan said, chuckling.

They returned to Nathan's truck. He glanced at the clock. "You might have to explain our tardiness to your parents. We only have an hour."

"Swell." Mac muttered as her phone rang. "Too late. Dad knows."

"Hey Dad. Before you start, I'm fine."

"What happened? I was calling about Professor Gregory."

"My apartment building burned to the ground. Tyrone was there. He said hello, and he's working on the fire. Apparently, they have an arsonist that is partial to apartment buildings."

"Thank goodness you're okay. Is Nathan with you?"

"Of course." Mac reached over, grabbing Nathan's hand. He lifted hers and kissed them back.

"Joe Rogers asked us to continue the investigation. We are full steam ahead.'

Mac sighed. "That's great to hear. Look, we're going to be a few minutes late. I need clothes and personal items. We'll be there as soon as we can."

Nathan grinned. "I'm glad Joe is on our side. Now, to find out who isn't."

Mac stared at Nathan as his comment cemented itself into her mind. Then she nodded. "You're right. We're bound to make someone mad."

After shopping, Mac was tired, but she knew her parents were waiting for them for supper, so she knew she couldn't cancel now. So, they traveled north of Atlanta to her childhood home. "I'll stay with my parents tonight. Dad will bring me to work."

"It's your choice, but you know I have a two-bedroom apartment. I never moved when Travis and Margot moved in together."

Mac tilted her head. "I didn't know that. If you're up for company, try it. If all goes well, we may find us a place closer to work." That statement brought a smile to Nathan. Even his eyes sparkled.

Mary, Mac's mom, greeted them at the door. "Thank heavens you weren't at home, Mac."

"I agree." Mac said.

"Ditto here." Nathan said, bringing a round of laughter.

Dinner was splendid, as always. Afterward, Myles asked Mac and Nathan to join him in the loft. Mac took Nathan by the hand and whispered. "This is where dad turns business."

Once in the loft, Myles ushered the duo into the leather seats surrounding the gleaming mahogany table. "I want to discuss the university case with you both. Joe described Professor Gregory as a brilliant mind. They got along great and the last thing Gregory said to Joe was 'things aren't always what they seem', but he failed to elaborate and Joe didn't push him."

"Oh man. That must be hard for Joe. Hearing those words from a friend and colleague and then the death." Nathan said as he shook his head.

"What's your game plan? Mac, I know you have one. You always do."

"I haven't discussed it with Nathan yet, but I'll share my ideas. The first being the fingerprints recovered from the solo cups. Once we get them identified, I'd like to speak with those that attended the same rooftop meeting."

"Absolutely. Especially since the blood you swabbed on the roof matches Gregory. We need to search for Gregory's black notebook. His wife told us he carried it with him everywhere. He started this about six months ago." Nathan saw something flicker in Myles' eyes.

Myles jotted a note. "I hadn't heard about the black notebook."

"We just found out about it at Mrs. Gregory's interview." Mac explained as a cell phone chirped.

Everyone checked their phones. Myles answered his as he stared at Mac. Then he thanked Tyrone for reaching out.

"Unfortunately, your apartment is a total loss."

"We figured it would be. I've already been to the store and dropped some things at Nathan's. Since Travis left, he has a spare room." Mac explained even though she felt weird telling her dad she'd be sharing an apartment with a guy. Which is something she's never done. She's unsure if she can live with another person, let alone a guy. But she's willing to try.

Myles never faltered, saying, "Nathan, she's in your hands. Take care of her."

Nathan glanced at Mac. "Always."

Then they jumped back to the case. They tried on different scenarios as to what Professor Gregory found. Was it money discrepancies? Enrollment numbers askew? Nothing made sense as to why someone would go the distance to kill a faculty member and professor.

Mac paced. "I need my cards, but they burned up in the fire. I'll start on a new set tonight. Then I'll have a better feel for the case. My bet is money. Professor Gregory had a brilliant mind, and he taught finance. Something about the money was off and he found it. But my question is, did he find out the source of the funny money or was he still working on it?"

"Maybe he just got too close." Nathan added.

"I like the way you two think. You're good together. Now, go home, rest, and I'll see you in the morning. You'll get a lesson on the fingerprint machine."

The following morning began with Mac reporting the fire to her insurance company. When she finished, she found Nathan at her side with a steaming cup of coffee and a grin. "So, how did you sleep?"

"For someone who lost all their earthly things while working a murder case, I slept great. Thanks for letting me stay here." Mac said as she sipped her coffee. She took another sip. "What kind of coffee is this? It is delicious."

Nathan grinned, then explained the coffee was from overseas. He found it while stationed in Germany.

"We need to sell it here. It is phenomenal."

"It would have to be packaged in a name, I can say. The only way I get it is to call the store and tell them my name and say Kaffee. They have me as a standing order. After a yearlong stint in Germany, I still can't pronounce it."

Mac finished her coffee in silence. Then they left for the office. Nathan was anxious to see the fingerprint machine while Mac wanted another cup of coffee.

Myles was true to his word. He stood at his door speaking with George when the duo stepped off the elevator. "Good morning. Meet us in the lab in ten minutes. George and I have a conference call in thirty minutes."

Nathan nodded as Mac entered her office, placing her stack of index cards on her desk. She already had enough information to separate the cards into groups. But as soon as they find the fingerprint owners, she'd have another stack.

The duo met Myles and George in the lab. They had the fingerprints from Ionna already loaded into the machine. George gave them a rundown on how to get the prints to the machine. It was easier than expected.

Then George began steps to operate the machine. After he entered the batch of prints to the query, it was a waiting game. "Sometimes prints come back quickly while others it takes a while. Now is a good time to get coffee."

"Speaking of coffee, Nathan has a German coffee that is out of this world. You should try it." Mac said, then she added, "I'd like to sell it in the states."

All eyes turned to Mac. "You've never mentioned selling anything. This must be some coffee. How can get some, Nathan?"

"I can call the store and re-order. They have me on redial." Nathan chuckled.

"Please do. I'll pay for the office coffee." Myles informed Nathan, but Nathan would have gladly paid for it after what Myles had done for him.

When they returned to the lab, they had the names of every fingerprint. Mac beamed with excitement. Now, they had interviews to conduct. Nathan pulled up the university's website and every name on their list was a professor at the school. Clarence Wright, Lydia Bellew, Maureen Culvert, William Mack, and Carlos Goya were the people on the roof with Professor Gregory. So why haven't they come forward with information?

Nathan asked, "Why didn't the police collect the trash like you did? Were they so blinded that they immediately thought of suicide, or did someone help them think that?"

"What? Like a payoff or something?" Mac asked.

"Think about it. If they had investigated thoroughly, they would have the same information we do. So why not go after it? Why assume someone jumped from the roof?" He paused, then added. "There's a lot about this case that makes little sense."

"I agree. I'll start calling these people for interviews. Can you check with Ionna on the cigarette you found?"

Nathan nodded and stepped from the office as Mac started at the top of her list, calling and leaving messages. Then she figured everyone was in class. Just as she laid her phone down, hers rang. She answered and Carlos introduced himself. He agreed to an interview later in the afternoon. When Mac explained that she wanted to speak with his peer, he offered to have everyone together. He suggested meeting off campus, offering his home as the meeting place around five. Mac agreed.

When Nathan returned, Mac explained about the interviews with the group. Nathan offered, "That would be nice to see them all at the same time and place. But if someone wants to talk outside of the group, they need to be able to reach us."

"We'll share that this afternoon." Once Mac finished with her notes, she asked Nathan, "Did Ionna find anything on the cigarette butt?"

"She's still working on it. When someone ground it into the roof, it was destroyed. But she's hopeful of DNA recovery." Nathan said with an eyebrow lifted.

"That would be incredible. Let's remember to check the folks at today's meeting and see if any of them smoke." Mac pointed out as she jotted another note.

Mac and Nathan studied the company's software, then they spent time in the lab with George. Finally, it was time to head north. Mac was eager to speak with this group. If they were on the rooftop before the incident, then they held the most information.

Nathan pulled alongside the curb of Carlos' home since the drive was full. "It looks like everyone made it. Let's do it."

Mac exited while checking her surroundings. She spotted a car at the next intersection facing them. It was a dark-colored sedan with tinted windows. Instead of pointing to it, she asked Nathan to glance at her and look over her left shoulder.

He did and laughed, like Mac made him laugh. He caught a glimpse of the car, then muttered, "I got it."

They entered the house with solemn expressions. Both ladies held tissues as the duo was introduced. Carlos offered seats in the family room. Mac and Nathan sat in the kitchen chairs facing the group.

Mac began the interview by explaining their presence and what they hoped would happen. The group nodded their heads. "Who would like to begin? We need to know what happened at that rooftop meeting."

A gentleman raised his hand. "I'm Clarence Wright. I was probably closet to him. We joined this university together. We were on the rooftop the same night as Professor Gregory's death. He called the meeting, saying he needed to discuss something with us. But he never got the chance. When it started raining, we left. Professor Gregory said he would follow."

"Did you see anyone there that wasn't invited to your meeting?" Nathan asked.

"Not a soul. It was cold and wet, but when your best friend asks you to do something, you try to make it happen. That's what I did. He would have been there for me." Clarence said as his eyes welled up with unshed tears.

Mac continued the questions, "Did anyone else notice anything or anyone?"

All heads shook. Mac felt deflated. But she asked, "Did anyone see a black notebook that Professor Gregory carried with him?"

"Yes. We all did. He carried it everywhere he went. But I'm unsure of its location now." Lydia replied.

Carlos said, "He bought a small safe not too long ago, but I've no clue where he stored it. Or if he kept the notebook there."

Maureen blurted, "Why would someone want to kill Professor Gregory?"

"That's what we're trying to find out. Did he say anything to any of you about suspicions he had regarding the university?"

Clarence and William nodded. William shared. "Yes, he did. When they offered James the faculty spot, Joe asked him to investigate the financials. Other Board of Trustee members had questioned several lines in the financial reports. With James' background in financial management, he was a shoo-in."

Nathan glanced at Mac. They wondered why Joe never mentioned that tidbit of information to them.

"Did he share anything with any of you?" Nathan prodded.

"No. We suspected that's why he called the meeting. He'd been working on it for months. Have you spoken with Paul?" William asked.

In unison, the duo asked, "Who's Paul?"

Clarence replied, "He's the president of the university, Paul Drummond. He was hired because of his expertise at growing university enrollment. So far, he's done that. We have students coming here from across the country." Then Clarence tilted his head, "Who hired you if Paul didn't?"

"Joe Rogers." Nathan stated.

"Ah. I imagine Joe suspected something. I'm glad Joe hired you. He won't give up on finding out. Joe spent time in the army where you never left a soldier behind. I already suspected foul play but now with Joe involved, I'm convinced. So, it's time we find out what really happened on that roof." Clarence said.

The group spoke about Professor Gregory and his habits around the university. They shared places they would go to unwind, then Carlos asked, "Did you find his cell phone?"

"No, we haven't. We're hoping the police department has it in evidence."

Carlos added, "He typed on that thing all the time. There might be something there for you."

Chapter 3

Once Mac and Nathan closed their vehicle doors, they sighed. Mac was the first to admit it. "This is turning into a lot more than we expected. Should we track down Paul Drummond while we're here?"

"Absolutely. I'll see if Carlos or anyone has a phone number for him since it's after working hours." Nathan jumped from the truck and trotted back to the house. Mac watched him knock, then glance back at her. The door opened, and he stepped inside.

While Mac waited, she worked through what they knew. It seems Professor Gregory was definitely onto something, and he might have gotten a little too close. But who would have the most to lose? Would it be Paul? Or someone else?

Nathan slid under the wheel within a few minutes, holding a sticky note. "I have his cell phone number. Want me to call him?"

"Sure." Mac leaned her head back and listened to the one sided conversation. The way Nathan looked at her, she expected news.

"He'll meet us, but he wasn't happy with the call after hours."

"Really? Like murder investigations only happen from 9 to 5. I can't wait to meet this one. Where is he?"

"That's the odd thing. He's still at the university."

Mac had no words. She stared at Nathan, trying to understand why Paul commented about the meeting time when he was still there. Were they interrupting him, and if so, what was he doing at work this late?

Nathan drove them to the university without a map. That's impressive. He learned about new towns quickly, maybe from his days as a state trooper.

Paul met the duo at the front door of the administrative building. Nathan thought he saw movement on the building's side, but they kept moving forward. Paul shook hands with the duo, then led them into his office. The building was dark, except for the lobby and Paul's office.

Mac asked, "Do you often work here alone?" She wanted to get a feel for the man.

"Yes. I get more done when there's no one here. Especially on those projects requiring concentration." Paul explained. Then he asked, "So, what's this about Professor Gregory's unfortunate demise?"

Nathan started the interview while Mac sat back and watched Paul's facial expressions. A few times, his eyes darted to the lobby and then they moved upward to the right. That always makes Mac curious about answers.

Paul claimed he knew nothing about James' investigation into the financials. He thought James was fine and had no reason to be concerned about him. James never brought his concerns to him.

When the duo asked to look at James' office, Paul declined because it held confidential information on students. So, without a warrant, that was off limits.

The interview ended shortly after, and Nathan made certain that Paul knew they would be in touch. Nathan didn't trust Paul. Mac saw that. They dropped their business cards on Paul's desk as they showed themselves out the office door.

On the way to the truck, Nathan walked to the building's edge, looking down the side to the back. There were cars back there, but he couldn't tell the make or model. He wanted to find out.

Once inside the truck, Nathan explained about the vehicles in the back of the administration building. They devised a plan to get closer. Nathan left the lot in case Paul watched them. Then they circled around another building, which was down the road from the administrative building. There would have been no way Paul could see them from his location.

Mac and Nathan grabbed cameras from the back of the truck, changing the lens to a long distance. Mac asked, "How do you want to do this? Are we separating?"

"No. We're together. Take photos of the car tags, and anyone you see. We might have duplicate pictures, but at least we have them. Let's walk that way, away from the buildings, then go right. We should see the building to our right about 250 yards down."

Mac nodded as they closed the back of the SUV quietly. Since they were traversing unfamiliar territory, they wore their night googles. It made snooping easier and safer. They could stay out of holes in the ground, which led to sprained ankles.

Nathan led Mac to the back of the building, glanced around, then headed into the woods. The woods were thicker than expected, which slowed them down. But it was worth it. As they got closer, a few cars left the lot while others came in. They hid during this time. Especially since they had no idea what was going on.

The building lot became quiet, and the duo made their move. They exited the woods together, taking photos of the license plates of each vehicle. When they were close to the end of the row, they heard voices. The duo dropped behind a truck, hoping no one spotted them.

They figured the guys were on a smoke break because a few minutes later, they reentered the building. Mac and Nathan quickly finished their photo taking and escaped into the woods for their trek back.

Surveying the lot before stepping out from the wood line, Nathan pointed back towards the administrative building at more headlights. "What's going on there?" He whispered.

"Something that requires nighttime work."

Nathan didn't respond, instead he walked to the truck removing his night googles. He opened the back, placing his camera back in its case. When Mac returned hers, he asked, "What type of work requires nighttime hours? Other than cleaning crews."

"None." Mac said as she leaned against the truck. So, what's happening in that building? There were no lights on that the duo saw other than the lobby and Paul's office. So where are those folks?

They climbed into the truck and drove to Nathan's apartment. Mac realized she would need another shopping trip in the next few days. She needed to replenish her wardrobe and contact her insurance company since they never contacted her today.

"Want to grab some supper before going home?" Nathan asked.

"That sounds good. I'm hungry."

Halfway home, they stopped and had a quick bite. Both were tired and eager to get home. Before they made it, George called Mac for an update. Mac wondered why her dad didn't call, but she didn't question it. She described their meetings tonight with the group, then with Paul Drummond, ending the update with the car photos.

"I'm with you two. Something isn't right. Why would those people be there at night unless they were on a cleaning crew?"

"That's the same thing we thought. The people were only at the administrative building. All the other buildings were dark. Another strange thing was the lobby and Paul's office were the only lights on when met Paul. The rest of the building was dark."

George paused before asking, "Where were the people, then?"

"We don't know. While we watched them, cars came and went. We're unsure if it's a shift change. Actually, we don't know what it is yet," Nathan explained.

"You have yourselves a puzzling case. Do you think Professor Gregory's death is part of what's going on at the admin building?"

Mac and Nathan glanced at the other. "That's a possibility." Nathan answered.

Then Mac offered, "We'll be at the office in the morning with tons of photos."

"Ok. See you then," George said as he ended the call.

Mac plopped down on the sofa with her cards and notepad. She needs her cards more than ever now. Nathan sat beside her and watched her work through the information.

"Do you think Mrs. Gregory would help us get the cell phone data from James' phone?" He asked.

"I would think so, especially since she wanted us to find out about her husband's killer." Then Mac looked at Nathan. "This private investigator gig is different that the FBI, huh?"

"Yes, it is, but only for information issues. Before we just got warrants for everything. Now we must use family or friends for information. I'm still glad we made the switch. Are you questioning your decision?"

Mac shook her head from side to side. "Not really. Getting information was just easier on the Federal side. But I'm with you. I like this side too."

Taking her notepad, Mac jotted a note to ask Mrs. Gregory about their cell phone information. Then Mac remembered, "We didn't call Detective Chinni about the black notebook."

"Add that to the list for tomorrow. I suspect he won't confess to having it, anyway."

Something in Nathan's tone caused Mac to pause. "Are you struggling with Chinni's investigation?"

"Was I that obvious? I just have my doubts about his truthfulness. Sometimes I feel he's on the up and up and other times, I think he's lying to us," Nathan shared.

Mac nodded. "What if I told you I feel that way about Paul Drummond?"

Chuckling, Nathan said, "There is no surprise there."

After Mac finished her cards, she and Nathan parted ways. She lay in bed pondering the case and her relationship with Nathan. Why is she hesitant to move forward with Nathan? She knows it will be long term. He's her rock. She decided she doesn't want to do life without him, so what's her hold up?

She drifted off to sleep when her cell phone blared. "Dad?" Mac answered as she wiped her eyes.

"Mac. Mrs. Gregory was just attacked in her house. She called the office because she couldn't find your business card. Can you speak with her?"

"Of course I can. What's her number?" Mac jotted the number on a small pad she kept beside her bed. "I'll call now. Okay, then I'll call you back."

Mac walked across the hall to Nathan's door, but he opened it before she knocked. "What's wrong?"

"Dad called and said that Mrs. Gregory called the office for us. Someone attacked her in her some."

"Call her. Let's see what she says. It sounds like someone is looking for something." Nathan said as he walked to the family room.

Mac dialed the number her dad gave her and waited. No one answered, so Mac left a message. Sixty seconds later, Mrs. Gregory called. Mac placed the call on speaker so Nathan could be a part of it.

Mrs. Gregory sniffed, "Mac and Nathan. Thank you for calling me back. I couldn't find your business cards in all the mess."

"Tell us what happened," Nathan prodded.

"I had gone out to dinner with a co-worker from school. She thought I needed dinner out. When I made it home, I parked in the garage and entered through the kitchen. The mess was unbelievable. There was nothing left in the drawers. Everything was on the floor. It's like someone opened the drawers and dumped the contents."

Mac and Nathan nodded because it sounded like Nathan was right. Someone was looking for the missing black book.

"Mrs. Gregory, was the upstairs in the same condition?" Mac asked.

"Yes, but worse. Whoever was in my house was still there when I entered the bedroom. They knocked me into the dresser, hitting my head in the mirror. I'm in the hospital, waiting for a CT scan and stitches."

"Is anyone there with you?"

"No, I drove myself to the hospital because I didn't want to stay there alone. I'm thinking about going to my sister's house in Florida."

Nathan replied, "That might be a good idea." He paused, then asked, "Have you thought anymore about the black notebook that James carried?"

"Yes, I have, but I've come up empty-handed. I've no idea where he hid it."

"Ok. We'll keep looking. We would like access to your husband's cell phone records. Would you be willing to grant us that privilege?" Mac asked. "The cell phone might hold valuable information, which could help us find his killer."

"Of course, I will. Tell me what I need to do." Mrs. Gregory said.

Then Nathan said , "We'll get the paperwork together tomorrow. You take care of yourself tonight. Let us know where to find you in the morning."

"Thanks for calling. I knew I could trust you." Mrs. Gregory said, as she choked up with tears.

The call ended with Mac muttering, "She could have been killed tonight."

Nathan took her hand in his. "But she wasn't. She sounds like she might have a concussion. I hope the hospital keeps her overnight. At least she'd sleep easier knowing there were folks around if she needed anything."

"I agree. I need to call Dad back and explain the call." Mac tapped Myles' speed dial button, and he answered on the half ring. They spent several minutes discussing the situation. Myles explained since Mrs. Gregory wasn't their client, they couldn't protect her. But the police could.

When he said that, Nathan dialed Detective Chinni. Chinni answered with sleep in his voice. Nathan identified himself and Chinni groaned ever so slightly. The hair on Nathan's neck stood up. Something about this guy didn't seem right, but he pushed forward, wanting Chinni to protect Mrs. Gregory.

Mac sat back on the sofa and listened to Nathan explain the situation. A few times she wanted to unleash her wrath on that guy, but she refrained. She didn't want to interfere with Nathan's conversation. By the time Nathan ended the call, Chinni agreed to go to the hospital for Mrs. Gregory.

Nathan's eyes met Mac's, and they shared the same emotion. How could a detective be less caring about people and do a decent job?

Mac was unsure if they could sleep, but they returned to their beds to try to get a little more before their day started. When Mac laid her head on the pillow, she struggled to shut her mind down. She worked on scenarios about Professor Gregory's murder. By the time her alarm rang, she still had no answer.

The duo met Myles and George at the office. Mac shared about the cell phone data and Mrs. Gregory's okay to obtain it, but they were uncertain how. So, over the next few minutes, George showed them the forms required to get the information.

Once they had them filled out, they dialed Mrs. Gregory. She answered on the first ring. Mac identified herself and asked about her injuries.

"I have a mild concussion, along with 18 stitches in my head. The doctor kept me overnight for observation and I'm waiting to see if he'll release me."

"We have the paperwork that needs your signature for James' cell phone data. We'll be there in two hours." Mac advised unwilling to give Mrs. Gregory the option of backing out. She was afraid she'd change her mind.

When the duo entered the interstate, Nathan said, "We still need to pull tag numbers from our photos last night."

Mac nodded, then said, "We'll do that when we get back. I hate this university is two hours away. That takes a lot from our day."

"I agree, but it will be worth it if we recover something valuable from his phone. Do you know if Ionna handles the tech stuff too, or is she blood and stuff?" Nathan asked as he guided them over to the next lane.

"You know I didn't ask about that. Something else for our list. One day, we'll know this stuff like we did at the FBI." Then Mac leaned her head back on the headrest and let her mind wander. She thought of Williams, Spencer, and Travis and Margot. She thought Travis and Margot might want to join them at her dad's company, but so far, they've said nothing.

They entered the hospital lot and headed to room 212. Mac knocked on the door and entered. Detective Chinni sat in the recliner between the door and the bed. He grinned when he saw us.

"Mac, Nathan, glad to see you," Chinni said in an almost chipper tone.

"Thanks for being here, Chinni." Nathan said as they shook hands.

Mac and Nathan discussed how they should handle the request and they didn't want Chinni to be a part of it. Nathan asked Chinni to meet with him in the hallway. Once they left, Mac brought the papers out.

Mrs. Gregory didn't even read them. She signed quickly. "Thank you for speaking with me last night. I don't know what I'd do without you two."

"Thank you for this. We're getting closer to figuring things out. Stay in touch with us. Let us know where you end up staying." Mac said, then a thought struck. "One more question. Did you happen to see your attacker? Like hair color, skin color, anything that might help us identify him."

"He hit from behind. I never saw him. All I remember is black boots. But that's it." She reached up, touching her bandage as memories flooded her mind.

Mac walked to the door, then glanced back. "Take care of yourself."

Nathan stood next to the door when Mac exited Mrs. Gregory's room. She gave Nathan a slight nod as they accomplished their goal. Nathan bid farewell to the detective, thanking him again for helping.

When they walked outside, leaves blew across the lot. Mac pulled her jacket tighter, hoping to ward off some of the breeze that had begun to blow. "It's cold up here." She stammered as Nathan chuckled.

On the return trip, Mac approached the subject of Margot and Travis. Nathan was unsure how they felt since he hadn't seen Travis since they left the FBI. Mac suggested meeting them for dinner. Before they could discuss it, her personal cell phone rang with an unfamiliar number.

She answered, then waited for the caller to identify themselves. When they did, she released the breath she didn't know she held. Her insurance company finally called and offered to pay her for her loss. She gladly accepted. "Looks like the fire was arson. Tyrone spoke with my insurance company, giving the details of the investigation."

"That's great. Now, you get to shop again." Nathan grinned because he knew Mac hated clothes shopping.

After a few miles passed, Mac noticed Nathan never returned to their conversation about Travis and Margot. While she didn't want to pry, she didn't want to be the reason Nathan and Travis lost their friendship. They had been friends for far too long for that. She waited to discuss it at home. There had to be a way to get them together.

Myles was away when they entered the office. But George was there. He spoke to a group of folks in the conference room. When he saw the duo, he invited them to the meeting. Mac was somewhat skeptical, but agreed.

As soon as they cleared the door, George introduced Mac and Nathan to the group. It turned out that the group were other investigators, so Mac and Nathan needed to meet them, and George knew it. Questions flew at Mac when they recognized her last name. She beamed but refused to answer questions during the meeting.

George picked up on her cue and he resumed. The company had grown and was splitting into different departments. Over the next month, each agent will receive their assignment. If they had issues with it, they would meet with George and work to find a solution. He reiterated no one was losing their jobs. In fact, they may need to hire more.

When the meeting ended, George asked to see Mac and Nathan. Mac assumed it was the signed cell phone information , but it wasn't. She laid the signed form on the table, waiting for George. He glanced at it and said, "I needed to see you two for something else."

Mac and Nathan straightened up in their chairs. Unsure what to do or say.

"Relax. This isn't the FBI, so there's no need to be tense. Myles is out of the country on an assignment. But he wanted to move forward with our next step in our business plan."

"Where is Dad?"

"He is in the UK. He's meeting with prospective clients who have offices in the USA, too."

Mac nodded, giving George notice to move along. George plucked two pieces of paper from his folder, sliding one to Nathan and the other to Mac.

"These forms are notices you're being moved into a leadership role. You'll still investigate cases, but you'll also supervise new agents."

"Wait. What? We just got here. How can we supervise new agents if we don't know anything?" Mac stammered.

"You will know everything I know by the time you get your first one. We're not here to throw you into the deep end without a ladder." George snickered. "I thought you knew us better than that."

Mac glanced at the form, then to Nathan, ending on George. "I know, but this is so unexpected. We thought we'd have time to learn your way of doing things before any changes happened."

George looked at Nathan. "You haven't spoken. Can you share your thoughts?"

"I'm ready."

Mac's head spun to face Nathan. "Really? You know nothing, either."

"But George said he'll teach us. As long as I have that, I'm good and you will be too. Thanks for the opportunity, George."

George smiled. He knew he had them right where Myles wanted them. Then he said, "Follow me. We'll submit your cell phone form." He picked up Mac's form and glanced over his shoulder, chuckling.

Nathan stood first, then Mac. She followed him out the door.

George sat in front of his computer, scanned the document, then submitted it online. "See. That wasn't so hard. The hardest part is getting folks to sign it. I will share that if she didn't sign it, we can still get the information, but it won't hold up in court. That's for another day."

"So, now, we wait. While that's processing, we need to start on the photos we took in the parking lot. We know how to run car tags. Thanks, George." Mac patted him on his arm as they left.

Mac had so many things swirling through her mind, she was unsure where to start. Wonder why Dad didn't give us a heads up on this change? How many agents are they looking to hire? Is business that good?

Nathan had his photos loaded into his computer already, so he waited for Mac. Once they had them side by side, they divided the list. There were twenty-one in all. So, it shouldn't take long to pull the tag information.

They separated to work on the tags. Mac and Nathan worked in silence as they typed their queries into the system. When the results came through, the duo felt frustrated. Mac spouted, "That was a waste of our time."

"Not exactly. Look here." He laid the results on the table. Then he pointed to his find, saying, "We have vehicles registered to two LLCs and three rental car companies. Why do you suppose that is? Cleaning crews wouldn't need rentals, now would they?"

Mac perked up when she saw Nathan's eyes. He was onto something. Now, to dig deeper. "We need to find the owners of the LLCs and the contact rental companies for the renter's contact information, if they'll share it."

Nathan offered to contact the rental companies while Mac worked on identifying the LLC owners. She immediately pulled up the secretary of state's website and entered the company's name into the search box. It gave no results. That indicates that the company did not incorporate in Georgia. There has to be a better way to find this. Instead of searching for George, she went back to her desktop and found an app that she needed. She clicked into it, entered her search, and waited.

Five years ago, they established the first LLC in Nevada, while they established the other one in Utah three years ago. Mac remembered the university being new, but she couldn't remember how new. She pulled her notes and found it. Coincidences don't exist in murder investigations. It must mean something since the university and the LLC formed in Nevada five years ago. The agent of record for the LLC is an attorney.

Mac wants to know the LLC's owner, but that will wait. The business operates as an import-export. That title covers a lot of possibilities.

With the second LLC entered, Mac pondered the information she found. When the second one popped, it also gave an attorney's name for the agent of record. Different attorneys and different states. What did James stumble into?

Mac grabbed her things and met Nathan in his office. When she stepped to the door, he ended a call. "Hi Mac, what did you find?" He asked.

"I have an LLC from Nevada that incorporated the same month and year that the university opened. The second LLC was incorporated in Utah three years ago. Both have attorneys as agents of record. But I still have no idea who the business owners are."

"George may be able to help us through that. I have two rental agencies emailing me photos of the guys that picked up the rental. All the rental paperwork was done online, so they have nothing on the driver. We'd have to gain access to their system for a photo ID of the driver."

Mac shook her head. This private investigation stuff was hard. Being an FBI agent, information flowed freely. But on this side, we had to fight for it.

"We'll get it, Mac. I see your struggle. It's written all over your face. Let's find George." Nathan dialed the in house number for him. Instead of answering, George appeared at the doorway.

"Why the sad face, Mac?" George asked as he glanced at Nathan.

Mac looked at Nathan for help, so he obliged. Nathan explained their conundrum and George nodded. "Here's your lesson for today. Turn your laptop toward me." When Nathan did, George tapped an icon, and it opened. "This is the best thing. It has all kinds of searches for you that you would not otherwise have access to."

George looked at one of Mac's LLCs. He pulled the LLC in Nevada first. The owner is listed as PPD Enterprises. "Do either of recognize that?"

Both shook their heads from side to side. Then Mac shouted, "Paul Drummond. He could be PPD. He's the university president."

"Ok. That's a start. Now for the second LLC. It's registered to the attorney, Kyle Durlin. So, now we go deeper into Durlin." George backed out of that application and tapped another. He waited until it loaded. Then he added Kyle's name to the search bar.

He whistled when the information came back. "Kyle's had issues with the bar association on many occasions. It appears he has a gambling problem. He moved to Utah from Nevada right before setting up this LLC."

"So, whatever James Gregory stumbled into, it was big and worth enough money for someone to kill him." Nathan stated.

Chapter 4

George and Mac tilted their heads as they considered Nathan's assessment. Then Mac asked, "That's it. We follow the money. Wasn't Professor Gregory a finance teacher?"

"Yes, he was. Somehow, we need the university's financial records. If James could find the discrepancies, we should, too."

Now, Nathan and George tilted their heads as George said, "I'm no finance wizard."

"Ditto." Nathan muttered.

"Well, someone here must know someone that can help us." Mac turned her attention to George. The duo watched as ideas raced through his mind.

He raised his hand, then said, "You might be right. Let me work on it."

George left Mac and Nahan alone. They stared at each other. "So, where are we? We have two LLCs that rented a bunch of cars. Attorney's names are on the secretary of state site, so we still have no idea of the owner's name, and I'm certain that's by design. The rental agency is sending a photo from their office."

"That sums it up. What could a group of people do in an administrative building in the overnight hours to make money?" Nathan asked, more to himself. But that didn't stop Mac from replying.

"I've been pondering that same question. There's only so much room in the building where they could hide. So, you're looking at a half-dozen rooms. That's not a lot of space to work in with that many guys we saw the other night."

They took a few minutes to work on the idea, but nothing came to fruition. The amount of space and the number of people stumped the duo.

Nathan checked his email after receiving an alert. "We have our first picture of a rental car driver."

He clicked it open and stared at the picture. The driver was a typical guy with brown hair, Caucasian, and no visible tattoos. His eye color was unknown due to the camera angle. "That's not much help."

Mac stood. "I'm going for coffee." Nathan grinned because he knows she likes to drink coffee while thinking. She always says it helps her. He stood and followed her out the door.

Halfway through her coffee, she said, "I failed to check for the cell phone information."

"It will be there." Nathan reminded her.

When they returned, Mac tapped her computer. "We have it, Nathan." She said loud enough for him to hear her, since he went to his office.

"Show me what we have. I have high expectations for this."

Mac clicked it opened then stared at it. "It's 101 pages of information. I'll print that and we can split it."

They chatted about nothing while the printer worked its magic. Then when it delivered the last page to the tray, Mac said, "They sent over texts and call numbers."

"Look at this. I have James' notes. Let's read through it, then we'll get together to discuss and swap stacks." Nathan suggested.

Mac agreed by taking the first fifty pages. She sat down with her notepad to the right of the stack and began reading the information. The text messages were enlightening. There were multiple texts from the same number, so she jotted the number on her pad. James and the phone owner were not friends, that was obvious, plus the unknown text sender became increasingly agitated.

Unfortunately, the texts were vague, so Mac had no idea what they referred to. But James had information when he died. There's something illegal happening at the university, that much Mac knows. Now, she needs to find out who owns the phone number that sent James the text.

After reading her stack for the second time, she walked to Nathan's office. he had a page full of notes and she had one phone number. "Looks like you hit the jackpot."

"I did. Clarence was right when he said James typed on his phone all the time. If James used a cloud account, I could find more. The bad news is that he typed in shorthand, with a lot of numbers. Then, I have texts from someone that was clearly upset with James, but there were no direct threats to his life, just subtle hints."

"So, we need help to get the university's financials and now we need someone to help break a code." Mac reached up and rubbed her neck. Mac wanted to reach out to Margot, her go to FBI counterpart, but she knew she couldn't.

George stopped by Nathan's office. "They you are. What's new on the case?" No one offered to speak, so he continued, "What's with the long faces?"

"We need the university's financials, and we need help to break a code." Mac blurted.

"Ok. I'll call Joe, from the Board. He'll produce the financials. Now, where's the code?"

Nathan handed it to George and George sat in the chair next to Mac so he could concentrate. "This looks like some sort of shorthand, but this is definitely a code. Let me find the guru. Back in a few."

The duo shared a glance. "Are you analyzing this too much? George seems to have an answer for everything we ask."

Mac nodded her agreement, but something bothered her. Was it the fire? Was she missing the FBI or just the people that worked with her? When she looked up, Nathan stared at her.

"Mac, what's troubling you? And don't say nothing."

"I can't put my finger on it. At first, I thought it was the stress from the fire, but that's over. Now, I'm wondering if I miss the FBI or just the people we worked with." Mac tilted her head and lifted her shoulder.

George returned with a guy wearing skinny jeans and hair dyed the color of a yellow Easter egg. "Mac, Nathan meet Raymond Dollar. The best code cracker money can buy."

"That's a good one, George." Nathan slipped in.

"Raymond, it's nice to meet you." Mac offered as she shook his hand.

"People call me Raymond. Now, show me what you have." His eyes bounced from person to person, finally landing on George.

Raymond accepted the papers and studied them. "This shorthand is typical for a financial person. Colleges teach them this shorthand. This second piece is a little difficult. It appears to be a list of financial transactions, but I can't say what yet. I'll have the first part transcribed by the end of the day."

"We'll take it. Here are our cards. You can reach out to either of us," Nathan stated.

Raymond accepted the cards, then asked, "Can I keep these papers? And do you have them in digital form??

"Yes, and yes. What's your email and I'll send them to you?" Mac offered.

Once they handled that, Mac and Nathan waited for the results. George was working on Joe for the financials, but they've received nothing yet. So they slipped away to a clothing store for Mac to replenish her wardrobe.

When the pair returned to the office, George caught them at the coffee machine. "I've left Joe a message. He usually calls right back from a quiet place, but he hasn't yet. I'm feeling uneasy about this, but I'm not ready to move on it."

"Would Clarence or any of the others have access to the financials?" Nathan asked.

"That's a good question. Why don't one of you call him and ask?" George suggested.

Mac sat in the corner chair of Nathan's office while he dialed Clarence's number. He left him a message, too. Then he dialed Carlos, with the same result.

Nathan looked at Mac. "What are the odds that we left three messages for three different people? Tell me nothing has happened to them."

"I wish I could. We'll wait for a return call because they may be in class. But if we haven't heard from them by morning, we're going up there." Mac stated in a terse tone.

"You're right. It would be too late to help them if they're already dead. And we are two hours away." Nathan said, as a way of making himself feel better. "Let's call Ionna and see if she can help with phone number. We need to find out who owns it."

"Good idea. Go ahead." Mac said to Nathan as she winked at him.

He grinned as he picked up his phone. Ionna answered on the first ring. Nathan explained their predicament, and she asked him to come to the lab. He stood, grabbing the phone number, and walking to the door. Glancing back, he said, "Aren't you coming, Mac?"

"She didn't invite me." Mac said, snickering.

"That's cute. Come on. I need protection." Nathan retorted with a laugh.

"Oh, so now you don't think I can protect you. Is that why you're laughing?"

"Let's back up and start over. I asked you to come with me and you started the banter. Mac, I know you have my six." Nathan leaned down and kissed her.

"Always." she said as she followed him out the door.

Ionna waited at the door for them. "Where's the number? I have the search cued and ready."

Nathan passed her the number, but not without their fingers touching. Mac watched the exchange, then chastised herself for not coming with Nathan when he asked. He knew what would happen.

Ionna met Nathan's eyes, but his phone rang, breaking the connection. "George, we're at the lab. We'll be right there."

"Call us with the results. Gotta run." Nathan held the door for Mac as Ionna watched them leave.

"You knew, didn't you? You knew Ionna had feelings for you."

"Not really. She'd said nothing to me," Nathan said as they trotted up the stairs.

George stood at the elevator when the duo rounded the corner. "You took the stairs? There's no need for that." He shook his head, then said, "I'm leaving for the day, but if you hear anything from Joe or Clarence, I want to know about it. I have an uneasy feeling about this."

"We do too. If we hear nothing overnight, we'll return to the university and do some digging on our own. Joe hired us, right?"

"He did, but for the university. If something happens to him, our contract would fall to the one next in line on the Board." George explained.

"Does the president have anything to do with our contract?" Mac asked.

"No. Why would you ask that?" George inquired.

"Just thinking is all. Nothing concrete yet," Mac replied with a shoulder shrug.

George pushed the down button for the elevator, and when the doors opened, Raymond stood there staring at us. He said, "Do you always congregate at the elevators?"

"No. Perfect timing." George said. "Did you find anything?"

"Yes, and no. The no part is still working, and that's the code. The yes part is the shorthand. I have that decoded for you and I emailed it before coming here. There is one detail that's a little harder to decipher in his shorthand. It looks unfinished because there are a handful of words that I can't figure out. That's a work in progress."

"That's great, Raymond. Thanks for getting it to us so fast." Mac said.

Then Nathan, "We'll look at it. George, go on home. We've got this. We'll touch base in the morning." George nodded as he pressed the down button.

Mac and Nathan headed into Nathan's office to view the email. "I hope this shorthand makes sense to me."

"I agree. If this guy was so smart, he may be way over my head." Mac added.

Nathan clicked his email open. Raymond was the last one received. He opened the attachment and printed two copies. It took a minute for the entire document to print. "How could James get all of this information on a phone?" Nathan said to himself while Mac chuckled.

Once Mac had her copy, she slipped off to her office. She needed quiet time to dig into this. As she began, she noticed a pattern in the sentences. One or two words seemed to be out of context, skewing the sentence. She jotted the odd words down on a pad, hoping to find the meaning.

Nothing seemed to make sense. They were in no order to form a sentence. Did Nathan find this? Mac leaned over and hit the interoffice call button for Nathan. "I found something."

Before she ended her call, Nathan stood at her door. "Did you find a bunch of strange words tucked into sentences?" Nathan asked with a head tilt and an eyebrow raised.

"Yes. So, if you have it, it means something. Did you keep a list of words?"

Nathan trotted back to his office, returning with a piece of paper. "I don't read at fast as you, so I haven't finished it yet."

"Let me have it. I'll finish yours, then we'll write the words on the whiteboard. Maybe that will help us understand James' meaning." Mac shared.

While Mac worked on the rest of Nathan's documents, Nathan scribbled the words on the board. When he finished, he stepped back to study them. So far, then meant nothing. As he stood staring at the board, Mac produced Nathan's list. "Add these, please."

Nathan wrote the words on the board while Mac leaned on her desk, saying the words out loud. Sometimes that helps her hear something when she has a hard time figuring it out.

He joined her as she continued studying the words. A few of the words include asset, plan, model, budget, ratio, management, holding, currency, and capital. These are parts of something larger. They just didn't know what yet.

Nathan checked his phone as it rang. "It's Clarence." He told Mac before answering.

Clarence explained he'd been teaching class, but he hadn't spoken to Joe in a couple of days. The others are staying in touch with one another twice a day as a precaution. Joe's friend on the Board is Harrison Morelli. Clarence doesn't have Harrison's number, but he could get it for Nathan and call him back.

When Clarence mentioned he hadn't heard from Joe in a couple of days, Nathan's insides twisted. Could something have happened to him? Why hasn't anyone called?

Mac watched Nathan's facial expressions as he finished the call. Then he said, "Clarence was teaching, and he hasn't heard from Joe in a couple of days. He's getting me Harrison Morelli's phone number, who is friends with Joe. Harrison is also on the Board. He might be our next contact if something happened to Joe."

"Do you think something happened to Joe?" Mac met Nathan's eyes.

"I'm unsure, but every time it's mentioned, my insides twist. I hope my gut is wrong. Do you still want to wait until tomorrow to go to the university?" Nathan asked.

Mac paused, then said, "Yes. It will be easier in the daytime and the teachers will be on campus. It's time to let them know we're investigating James' death."

This time, Nathan paused. "You're putting us in the middle of something huge. Are you willing to risk your life?"

"It's nothing we didn't do for the FBI and these folks deserve it, too." Mac shared.

Nathan agreed. "Ok. Tomorrow morning it is then. Does Joe have a family? If so, I wonder why we haven't heard from Chinni. Surely, he would call us if someone reported Joe missing.

Mac's head snapped around. "Call Chinni. Ask him."

So, Nathan did. Chinni didn't answer his cell phone, so Nathan left a message.

Until they had confirmation, they waited. Mac took a picture of the whiteboard. So she'd have the words with her, and could review them again before bedtime.

The duo ate a bite before heading home. Mac still had to prepare her new clothes to wear. They still sported price tags and wrinkles.

The following morning, Nathan checked his cell phone first thing. He had no messages or calls from Joe or Chinni. Now he was officially worried.

When Mac came from her room, he shared. "We'll call George and head straight to the university. There's no need prolonging the inevitable. I'm changing into jeans as a precaution." Mac advised, as she tilted her head.

Nathan was already wearing jeans. If the case took him back to the woods, he wanted to be in jeans instead of cotton slacks.

Mac called George from the car, and he agreed with their assessment. Joe was a major player in their investigation, and they needed to know his whereabouts.

Chinni called a few minutes afterward. He'd heard nothing of Joe's disappearance. Nathan explained they were headed to the university and Chinni volunteered to meet them there.

Apprehension filled the truck as they got closer. Joe is being held somewhere, or he's dead. They needed to know which one quickly. If he's being held somewhere, they'd work to find him. If he's dead, then they would add his death to their list.

Mac's mind returned to the activity at the admin building when they took the pics of the vehicles. "I still do not understand why so many men were at the admin building after hours."

Nathan changed lanes before adding, "We know it's not cleaning people. There were too many for that one building."

"And the lights weren't on in the building other than Paul's office and the lobby. So where we they?" Mac questioned.

"I'd like to know that myself." Nathan replied as his cell phone rang. He tapped the button on the dash, then answered.

Clarence called with Harrison's number. Mac jotted in her book. When Clarence said he called Joe's cell phone again and now it goes straight to voicemail. It's like he's turned it off. Then Clarence said, "I'm going to Joe's house. I'll call you when I get back."

"Clarence, don't do that alone. We'll meet you there. You have no idea what you'll find. What is Joe's address?"

Clarence recited the address from memory. "I'll wait in the driveway."

Mac entered the address into her phone. "We're twenty-eight minutes away."

Neither spoke as they feared the worst. In times like these, the duo could have used their dash lights. Instead, Nathan pushed the pedal as far as he dared. Luckily, there were no car accidents to impede their way, and they arrived on time.

Clarence still sat in the driveway, but he jumped out of his car when he saw the black Suburban pull to the curb. On the walk to meet Clarence, Mac and

Nathan unsnapped their holsters. They wanted to be prepared for anything.

"Glad you waited, Clarence. Did you see anyone coming or going from the house?"

"No, Nathan. I saw nothing. The house is dark, and the blinds never shifted, that I saw. This is bad, isn't it?"

"Well, things are changing, that's for sure. We hope nothing happened to Joe of because of his involvement with us."

With a tilted head, Clarence replied, "Me too. We need to know what's going on here for the students' safety."

Mac and Nathan nodded as they approached the front door. It was locked. "Do you have a key?"

"No. But I know where he hides one. It's on the back deck. This way." Clarence waved to the pair to follow him. They did, but not without looking over their shoulders.

The backyard was nice, with a greenish lawn and tons of leaves. Mac thought about sitting outside on the deck to enjoy the foliage during the fall, but then the thought of raking the leaves changed her mind.

Clarence found the key next to the door in a fake bottomed pot. He handed the key to Nathan so the pair could enter first. Nathan slid the key into the lock and opened the door slowly. No sounds came from the home except the hum of the refrigerator.

Nathan stepped inside first, then invited the others inside. "Clarence, stay here while we clear the house." He nodded.

Mac tapped Nathan on the shoulder like they've done countless times and proceeded deeper into the home. They entered each room, opened every door, and came away empty.

"Clarence." Nathan called. "It's all clear."

Breathing a sigh of relief, Clarence joined Nathan in the living room while Mac searched upstairs. "There's one car in the garage. Did he have two?"

"Not that I know of. I only saw him in a Chevrolet Silverado."

"That's what is in the garage. So, either someone picked him up, and he hasn't checked in yet, or someone kidnapped him." Nathan looked around the house. Nothing stood out. Everything had its place. When he glanced into the kitchen, he saw no dishes in the sink or the counter. It's like Joe knew he was leaving. Otherwise, there would be things sitting about, like mail, coffee cups, and coats.

Mac joined them a little while later, saying, "I found nothing indicating Joe was kidnapped. But I also found a small suitcase too. He might have had a larger case or he may have left with nothing."

Nathan asked Clarence, "Did Joe have a home office?"

Clarence shrugged his shoulders. Mac found that odd. A man holding a position such as Joe would need a place to work. Mac walked down the hallway toward the garage. She opened the door to the laundry room, paused, then walked deeper into the room. There was what appeared to be a closet inside the laundry room.

"Nathan, can you come here? Clarence can come too."

Both guys trotted to Mac's location. "Did you open this door?"

"No, I didn't see it. There are no knobs on it. How did you spot it?" Nathan inquired.

"The recess." Mac pointed to the recessed panel.

Nathan walked over with his gun drawn, sliding the barn door open. He exhaled when he found it empty. "Here is Joe's office. This is a great space for an office. It's also very tidy."

Mac and Clarence walked over to the closet and peered inside. This is where Joe kept his paperwork and bills. They were standing up in a bin, waiting to be paid. But none were due right now. These due dates were a month away. By all appearances, it seems Joe left on his own volition.

Clarence was thinking the same thing. "If Joe knew he was leaving, why didn't he call someone? He knows how important this investigation is to us and the university."

Nathan placed his hand on Clarence's shoulder. "I'm sure he had his reason."

Mac tried to enter Joe's laptop, but it was password protected, so we searched for a calendar, finding nothing. Glancing at Clarence, Mac asked, "Has Joe mentioned having a family somewhere? Or maybe somewhere he likes to vacation."

Clarence worked to recall past conversations with Joe. "He mentioned something about visiting Tampa, Florida, a time or two. But I don't recall him having family there."

Mac and Nathan's eyes met. "Does Joe gamble?"

"I think he does some. We had a conversation where we discussed ways to relax. He described slot machines. They gave him a chance to think. For me, it's a good book and a beach."

Nathan nodded his head because the beach was his choice, too. Mac confirmed hers, too. Nathan grinned when they shared the same idea.

"Can Ionna check out hotel reservations in the Tampa area like Margot could for the FBI?" Nathan asked.

"No idea. But it doesn't hurt to ask. It would save us tons of time."

Nathan tapped his speed dial for Ionna while Mac watched and listened. He described their dilemma, and she agreed to find out if Joe was registered in one of the casinos.

So, now they wait for a word. Where else could Joe be other than Tampa or sitting on a beach? If he's not in Tampa, where do they look next? Florida has thousands of hotels along their shoreline.

Nathan's cell phone rang with a call from Chinni. "Detective. Yeah, I know. We're at Joe's house. Clarence met us here. He's very concerned about Joe's disappearance. Have you heard anything?"

Mac and Clarence waited for Nathan's conversation to end and when it did, it was a letdown. "Chinni has heard nothing about Joe. No one has reported him missing. He's at the university waiting for us."

Nathan looked to Mac. "Are you ready to go over there?"

"Sure." She glanced around the office space once last time and slid the door closed.

When the threesome was outside standing by their cars, Clarence asked, "Were you able to speak with Harrison?"

The duo shook their heads. "Not yet. That's next. Stay in touch with Clarence. If you feel uneasy about anything, call us."

He nodded and entered his vehicle with his shoulders slumped. He was clearly worried about Joe.

When he backed out of the driveway, Mac and Nathan walked to their vehicle, entering it in silence. "So, do you think Joe is safe?"

"By all appearances, he left for a trip telling no one. That may be out of character for him, but it might be the smartest thing he could have done." Nathan explained, as he tapped Harrison's phone number into his cell phone.

While it rang, he stared at Mac. He left a message asking for a return call.

Mac's head tilted. "Could Harrison and Joe be together?"

"Anything is possible."

Nathan pulled away from the curb, driving to the university. Just as they pulled in, Ionna called Nathan.

"Hi, Ionna, We're here." He said, giving Ionna the heads-up. Mac was listening.

"There are no records of Joe or Joseph Rogers in any Tampa hotels or casinos." Ionna said.

Mac shrugged her shoulders. Then she asked, "Can you check for a Harrison Morelli?"

Nathan grinned. Mac was a great investigation, never leaving a stone unturned.

Ionna promised a return call.

Nathan pulled up next to Detective Chinni. When they met at his trunk, he asked, "Did you find Joe?"

"No, we didn't, but we're still looking." Nathan explained. "We're here to speak with other professors that worked with James Gregory. Can you make that happen or should we visit with Paul Drummond first?"

Chinni stammered. "Sure. I can help with that." He stepped away from the duo and made a call. The conversation sounded heated as he tried not to yell at the other party. Mac wanted to know who was on the other end of that call.

They waited until he finally returned to them. "Where do you want to start? The professors that are in class are of course off limits until class ends."

"Of course. We have no intention of disturbing a class. At this stage, we're still learning everything we can about James since no one feels he killed himself."

Chinni nodded but Nathan and Mac witnessed his jaw muscles working. It's like he gritted his teeth on Nathan's last statement. How involved is Chinni in this coverup? What information is he keeping from the duo?

Chapter 5

Chinni suggested they start in James' department. Nathan and Mac simply nodded as an acknowledgement. They studied Chinni as they followed him to the Financial Building. The building was five stories. It was like the administration building, but shorter and a little lighter. The building was a flourish of activity. People milling about on the front lawn dressed in jackets, scarves, and hats.

Mac realized it was colder at the university than it was in town. Maybe the mountains hamper the temperatures, she pondered, glancing around the area before entering the front door.

Students rushed into classrooms just as a tone sounded. When Mac and Nathan were in school, they had a bell. Now it seems someone has replaced that too.

Chinni turned to face the pair, then he offered, "We have several floors to cover. Since I don't know which teachers are teaching, we'll have to walk it."

Nathan replied, "That's fine by us. Let's get started."

Mac noticed the tense tone coming from Nathan. She looked at him and tilted her head. He nodded, but said nothing.

They came across several professors in the lounge and Chinni introduced the pair to the professors. He stepped outside the door while Mac and Nathan spoke with the others. No one offered new information. People held James in high regard, and no one believed he killed himself. He had too much to offer others.

When they finished the interviews, they stepped to the door, finding Chinni in a deep conversation with Paul Drummond. Paul's face was in a scowl. Mac whispered, "Looks like we stepped on someone's toes."

Nathan chuckled. "I think you're right. Let's interrupt." Nathan and Mac walked over to the two men.

"Thanks for waiting, Detective. We're ready for our next stop."

Paul Drummond spoke quietly, "Do you really need to do this? I mean, we are in class."

"Yes, we do. We're finishing up our investigation into James' death and this solidifies our findings. We'll turn our report on you as soon as it's ready."

Paul nodded because he's the one that hired the duo. There was no way he could question the investigation. Mac looked at his face and saw a faint tick in his right eye. Wonder what causes that? Does it happen during stressful times? Or is it involuntary?

Chinni said, "We'll go up to the second floor and work our way to the top." He walked over to the stairwell, entering first.

When the threesome stepped into the second-floor lobby, it was quiet. Class had begun, leaving the hallway empty. It was eerie how it can bustle one minute then completely empty the next.

Chinni steered them to another lounge at the end of the hallway. This one mirrored the first-floor lounge, except there were only two folks in it. Chinni introduced the pair, and Nathan immediately saw trouble in the man's eyes. Nathan waited for Chinni to step outside before asking questions.

The man, Jerry Sorenson, said, "Have you found out who killed James? I've been worried sick since his demise."

Mac asked, "What do you know about James' death?"

"All he told me was that he was meeting with several other financial professors on the rooftop. It's where a lot of us go when we don't want students around. He mentioned he's been working on something, and he thought it was time to share." Jerry explained.

"Did he elaborate on what he had been working on? This information is critical to the case, Mr. Sorenson." Mac stated.

"I tried to pry it out of him, but he said I would have plausible deniability if anything happened. I guess he suspected something might happen to him. But why didn't he involve the police if he felt threatened? I don't understand." Jerry looked at the duo with sad eyes, holding unshed tears.

"Did you see James carry a black notebook?" Nathan asked the professors.

Both nodded yes. Then he asked, "Do you know where James would stash the book for safe keeping?"

Jerry replied, "No. But I know he protected that book from prying eyes. He never let go of it."

The other professor didn't offer anything, as they were new to the university. But the duo left handing business cards to both.

Chinni rested against the wall this time and he was alone. "Okay, Chinni, next floor."

The next three floors delivered the same information. So the duo thanked Chinni and left him standing in the lobby. When Mac and Nathan walked down the front steps, Mac glanced at Nathan and said, "James did not commit suicide. Our case is over."

"But are you willing to leave the murder unfinished?" Nathan asked her.

"I don't want to, but without Joe, no one has offered to pay us for our services." Mac stated.

Silence followed for a few minutes. Then Nathan said, "Let's turn in our report to Paul, who probably will do nothing with it. Then submit it to the Board of Trustees. That would give Joe the opening he needs to finish the investigation, if we can find him."

Mac nodded as they climbed into the truck. Movement caught Mac's eye. "Look at the vehicles driving behind the buildings."

Nathan's eyes lit up. "Care to enjoy a nice dinner, then we'll take a nighttime stroll through the woods."

"I thought you'd never ask."

They left the university so Chinni would think they were traveling to Atlanta. But Chinni had another idea. He followed them from three cars behind.

It took Nathan several minutes before he noticed the tail. "Uh, Mac. Chinni is following us. He's three cars behind."

Mac pulled her visor down and used the mirror to spot Chinni. "Um. Very interesting. Obviously, he doesn't trust us now. Wonder what changed?" Mac paused. Then added, "Take the interstate for a little while. Let's see what he does."

Nathan stopped at the traffic light and turned left to enter the interstate. As he entered the interstate, he glanced into his mirror. "He didn't follow."

"Interesting. Wonder where he's heading?" Mac asked.

Mac's question met silence. When she looked over at Nathan, his eyes were mere slits. That's his tale, that he's in deep concentration.

He exited the interstate at the next exit and, without speaking, he turned toward the police department. The duo drove around the block, searching for Chinni's vehicle. Mac spotted it backed into a parking space in the rear lot.

"So, what do you think now? Why would he follow us? He couldn't have heard the comment about dinner and the stroll through the woods. We were outside when I mentioned that."

Mac's head swung from side to side. "It must be our involvement in James' death investigation. Wonder if he feels we're in too deep? Or is Chinni part of the coverup?"

"That's my vote," Nathan said as he turned right from the lot, heading to town. They pulled into a parking lot full of cars, hoping to hide theirs.

Over dinner, they discussed their plans for tonight, which stayed the same as the first time they ventured into the woods. They would take more photos to see if other vehicles showed. If the same ones are there, then it's planned meetings or working hours.

"How can we find out where the people are in the building? I'd rather not ask about Chinni or Drummond. Would Clarence know?"

"That's a good question. We'll call him once we finish our meal."

Neither spoke as they cleaned their plates. Nathan paid for their meals and kept the receipt for the business meeting.

They surveyed the lot before walking to their truck. Once inside, Nathan dialed Clarence. When Nathan asked about the cars, Clarence said he had no idea why the cars would be in the lot. At that time of day, most of the faculty and students have long left the grounds or are in their dorms.

"That proves the cars are there for no good reason."

"But what's the reason? Is that what James found?" Nathan asked.

Mac shrugged her shoulders as a reply because she had no clue what James knew. If they did, the case would be solved by now.

They parked in another parking lot closer to the university and checked their gear. The night vison googles were a must, plus their ballistic vest and a jacket. A breeze picked up this afternoon, continuing into the evening.

Once darkness fell, Nathan drove the truck, parking it in the same place as before. It was convenient for them and hidden from view from the university. Just as Nathan put a foot on the ground, his cell phone chirped.

He grimaced. When he plucked the phone from his pocket, he quickly answered, as he didn't want the call going to voicemail. Then he tapped the speaker button. "Harrison Morelli, here. I'm returning your call."

"Hi, we got your name and number from Clarence, Joe's friend. We're trying to find Joe. It seems he left the area, and we desperately need to speak with him. Can you help us?"

There was silence on the other end of the phone. Nathan thought Harrison had ended the call until Harrison replied, "Let me see what I can do. I'll be in touch."

Mac titled her head and asked, "Is Joe with him?"

"I've no idea. The long stretch of silence is puzzling, and we wouldn't know if Joe spoke with Harrison." Nathan shook his head. How were they ever going to find out who killed James if people kept secrets?

Nathan turned his phone on silent for fear of another interruption and this time he didn't want to give away their hiding places. They surveyed their surroundings before proceeding into the woods.

They followed the same path as their first visit, which made this trek easier. Everything looked the same. Mac noticed headlights glowing through the woods as they got closer to the admin building. Then she realized. If the headlights face the woods, the vehicles are backed into a space.

Mac tapped Nathan on the shoulder, then whispered her idea. He agreed, and they moved a little faster because they didn't want to miss anything. When they reached their hiding spot, they stopped, checking their surroundings.

Both investigators pulled their binoculars to their faces. They watched as an 18-wheeler backed into the loading dock with another one waiting to take its spot. The lot was a flurry of activity.

Nathan whispered, "I'd love to see what's on that truck."

"Me too. But we're not getting any closer. Promise me." Her request didn't garner an answer, so she tapped on the arm.

He muttered, "Promise." But it sounded forced. Nathan had worked out a plan to join the guys on the docks. He thought he could act like he belonged to loading goods on the truck. But since he promised Mac, he knew that was off the table.

Mac snapped photos of the truck's side panels with DOT information. She'd track the trucks that way and hopefully the drivers would talk.

The only sounds in the woods were the cameras as the duo photographed the vehicles and people in the lot. Last time, they never saw a soul, but this time, people were everywhere.

Nathan and Mac took a break when the activity slowed. They drank water and whispered about what they saw. Mac asked, "Where are they storing the pallets they're moving?"

"I was thinking the same thing. To fill up two 18-wheelers, it would take a lot of cargo. Are they using unused offices or classrooms?" Nathan stopped, then asked, "Should we show these to Clarence and see if he has any idea?"

Mac gave Nathan's question some thought. "Let's hold off. I don't want to put his life in the crosshairs, anymore than it already is."

They finished their surveillance at 2:00 am when the last truck pulled away. The duo tried returning to their vehicle in time to follow the truck, but they never found it.

Mac texted George about their surveillance, then stated they would be in office at 10:00 am and would like to meet with him. Mac laid her head back on the headrest, letting the case run through her mind. The thoughts stopped when she landed on the whiteboard and the words. She promised herself she'd review them before bedtime.

Before they made it home, George replied, "OK."

Chuckling, Mac said, "George must never sleep."

Nathan parked the truck. "How could he? He has us now." Then they both laughed.

They entered Nathan's apartment and never turned on a light. Instead, they walked to their rooms, each collapsing into bed. Mac didn't move until her alarm sounded. When she had showered and dressed, Nathan stood at the stove.

"Are you cooking?"

He glanced over his shoulder. "Yes. I was starving when I got up. Here you go."

The plate on the counter astonished Mac. It held a perfectly cooked egg, two strips of crispy bacon, and one piece of toast. Then he placed a steaming cup of coffee beside it.

"Wow. I didn't expect this. This is fantastic." Mac didn't raise her head until she'd consumed every morsel.

"I'm glad you liked it." Nathan said as he swallowed his last bite. Mac rinsed the dishes, placing them in the dishwasher. Then they headed to the office to meet George.

George wasn't in his office when they arrived, so they headed to the lounge for coffee. When they entered, they found Myles sitting across from George. Myles stood when he saw the duo, hugging Mac and shaking Nathan's hand.

"It's great to see you two."

"Hey, Dad. Glad you're back. Where did your trip take you this time?" Mac inquired.

"Oh, here and there. Drumming up new business." Myles said as he glanced at George.

Nathan saw it too and looked at Mac. Was Myles hiding something? Nathan worried that the mistake would harm Mac. She finally got over Myles, keeping the business from her. Now, he didn't know how she would react.

Mac stared at her dad. Then she turned to George. "Can we meet now?"

She gave her dad a quick hug, turned and walked from the room. Nathan's insides twisted, but he refrained from explaining things to Myles. It wasn't his place yet.

George and Nathan followed Mac to her office. Nathan's things were already in there. Mac pulled a notepad from her backpack. She started at the top and finished talking some thirty minutes later.

The abundance of information left George unprepared. "Joe is still missing, but you contacted Harrison. We're hoping that pans out. Then you have more photos showing transfer trucks backed into the loading docks. Now, you suspect Detective Chinni is part of the coverup."

George took a minute to review his notes. "Any word on the phone number that texted with James?"

"Ionna has that. We'll follow up today." Mac stated.

After he flipped a few more pages, he asked, "Any progress on the words list?" He pointed to the whiteboard as he spoke.

Nathan replied, "That's still in progress."

George pondered the information, including the professor's interviews. He offered, "Work on the photos from last night's surveillance. Mark the same vehicles, then new ones. Have tech track down the transfer trucks. That might lead us somewhere."

"If Joe is dead, who do we work for?"

"Nathan, that is a good question. I'll read the university documents that Joe sent when he hired us. We might work for free. If that's the case, decide if you want to keep going or let it be."

Mac and Nathan looked at the other. Neither wanted to see this end without finding out who killed James.

George watched the pair, knowing their decision. "We have money set aside for this predicament. You don't have to stop if you don't want to. Now, it can't go on forever, but you're good, even if it takes a few months."

"What about other cases?" Mac asked.

"If the leads dry up on this one, you can take another case and work this one too. Your choice."

They nodded in understanding. George stood. "Let me know if you need anything."

When George left, Mac said, "I don't think I can walk away right now. There is something happening at the university, and we need to find out what it is."

"I agree."

They uploaded the photos from overnight onto their computers and marked the duplicates. Then highlighted the new ones. "There are several new vehicles here. What about for you?" Mac asked Nathan without looking up from her computer.

Nathan replied, "Same here. I wonder if Ionna can track the transfer trucks. George never mentioned a name, only tech."

"Call her and ask. We need to follow up on the phone number, anyway."

Nathan tapped Ionna's speed dial button. She answered, "Great minds think alike. I was getting ready to call you. The phone number from James' phone traced back to a burner phone. I don't have the owner's name, but I have the store where it was purchased."

"That's great. Send me whatever you have on it. Now, I have something else for you, but if this isn't in your wheelhouse, just tell me. We have DOT numbers for two transfer trucks. We need to find the owners. Can you help?"

Ionna clicked a key on her laptop and said, "The email should be there for the phone. Yes, I can do that for you. Send me what you have on the trucks."

"Two photos are coming your way. Thanks, Ionna." Nathan said as the call ended.

Nathan opened the email from Ionna and then clicked the document. It showed a barcode from the burner phone, then it gave the duo an address where the burner was purchased and when.

"I'll call the store and see if they'll give us the information. Otherwise, I'm unsure how to get it," Nathan said with a shoulder shrug.

"That's the only way I know, too. Maybe use the word murder. Sometimes pleading works too." Mac offered. With no direction, Mac stared at the whiteboard, covered in random words. Why would James include these words in sentences? As a single word, no one saw a meaning. Did James write sentences with the words?

Mac took paper and pen and started jotting words from the list. She iterated the sentences into something useable, but it still made little sense. Then she had the idea of including words like the, is, a, or an. Thinking it would help construct a sentence. After a few minutes, she got flustered, coming away with nothing.

"Should we finish our report on James' death? Then we can see where things go from there," Mac asked.

"We can do that. Let's tackle that first, then I can make our call to the convenience store where someone purchased the burner phone. I mapped the address, and it's thirty miles from university in a small northeastern Georgia county. If the store isn't busy, it should be easy to find the manager."

The two sat shoulder to shoulder as they worked on James' investigation. It took the better part of two hours to finish it. They discussed what to include in the report and what to hold out. If Paul or Detective Chinni got hold of the report, they wanted the two men to know they have little information on the killer. It's better if they don't know they are suspects.

When they sat back in their chairs, Mac asked, "What reason would Paul have to murder James?"

"If James found Paul doing something illegal on the school grounds, that might push Paul. But otherwise, I can think of nothing."

"Until we can find out what happens in the overnight hours, we're stuck." Mac stated. Then she added, "I thought Joe would call by now."

"Me too. Why don't you deliver the report to George while I call the store for the phone?"

Mac stood, reaching over to the printer for the report, then leaving. George was headed to the lounge for coffee when mac turned the corner, so she tagged along.

"George, here's our report on James' death. We've concluded his death was not a suicide. Included in the report, is our interviews and their beliefs as well."

"Are you sure you want me to turn this into the university? We still have no idea of Joe's whereabouts. Clarence was second in line, and he would be the one receiving the report. Would that put him in danger?"

Mac pondered the question. "Hold on to it until we hear from Joe. We can't chance Clarence being in someone's crosshairs." George nodded as she left, holding two cups of coffee.

When she returned to Nathan, he was still on the phone. Mac perked up when it sounded like the convenience store still had the video from the purchase date. Sipping coffee, and waiting for a word, Mac stared at the board. Something niggled when she saw two words. Wash and ink.

But as Nathan ended the call, she focused on him. "The store still has the video from the phone purchase. We just made it too. The store manager was more than helpful as he agreed to send the photo to me."

"Fantastic. I gave the report to George, but he found out that Clarence's second in line, and I couldn't put his life in jeopardy, so I asked George to hold the report until we found Joe." Mac explained.

"I'm with you. Clarence is already a bundle of nerves, so I can't imagine what this would do to him." Nathan said.

Then Myles stood in the doorway. "Are you two at a stopping point on the professor's case?"

"We can be. Why?" Mac asked.

"We found one of the transfer trucks in Florida. Someone parked it at a Miami dock and left it," Myles said. "The dock supervisor is on video with me showing me the truck and I thought you'd like to see it too."

"Let's go." The threesome walked to Myles' office and found the supervisor still on the video. Myles introduced the duo and gave him a generic reason for wanting the truck to be found.

The supervisor turned his phone so they could view the truck from outside to inside. Nothing looked unusual on the outside, other than someone leaving it behind mountains or shipping containers. They left it here for a reason.

When the guy opened the back door, he yelled, "Oh no! You're not going to want to see this. There's a dead guy in the truck."

Nathan said, "Yes, we do. We need a picture of the dead guy. Can you do it? If not, we'll call the police and have FDLE give us a picture."

"No, I can do it. I was in the service for years. I've seen my share of death." He walked closer to the front of the truck. The light grew dim.

Nathan engaged him in conversation about the service, as they had that in common. Then the guy stopped.

"Uh, you're not going to like this. But there's two people back here. Both appear to have been shot in the back of the head." The guy leaned over, snapping photos of the victims and the inside of the truck. He looked around at the interior, then muttered, "There's another smell in here besides death, but I can't describe it."

Myles stepped in, "I've notified the FDLE. They're sending a team your way. Thanks for the help with this. We're trying to find out what's happening at the university while searching for a killer."

"No problem. If you need anything else from me, you have my number." The supervisor didn't seem fazed by finding two dead bodies. He took it in stride and agreed to text Myles when the FDLE arrived.

Mac and Nathan looked at Myles as he ended the call, then Mac asked, "So, how did you find out about the truck?"

"Ionna put out feelers through our system using the DOT numbers you two found. We got the alert a few minutes ago. That was smart thinking to photograph the vehicles."

"We did it again two nights ago. That's when we saw the transfer trucks. It's so strange to see all the activity overnight at university. There are no visible lights on in the building either, which makes it stranger."

Myles nodded. Then offered, "Let's run the victims through facial recognition. We might get lucky."

Mac and Nathan agreed and headed off to their offices. "What are the odds these guys were at the university?"

Mac's head spun around as she looked at Nathan. "That's a great idea. Let's compare the photos to the ones we took. We can match him to an overnight worker. But if it matches, why did they kill him?"

"I have no answer to that question." Nathan said as he slid under his desk.

While Nathan submitted the queries, Mac walked to her office. She wanted to write each word from the board onto a notecard. They help her put things in order. She could move them around without wasting ink and paper.

By the time she finished, Nathan had submitted his search. He appeared hopeful when he heard his computer beep. "Could the system have found a match that quickly?"

The pair trotted to Nathan's office. He tapped the button, and a face popped up on the screen. It matched one of the dead guys. His name is Pedro Calderon. He was 54, living in Miami. The records gave them his criminal record, starting from before his 18th birthday. Pedro had been involved in gangs, murder, fraud, prostitution, and trafficking people across the border.

Mac stared at the face. "I think this guy was the truck driver. See the scar next to his eye? That's in a picture we have." Mac stepped away, returning with a photo. "Here it is. Isn't that him?"

"Yes, it is. The scar matches. We have our driver, so who is the other guy?"

"No idea. I'll compare it with our photos. Maybe we'll get lucky." Mac offered as she returned to her office.

The supervisor's words about another smell still resonated with Mac. What kind of smell remains after the products are moved? The truck was empty of cargo. Was there residue in the truck that the FDLE could test?

Mac called her dad, suggesting FDLE check for residue. When he asked why, she explained about the smell described by the supervisor.

"You've got the best investigative mind I've ever seen. I'll make the call." Myles said.

Then Nathan appeared at her door with his phone to his ear. He pointed to it and mouthed 'Joe'. Mac stood as she listened to the one-sided conversation. It sounded like Joe feared for his life after receiving a threatening call. The caller advised him to leave town or others would be in danger of losing their lives.

Chapter 6

Mac couldn't believe what she was hearing. Someone threatened Joe and his friends. They must protect those on the board and the faculty. No one is safe around here. But how can they do that? There are too many people that need protection. The next thing Mac heard was Nathan talking.

Nathan said, "Joe is safe bur he wouldn't tell me where he is. There was silence in the background, so if he's at the casino, I wouldn't know."

"We need to call George and explain about the threats. The faculty and board members need to know they could be in danger, even though I feel the folks closest to James would be the target."

Nathan paced as thoughts swirled. "Start with the people on the rooftop with James. If the killer goes after anyone, it would be them."

"We've spoken to them before about their safety. How should we proceed this time? There are too many to surveil with only two of us. But I will feel bad if one gets killed while we try to figure out what James discovered."

"I agree. We do the best we can. That's all anyone can do." Nathan said with a shoulder shrug. "It makes me happy to know Joe is safe. He wants the investigation to continue, and he'll update Clarence.

I confessed we entered his house with Clarence's help. He didn't seem to mind."

The duo stared at the board. They struggled with the random words. Mac got a niggle when she studied the words. There's something there that she can't put together yet. She's closer because she can feel it.

Mac left Nathan, returning to her office. She had the task of comparing the dead guy from the truck to their photos. While daunting work, if she could match it, that would tie both dead people from the truck to the university building. That would be a major lead.

She continued comparing the photo of the people they saw with the dead guy. About halfway through, her eyes grew heavy, so she opted for coffee. She wondered why she felt so sleepy. That's not like her, but she pushed through holding a coffee cup.

"Nathan." Mac called from her office. "I've got a match!"

"You do?"

"Our dead guy was at the admin building the first night we took pictures. I never found him in the second set, but he could've already been in the truck by the time we arrived."

Nathan's cell phone rang as he held the dead guy's picture. When he answered, he smiled, "Great.

Thanks for calling. I'll be waiting." He looked at Mac. "That was the store clerk where someone bought the burner phone. They are sending the video." Two seconds later, Nathan's email alert sounded.

Mac followed Nathan into his office so she could view the video, too. Nathan tapped the keys, and the video opened. They watched a man dressed in black with dark hair pay cash for several burner phones. The man never faced the camera. That proves the man had been there before because he knew about the camera.

Nathan emailed the clerk, asking for the bar codes on the other burner phones the guy had purchased.

"That was a great catch, Nathan. We could have Ionna see if the phones are operational."

Nathan's text message alert sounded. He slid the screen up and opened it. "This is from Joe. He spoke with Clarence. Joe is emailing the university's financials from a different email address and server." Nathan glanced at Mac. "Joe is scared and that worries me."

George popped into Nathan's office. "Why the worried looks?" He took the chair beside Mac and waited for the duo to unload. They did. He quickly realized he needed to take notes because of all the new information the pair had developed since they last spoke.

After the duo stopped talking, George said, "Let me ponder this for a minute. I can already tell you that offering individual protection to that many folks will be out of the question. But we can sequester James' rooftop friends into a single dwelling and handle their protection. Do we have any idea what's going on overnight?"

"No. I asked Dad to have CSI test any residue in the truck found in Miami. The supervisor that showed us the scene mentioned the odor. With two dead men inside, the other odor must be potent if it was noticeable over decomp."

"Good point." George spent a minute reading his notes. "Let me know when the financials come in. We'll get assistance unless you two are knowledgeable about financial mismanagement.

Both shook their heads. "We'd rather someone else take that." Mac said.

Then George suggested they follow up with CSI on the truck and discuss safety with James' friends again. They need to know the ramifications if they choose not to heed our advice.

While the threesome was discussing the case, Joe sent the university's financials for the past three years. "Here are the financials. He sent three of the five years. Whatever James stumbled upon is in this document." The printer jumped to life, and everyone stared at it. Once it had spit out three copies, Nathan handed Mac and George a copy.

"Anyone in particular we should send these too?" Mac asked George.

George glanced at the documents, then said, "Jackson Stroud." He flipped a few pages, then said, "How does a new university bring in this much money? I would assume grants and donations would be the primary source of funding."

Mac and Nathan followed George's lead, turning to the page he studied. Mac's eyes grew wide. Then she turned the page again. "The money grows monthly. They've never struggled with funding. That's impressive."

"Or illegal." Nathan muttered under his breath. "This place stinks. I'm unsure where this money came from, but I doubt it's legal."

All heads nodded in agreement. George couldn't take his eyes off the documents. "I'll stop by Jackson's office because I'd like a word with him before you send it to him. I'll be in touch."

Nathan was unsure how to react to George's statement. Why does he want to speak with Jackson first? George had never done that before. Mac never uttered a word because she focused on the papers.

A few minutes passed when a middle-aged black man stepped up to Nathan's door. "I'm Jackson. George sent me."

"Hi Jackson. Thanks for coming so quickly. This is Mac Morris, my partner." Nathan stated.

"Morris. Are you related to Myles?"

"Yes, he's my father." Mac replied, trying to keep her cheeks from turning red. There's something about working for the owner that makes it hard to keep from blushing. Mac hates it when her cheeks turn red, but she hopes in time they stop.

He shook hands with both agents, then said, "What do you have for me? George told me it was exciting. You don't hear that often in the financials department." Then he chuckled.

Mac and Nathan offered him a chair, and they shared their case with Jackson. He took notes and didn't ask questions until they finished their spiel. He reminded Mac of Tyrone with a wide smile and kind eyes.

"So, you're assuming someone at the university is using it for something illegal? Have you thought about money laundering? They take tainted money, deposit it into the university accounts, then remove it as washed money."

Nathan stared at Jackson while Mac stared at Nathan. Then Nathan turned to Mac. "We haven't

119

discussed the money yet because we don't have a starting place. Where does the university get the money?"

"That's where you two come in. I only handle the money, and I can tell you, just glancing at these papers, something is definitely amiss with this university. Watch your backs. With this kind of money, these folks play to win." Jackson stood and left the room with a promise to follow up with them when he had information.

Neither Mac nor Nathan spoke as they processed Jackson's words. Finally, Mac asked, "What kind of illegal activity could the university be involved in?"

"You name it from drugs, to gambling, to prostitution, to human trafficking. All of these take many people to handle the operation. My question is, where is it happening? There were no lights on again in the building when the trucks were there."

"That makes no sense to me, either. Could we get into the building for a quick look around?"

"No, Mac. That's way too dangerous. We know how they treat their board members and truck drivers. But there must be some way to find out where they are doing business?"

"I agree. We should see the building lit up if they use the classrooms, but then the students that stay on campus would see the building too. So, how are they using the admin building?" Mac asked as she rubbed her neck.

Jackson reiterated his warning about their safety. He strongly urged them to not take unnecessary chances until he got a handle on the financials. Jackson's eyes bore holes into Mac and Nathan until they agreed.

When they left Jackson, Mac said, "I believe he was serious."

"You think? I've never seen a stare quite like that." Nathan paused, then added, "I suggest we listen to him."

"Me too." George rounded the corner, almost bumping into them.

"Who, George? Where are you headed in such a hurry?" Nathan asked.

"I'm looking for you two. We have a client downstairs that I'd like you to meet. It sounds like a clean, quick domestic case. If you want something else on your plate, this might be a great start."

The duo looked at each other, and said, "Okay", in unison.

George grinned as he turned and headed back to the elevators. They rode down to the lobby in silence and exited to a flurry of activity. "What's going on, George?"

"We have several new cases, and investigators are leaving the office after their briefing. This happens regularly. Myles is a brilliant businessman. He keeps us busy with new cases." George opened a small meeting room door, letting Mac and Nathan enter first.

They met a petite blond-haired woman who has been living the good life. She had her hair and nails done to perfection. She wore diamonds on her fingers and her wrists. Beside her chair was a top-notch handbag worth more than Mac's wardrobe.

After the introductions, George asked Lizzie Van Deer to explain her situation. The last name caught Mac by surprise. The Van Deer's hold the titles to multiple high-rise buildings in Atlanta. That family is worth millions of dollars, if not billions. Mac wanted to ask if it was the same family, but she refrained. Instead, she listened to the lady speak.

"Over the last year, my husband, Frederick Corning, has been acting strangely. He stopped coming home from work, or he stayed out late. I want to know what he's doing and who he's doing it with. I refuse to have my name dragged out through TV stories over his escapades."

Mac and Nathan jotted notes, then Mac asked, "Where does your husband work?"

"He's a criminal defense lawyer."

Nathan jumped on the next question. "Has he received any threats from clients?"

"I wouldn't know. He's never shared his business with me. We've been married ten years, and I couldn't tell you one thing about his practice." Lizzie stated with a sadness in her eyes. "We've always trusted each other until now."

Lizzie handed George a piece of paper with physical addresses, emails, social media account names, and phone numbers for herself and Frederick. She asked the duo to start today.

Mac and Nathan left Lizzie with George. They headed to their office to dig into Lizzie and Frederick. The first internet search turned up pages and pages of articles about Lizzie and what she contributed to Atlanta. That answers Mac's question.

The strange part was there was hardly any information on Frederick. There were a few pictures of Lizzie and Frederick together at fundraisers and city events.

Nathan checked on Frederick's law degree because he wondered if he was truly an attorney. "I got something," Nathan offered. "Frederick has a law license, but I show no cases or winnings."

"So, what does he do all day when he leaves home?"

"Let's go find out."

They loaded Nathan's car with surveillance gear and headed to Frederick's office. The address led them to a swanky downtown high rise. Surveillance of a downtown building is problematic because of the parking situation. The duo parked across the street in a parking garage. The second floor was perfect for them, but they had to be extra vigilant because of the traffic.

Nathan backed the truck into the parking space, and they climbed over the seats until they reached the back. While uncomfortable, they would surveil the building from the back end of the Suburban. They had a few hours left of daylight and they hoped to find Frederick leaving the building.

While sitting in the truck, Mac checked Lizzie's information. "She didn't tell us what vehicles they drove."

"Call and ask her. That may solve our problem today since there's few vehicles left in the garage." Nathan suggested.

Mac dialed Lizzie's number and waited until she answered. When Mac introduced herself, Lizzie exhaled. Mac explained what she needed, and Lizzie recited the information from memory, but she failed to give them the vehicle's tag number.

Once she ended the conversation, Mac recited the information to Nathan. They scoped out the visible vehicles and realized they would need to ride the lot. After returning to the front seat, Nathan started the truck and pulled away, following the arrows to the right. As they traversed the parking garage, the higher they climbed, the fewer cars they saw. On floor four, they spotted two. One car was parked next to the stairwell door, and it matched Frederick's.

As they got closer, they noticed the interior light illuminated the area. Nathan muttered, "That's not a good sign."

Mac leaned forward as Nathan stopped several parking spaces away. Their hands rested on their holsters as they stepped from the truck. The only sounds they heard were from the street below. Nathan took the driver's side while Mac crept to the passenger window.

When Nathan reached the driver's seat, he said, "Mac, call an ambulance. Frederick is still alive, then notify George." Mac raced around the front of the car.

"He made someone angry from the looks of the beating he took. What does the note say?" Mac asked as she pointed to the paper poking out from under Frederick's arm.

Nathan snapped photos of the body and its position before plucking the paper from its spot. He held it up for Mac to read.

"That's interesting. 'You'll never learn.' What do you suppose that means?"

Chuckling, Nathan replied, "That our easy domestic isn't as easy as George thought."

Mac nodded. "Simple cases 0, George 2." Sirens grew louder the closer they got to the garage. A police car followed.

Officer Hairston introduced himself, then he asked for our licenses. We produced those, and he said, "I've heard I^2 does great work. Here's your IDs. Take me through what happened."

Nathan explained the circumstances of the discovery of Frederick Corning while Mac spoke with EMS. They suggested Mac call Lizzie so she could meet the ambulance at Grady Hospital Trauma Center. By the expressions on their faces, they question Frederick's survival.

The officer traded cards with the duo as George arrived on the scene. George went straight to Officer Hairston and listened to the duo share their findings. Officer Hairston's radio sounded, so he stepped away to listen to the call.

He returned to the group, saying, "Our CSI team is on the way."

While they waited, Mac and Nathan snapped photos of the car and the beating site. The front seat contained most of the blood, with blood spatter on the inside windshield and on the ground beside the car. They found no weapons in or near the car, leading them to think the attacker took the weapon with them, but a trash can never hurt.

The CSI van rolled up behind the victim's vehicle. A team of four folks exited the van, already dressed in white Tyvek suits. The suits kept the investigators from getting the victim's blood on them and cross contaminating the scene.

Officer Hairston found the duo at a trash can near the opposite stairwell. "CSI has asked for a tow truck. Do you need any more pictures?"

"No. We're good on that. There are no weapons in either trash can on this floor. We're headed to Grady to meet Lizzie, Frederick's wife. Stay in touch." Nathan offered.

"Take care." The officer walked off as his radio crackled.

Mac and Nathan returned to their vehicle as Mac's cell phone rang. "Hey, Dad."

"Yes, we're still in the parking garage, but we're heading to Grady to meet Lizzie. George should be there by now." She listened to her dad explain he had the test results from the transfer truck, and he would meet them in the office tomorrow morning at 9:00.

When the call ended, Mac shared the test results. "That's great. I'm hoping this helps push the investigation forward." Mac nodded her agreement.

Grady Hospital had been in the same spot for decades, situated right next to the interstate. As they rounded the Grady curve on Interstate 75, Mac said, "If I ever get shot, bring me to Grady. They've had the most practice with gunshot victims in all of Georgia."

Nathan's head swung around to see if she was kidding. She wasn't. "That's good to know."

He found a parking spot half-block away. They exited and made their way to the trauma center. George sat next to Lizzie as they waited for word on Frederick's condition.

George nodded to the duo that he needed a word. They stood at the coffee bar while George spoke softly to Lizzie. "She's a wreck. Now she feels guilty for not trusting her husband. We've heard nothing about his condition."

"We no found no weapons. Unless a camera gives us a lead, the attacker picked the perfect spot to deliver his beating." Nathan stated.

George nodded. "What are those odds? Have you ever heard of a perfect crime?"

Both shook their heads. "There are no perfect crimes." Mac repeated the statement she heard countless times at the FBI office. That just meant you had to work harder to find the attacker.

Just as the threesome turned to walk towards Lizzie, a doctor emerged from behind double doors. He made his way to Lizzie. They stood back so she could have privacy. She nodded, and then the doctor left.

George was the first to reach her. "How's Frederick?"

"In a coma. He may or may not recover." Lizzie sniffed, dabbed a tissue at the corner of her eyes, then looked up at George.

"You mentioned earlier you wish you hadn't involved us in your affairs. Do you want to end our agreement? There's no need for surveillance now," George asked.

She shook her head. "I want you to find out who did this to my husband."

George glanced over his shoulder, meeting Mac's and Nathan's stare. "You heard the lady."

"We'll be in touch." Mac said as she and Nathan left the hospital.

When they climbed into the vehicle, Nathan asked, "Why pay us to investigate when the police can do it?"

Mac thought a second, then replied, "Because she can."

Nathan nodded as he checked traffic before turning from the lot. "Let's stop at the office and run a background on Frederick. Since we're meeting Myles in the morning, we need a head start on this one."

"Can we grab supper somewhere? We can eat at our desks," Mac said as she rubbed her stomach.

With the query entered for Frederick's background, the duo ate their meals while discussing the case. Who would beat an attorney and then leave a note at the scene?

By the time they finished, Frederick's background was back. Nathan plucked two copies from the printer, passing one to Mac.

They read it line by line, and when they finished, they looked up with their eyebrows bunched. The pair had the same questions. "Who was Frederick before he became Frederick?" Mac asked first.

"No wonder Lizzie had trust issues. She should have. It looks like Frederick appeared eleven years ago, started courting Lizzie, and eventually married her. But what was his name prior to Frederick? We need to get his fingerprints."

"You're right, Nathan, but that's going to be difficult with him lying in an ICU bed. We can't just walk in there and take them."

"Maybe Lizzie will let us," Nathan offered, hoping he was right.

Mac struggled with her next thought, then it came to her. "Did the CSI team find any prints in the victim's car? They would certainly be Frederick's or whoever he is."

"Good idea. Let's ask." Nathan picked up his phone from his desk, dialing the CSI team leader. They spoke for a minute because the team hadn't run the prints yet. The team leader promised to call in thirty minutes as he would process them himself.

Thirty minutes to wait. They contemplated the note by asking, 'what didn't you learn, Frederick?' They couldn't answer that question because they didn't know the guy's true name. For a guy to go to that much trouble of taking on another identity, he must be hiding from someone. But who and why?

The CSI team leader called back at the twenty-seven-minute mark. "No luck on the prints. Whoever he is, he's not in the system. I'll keep the prints, so we have them for comparison."

"Thanks." Nathan muttered.

"So, we have nothing on Frederick. Now, we need a clean photo of him. Let's run facial recognition.

Maybe something will come from that." Mac dug through the folder on Lizzie, finding a decent picture of Frederick. For some reason, most of his photos are only side views.

Mac entered this query, and they waited again. She rubbed her eyes and her neck as the machine processed image after image.

Nathan brought her out of her drowsiness. "We need to call Clarence and the gang about their protection detail." Mac squinted at him as she tried to open her eyes. He chuckled. "I'll handle it."

Clarence answered on the half ring. Nathan explained their idea and the protection offer. Clarence didn't seem to want it, but he promised to call the others and get back with Nathan as soon as he could. That was all they could do. At least they offered protection. It was up to them to take it.

Mac's computer beeped with the completion of the facial recognition results. There were no positive hits. So, either this guy had never been in trouble with the law, or the photo was skewed.

Nathan asked, "So, we got nothing from that? Who is this guy?"

"I used the best picture we had. Maybe Lizzie has a better one, but I'd have to explain Frederick's background, and I'm not prepared for that yet. We need more information. Let's drive back to his office." Mac suggested.

Instead of sitting around stewing over the lack of information, the duo climbed back into Nathan's truck and headed back downtown. The streets were less busy, which yielded a parking space a half block from Frederick's office building. Nathan swore under his breath as he parallel parked the truck. Mac applauded him for getting it on the first try.

They entered the lobby without issue. No one sat behind the desk at the elevators. So, the duo checked the list of residents and found Frederick's name on the fourth floor. They pushed the button for the fourth floor and waited. The only sounds were the sounds made by the elevator descending to the lobby.

When they exited the elevator on the fourth floor, they stopped short. Something didn't feel right. Strange sounds came from around the corner. The same corner where Frederick's office would be.

The duo laid their hands on their hips atop their holsters. If someone was inside Frederick's office, they would want to know why. They turned the corner, Mac on the right, Nathan on the left. As they crept to the door, the sound faded. That was weird.

Nathan toed the door open, then they entered the office. The first room they entered was a lobby area. One small desk sat in the corner with a few chairs scattered about. The nighttime lights of the city bounced off the wall behind the desk, creating an eerie scene.

Then the noise again. The duo stopped, waiting ten seconds before moving toward the door. Nathan turned the handle, pulling open the door.

Mac entered with her gun drawn. She exhaled when she realized they were alone. "What's that sound?"

"The overturned printer. It's trying to print." Nathan walked over to it, and with gloved hands, he sat it upright but left it on the floor. The printer started printing, but since the ink shifted, the words were illegible.

"Wonder what that said?" Mac muttered.

"From the looks of this place, there is no telling what he was printing." Nathan glanced around at the office and the destruction. There was a piece of furniture that hadn't been overturned or sliced. What were these people looking for? They had dumped every book from the wall shelves onto the floor.

Mac and Nathan heard two male voices in the lobby. They plastered themselves against the far wall, which was out of eyesight from the door. Barely inhaling for fear of being heard, the duo waited.

When the two guys entered the office, Mac and Nathan stepped out, holding their guns in front of them. The two men charged Mac and Nathan. A fight ensued until one guy ran from Nathan after Nathan twisted the guy's arm far enough for his shoulder to pop.

Nathan raced to Mac's side when she hit the guy with a candle holder. Blood spurted from his head wound. Nathan reached out to capture the guy, but he kicked Nathan in the chest with his heel. The air went out of Nathan's lungs in a rush, stopping his approach. He leaned over with his hands on his knees, gulping air as the guy sprinted from the room.

Mac walked over, placing her hand on his shoulder. "Are you okay?" She rubbed his back.

"I am now. How about you?" He gently touched the red knot forming on Mac's forehead.

"I'm mad, but otherwise okay." Mac said as she looked around again. "Do you think the bad guys left anything of value?" She spotted no computer or cell phone in the clutter.

"It doesn't appear so." Nathan took two steps, then stopped. "Except this."

Chapter 7

Nathan pointed to the floor. "Is that what I think it is?"

Mac kneeled to take a closer look. "I think you're right. The carpet is dark, making it hard to differentiate. I probably would have walked over it. That's impressive you spotted it."

"My eyes are different from most. I can see camouflage easily where others struggle with it." Nathan took a few steps. "Here's another one." He continued walking, then turned back to Mac. "But I see no more."

"So, he stopped the blood flow with something, or his partner picked him up and left." Mac paused. "Do you think it punctured an artery?"

"I suppose, but we don't know which direction the guy went. Do you have the CSI kit in the back of the truck?" Nathan asked because he couldn't remember seeing her load it.

"Of course. I'll get it." She said as Nathan stopped her.

"I'll get it. We don't know what's outside." He started for the door but felt a presence. "Why are you following me?"

"I'm your partner. You're not going out there without backup." Mac winked as she held her gun at her side. Nathan sighed, knowing he couldn't stop her.

They returned to Frederick's office without incident, but they discussed feeling like someone was still out there. Mac swabbed both blood drops as Nathan searched for more. Then they searched for the object that caused the loss of blood. They found nothing with blood on it other than the floor.

"Do you think this blood is Frederick's and not our attackers?" Mac asked as she slid the last swab into the case.

Nathan lifted a shoulder, then said, "If it is Frederick's, then we might use it to trace his genealogy. Since he's not in the system, that would be the only way to find out who he is, unless he comes to and confesses."

They left the scene for home. Nathan called Officer Hairston and reported the damage to Frederick's office. He hoped the officer would handle it.

Mac's night was restless as she pondered the cases. Too many questions and not enough answers. She knows when someone suggests a case will be easy, it never is.

The following morning, the duo sat across from Myles in the conference sipping scorching hot coffee and eating a feast. They updated Myles on both cases in between bites. Myles shook his head. "Cases are never easy."

Mac chuckled. "I had that same thought last night. The university case was to break us in on our new role. Frederick's case was supposed to be surveillance only. Look where we are now." Everyone chuckled.

Myles stood from the table, grabbing his laptop from the side table. "Here are the results from the truck found in Miami. It is a hodgepodge of information. Use it how you see fit."

With notepads and pens ready, Myles began delivering the news. "The CSI team found ink, wood splinters, and heroin in the truck's trailer."

Mac inhaled. "I can see you have more."

Myles grinned, "I have some information on ink. CSI explained that ink stains are inorganic. They comprise a specific polymer that varies by manufacturer. These polymers could be styrene acrylate copolymer, a polymer resin, or others. The formulation, granule size and melting point vary the most. So, with that information, they are still working to identify the printer used. There was a vast amount of ink residue, but it some places the collection was so tiny, the computers didn't register."

When Myles paused, Nathan offered, "We can explain away the wood splinters because of the wooden pallets used to transport the goods. Ink and heroin are the two biggest finds. Do we think someone used the ink for labels on the heroin?"

Mac lifted a shoulder, "Isn't is weird if the label is on the top of the heroin brick that the ink made it to the floor of the trailer?"

Everyone stopped and stared at her. "Brilliant." Nathan said, beaming.

Myles grinned, "Yes, that's odd. The only way the ink made it to the floor was if the bricks were on the floor. So, are the wood splinters a byproduct of another job?"

"We watched guys load a trailer with wooden pallets." Nathan stated, explaining the wood splinters were supposed to be there.

"Ok. So now what? Where do you go from here?" Myles asked the duo.

Mac said, "Follow up with Jackson on the financials."

"Call Clarence about their protection. He never called back last night." Nathan said as he glanced at his phone. "Here he is now."

Nathan answered but stepped away, giving Mac and Myles time to chat.

"How do you like it so far?" Myles asked.

"We both like it. It's like the FBI without the rules. The only part we struggle with is information gathering. We can't throw warrants at people anymore. We're having to get information any way we can." Mac explained.

Before Myles could answer, Nathan returned. "Clarence and the others refuse our protection. They promised to call the police if needed."

"We've done all we can." Mac said with sadness in her voice. "But whoever killed James is not done. They will protect their enterprise no matter what."

Nathan looked at Mac with an idea. "Are they transporting heroin from the university? That would explain the residue."

"Is that what was on those pallets?" Mac asked with shock on her face.

Shrugging his shoulders, Nathan replied, "Whatever it was, it was in square boxes."

"We should've followed that truck." Then she chuckled. "Well, maybe not all the way to Miami."

Myles added, "I feel certain they would've spotted you before, Macon." Then he chuckled. Standing, he walked to the door, then turned to face the pair. "Do you think Paul is heartless enough to conduct his heroin business from inside a university building?"

In unison, the pair answered, "Yes."

No one laughed at that. Instead, Myles shook his head. "Then bring him down. Regardless of who's paying the bill. We need that stuff off the streets." Myles left the pair with their mouths hanging open.

Nathan asked, "Did he just say that?"

"I believe so," Mac said as she gathered her things. On their way to their offices, Mac suggested Nathan call Jackson for an update on the money. She wanted to dig deeper into Paul Drummond.

Nathan shared he wanted to run a background on Paul before contacting Jackson. He wanted more information. When he reached his office, he entered the search for Paul's background and the duo waited until they heard the beep. They were curious if Paul had a criminal past.

He opened the report and said, "Paul has no criminal past. He's married with no children. The only oddity is the number of times they've moved. They show nine addresses in six states, most of which are in the southeast. One stint was two-years in New Jersey."

Mac's head tilted. Why would Paul move so often? Do university presidents change that much? Mac didn't bother with questions because she didn't know which ones to ask first. She went to her office and started an internet search about university presidents. The search proved interesting, as most presidents stay on for years. So why did Paul move so frequently?

Then Mac had an idea. She plotted each address on a map. The universities seemed to be along an interstate system. "Does that mean anything?" She muttered to herself, thinking back on Paul's information. He said he changed universities to help grow their enrollment, but some already had a healthy enrollment. There's a word from our board. She turned and circled the enrollment.

Nathan offered, "Have you circled the words we've found in the investigation?"

Mac swung around toward the door. "No, I haven't, but that's a good idea." With a different colored marker, she circled the words they'd encountered. "That leaves only a few. These words appear to be in the financial field. Maybe Jackson could help us."

"Let's work on a scenario. Paul buys heroin to resell. Once his market hits the peak or the police come knocking, he picks up and moves. If he uses a few classrooms in an unused part of the building, who will suspect tit. Paul pays people to repackage it with his label, then to transport it. There's your ink and heroin."

Nodding, Mac asked, "When we were watching the building, do you honestly think all those pallets held heroin? That was an enormous amount."

Nathan thought about it for a second before answering, "How much money would that much heroin be worth?"

"I've no idea." Nathan left her to her thoughts.

Over the next few hours, Mac called references from Paul's past universities. One lady she spoke with claimed Paul was extraordinarily talented at growing enrollment, but no one knew how he did it. The moment she said their enrollment numbers dropped when Paul left, Mac's niggle was back. Mac asked a few more questions, then ended the call.

Two universities refused to speak with her about Paul. That leads Mac to believe that he left under suspicion of something.

She leaned back in her chair and pondered what she learned. Does Paul add fake students to the roster? If he did that, he would need money to go with it. Where does the money come from and what does he have to gain by spending money on fake students?

A word from the board jumped out at her. She turned her chair, spotting the word assumption. What did James assume? Did he call the same university and ask about Paul? What makes Paul leave a university for another one?

Nathan leaned against the door frame when Mac turned around in her chair. "Nathan, you know better than to sneak up on an armed person." She smirked.

"I didn't sneak. You just didn't hear me. But I have news." He explained Jackson's information. Paul has money in his personal accounts from a direct deposit from the university. But the kicker is the offshore account in the Caymans. It is staggering at upwards of fifty million. He traced it through the PPD LLC from the rental car. The offshore account has another company name on it, but Paul and his wife own it.

"That proves he is doing something illegal. I would think. How else could someone his age rack up that kind of money?" Mac reached up and rubbed her neck.

They sat across from each other at Mac's desk. Mac doodled on paper. She uses mind maps and notecards to help her sort scenarios. As she doodled, she scribbled questions on paper. Nathan watched her because he thought the process fascinating.

"Since we have the money trail, we can't alert Detective Chinni. He unnerves me to the point he might work with Paul. Do you think he pushed James from the ledge?"

"He's in my top two." Nathan stated in a matter-of-fact tone.

Then Mac mumbled, "I wish the others would let us sequester them for protection."

Nathan nodded in response, but they couldn't force the protection. So, he let it go when Clarence told him about their decision. They had enough on their plates with both cases.

Mac's cell phone rang. Glancing at the caller ID, she said to Nathan, "It's Lizzie." Then she answered. Nathan waited as Mac spoke quickly. He knew something had happened. Mac stood, motioning for Nathan to do the same. They walked to the trucks with Mac still on the phone.

Finally, Mac ended the call by telling Lizzie they were on the way to the hospital. "Step on it. Someone tried to kill Frederick in the hospital."

Nathan pulled them into the parking lot within fifteen minutes of the call. Lizzie met them in the ICU waiting room. Mac felt bad for her. "Lizzie, what happened?"

"I just spoke with the doctor. Someone entered the ICU and attempted to smother Frederick. An alarm sounded, and a nurse rushed into the room in time to see the attacker. He turned on her, sending her to the floor. Her head hit the wall on the way to the floor. While another nurse was on her way to Frederick's room to help, the attacker rushed past her. The first nurse has a concussion and will recover. Frederick had a setback with the lack of oxygen, but they stabilized him."

Nathan asked, "Did you call anyone else other than us?"

"No, Nathan, I didn't. Hospital security responded by searching for the guy, but he was gone by the time they arrived." Lizzie explained.

"Ok. I'll step away and meet with the hospital security. We know the leader from our past. I should be able to get video footage of the attacker." Nathan offered.

While he walked away, Mac directed Lizzie to a chair. She wondered if now was a good time to share what they learned about Frederick. Then she decided to wait for Nathan. Maybe Lizzie wasn't strong enough to hear the news.

The ladies sat quietly while Nathan was away. Every so often, Lizzie would comment about Frederick. She admitted to wondering about his past because he never mentioned family or friends. Her friends were his friends. But none of this mattered until now, because it was obvious Frederick had gotten himself mixed up in something.

Mac cringed as she listened to Lizzie ramble because she could answer a part of Lizzie's questions. They knew Frederick was a fake. But they still didn't know his given name. At that point, it concerned Mac that the background didn't offer any AKAs. If a person uses a different name, the background check would pick it up, but this one didn't. That's unusual. Mac filed that information for another time as Nathan entered the room.

"We should have the video within the hour. Although, no one identified him since he wore a surgical mask, scrubs, and a head covering."

"I'd still like to see. Maybe we could spot something else," Mac offered.

"That's what I said. I asked about entry to the ICU and the security leader admitted to not knowing how the attacker entered. He could have a badge belonging to someone else or he passed someone exiting the ICU." Nathan stopped for air, then he added, "No one said the ICU is a hundred percent secure. So, we'll have a guard outside of Frederick's room from now on until we solve this."

Lizzie looked at the pair. "Put the charge on my bill. I'll pay it."

Mac stepped away and dialed George. She explained their predicament, and he said a guard would be there in an hour. When she finished with George, Mac nodded for Nathan to join her at the coffee bar. While they poured their coffee, Mac asked Nathan about sharing Frederick's background with Lizzie.

He paused, looked at Lizzie, and shook his head. They needed something concrete to prove who Frederick is, and they don't have that yet.

The threesome sat shoulder to shoulder, waiting for the guard to show. Thirty-five minutes later, a block of guy showed at the door. Nathan greeted him first, just in case he wasn't part of the team. The guy was from an outside security firm, and he asked to be called Brice.

Nathan introduced Brice to the others. Lizzie was a little taken aback by his size, but his personality won her over. Brice had her laughing in no time.

The group met with Frederick's doctor, introducing Brice. Brice would be a family member who would stay in the room with him. This would allow Lizzie time at home to rest.

Brice took up his position, while Mac and Nathan escorted Lizzie to her car. They would follow her home as a precaution.

When the car doors closed, Mac asked, "Do you think Frederick's attacker would come after Lizzie?"

"It doesn't appear so, but who knows? I'd rather be safe than sorry. Lizzie certainly couldn't protect herself against an attacker. She falls apart at the thought." Nathan explained.

The trip to her house was uneventful. They never spotted a tail, so they assumed all was well. Until they turned the corner and spotted patrol cars in Lizzie's driveway.

Lizzie braked hard when she noticed the activity. Nathan drove around her car, entering the driveway first. She followed.

Nathan and Mac found an officer who called Officer Hairston from the house. "Ah. I wondered where you were."

"Someone tried to kill Frederick in the hospital a little while ago. That's how we showed up here. We followed Lizzie home because she was falling apart." When they looked at her, she sat in the car. "What happened here?"

"We answered a silent alarm. The back door was open, but no one was inside when we arrived. We assume the intruder left when he heard sirens as the first officer arrived within three minutes of the alarm."

Nathan asked, "Was anything disturbed other than the door?"

"Not that we can tell. We'd like your client to look around and let us know if anything is missing." The guys looked at Mac. She took the hint and walked to Lizzie's car.

Lizzie stood at her car while Mac explained the circumstances for the police presence. She asked, "What in the world is going on? This is too much." She looked like she would pass out, but she recovered enough to walk to the front door.

Mac stood on one side while Nathan was on the other. She held onto Nathan's upper arm for support. When they crossed the threshold, she exhaled. Everything was in its place. That made her feel better, so she released Nathan from her grip and walked away from the pair.

She checked every room in the house before returning to the foyer. "I see nothing missing. Evidently, something scared him away. I'll not stay here alone. I packed my bag and made reservations at a downtown hotel."

Everyone nodded because under the circumstances, that was brilliant. Officer Hairston finished his report, then muttered to Nathan and Mac that something was going on here. The duo nodded in agreement. Then Hairston offered his services in his off time. Nathan head tilted at that comment but didn't question it.

The pair followed Lizzie to an older hotel that had been in Atlanta for decades. The doorman greeted her, took her keys and bags from the trunk. Nathan explained their presence and gave the doorman his card. The doorman promised to keep a watch on Lizzie, and he would notify the others of the potential danger.

Mac and Nathan left Lizzie and returned to the office, where George waited for them. "I know you've had a long day, but I need an update."

"Gladly, because we need to discuss it anyway."

The threesome moved to the conference room after they stopped for coffee. Once settled, Mac asked, "Do you want to start with James or Frederick first?"

George's eyebrows shot up. "You've had updates on both."

"Yes. It's been a day." Mac and Nathan glanced at each other.

"Let's start with Frederick. His issue seems the most critical given the situation at the hospital."

Nathan started on the updates with Frederick's background, the attempted murder, then Mac jumped into the story when they followed Lizzie home. George's eyes grew wide by the time the story ended. "Does Lizzie know about Frederick's background yet?"

"No, we haven't shared. She had such a rough day that we decided we needed more information on him first." Mac replied.

"Ok. Now to James' case." George prompted.

Mac shared the test results from the residue, then added the information she garnered from Paul's past university jobs. George jotted notes as information came to him full force.

"What are you two thinking about James' death? Do you have suspects?" George asked.

Nathan replied. "We have two suspects right now. Paul Drummond and Detective Chinni."

George choked on Nathan's words. "Detective Chinni?" He titled his head and squinted his eyes as he studied the pair. "This isn't a joke, is it?"

"No joke, George." Nathan and Mac shook their heads in sync.

"What makes you suspect a detective?"

Mac took over, rattling off the reasons they felt Chinni was involved in some way. They suggested Drummond had Chinni on his payroll to look the other way, not necessarily the killer, but then again, he could have killed Paul.

As George listened, his mind worked on scenarios, placing Chinni in Drummond's back pocket. He glanced at the pair, then said, "Both suspects are plausible. Does Chinni have an inkling you suspect him?"

"No, we have no proof of either, yet. But we'll get it," Mac stated.

When the meeting ended, Nathan turned back to George. "Ionna is helping ID the blood at Frederick's office. She offered genealogy sites. Is that acceptable?"

"Absolutely. We've used it in the past. It's amazing to watch Ionna track the genealogy records." George shared.

The duo headed off to their offices before going home. They handled email and returned calls. Mac checked in on Lizzie, who was resting comfortably. Frederick would be lucky to make it through the night.

Mac felt bad for Lizzie, but when she tells Lizzie about her husband's past, it may be the best for both. She escapes the public scrutiny, and he finally escapes whoever chases him.

Ionna called Nathan, and she invited the duo to her office tomorrow for the genealogy lecture. She was ready to search for the ID, and since the blood owner wasn't in the database, they would use her genealogy skills.

Mac's body needed rest. When she stood from her chair, a wave of nausea overtook her. She sat back down and that's where Nathan found her. "Hey, Mac. Are you okay? You're pale."

"I can't answer that right now. When I stood, nausea hit me. Let me try again." With Nathan by her side, Mac stood without incident. "That was weird. I don't feel bad."

"It doesn't feel like you have a fever. Are you dehydrated?"

"That might be part of it. I haven't been drinking water today." Mac offered, but feared it was something worse than dehydration.

She stopped by the break room and grabbed a bottle of water and downed it before entering the elevator. Nathan chuckled, "You keep doing that and we'll have to stop for a potty break before we get home."

Mac smiled. "I think I can make it."

When they reached the parking lot, Mac doubled over in pain, throwing up her water. Nathan said, "We're going to the ER." Then he plucked his cell phone from his pocket and dialed Myles. Myles was still in the lab when he got the call. He and George raced to the parking lot with minutes of getting word.

"She had one nausea spell, then she finished a bottle of water in seconds, throwing it up here." Nathan explained the urgency.

"Take her Grady. We're following."

Nathan expertly drove their vehicle to the Emergency Department Entrance. Myles was already inside speaking with a doctor by the time Nathan arrived. A nurse met Nathan at the car door with a wheelchair. Mac looked at Nathan before sitting in it.

As the nurse rolled Mac through the double doors, he lifted a prayer. He'd never seen Mac sick, and he didn't like it. Nathan had barely turned off the truck before throwing open the door and running for the ER. When he reached the waiting room, he found Myles standing at a window with his back to Nathan. He spoke softly, so Nathan assumed he discussed Mac's situation with Mary.

George waved Nathan to a corner spot. "The doctor is with her. They will run tests and then let us know the issue. Did she mention feeling ill at any point today?"

Nodding, Nathan added, "Not at all. While we were busy, we had lunch on the run. She never spoke of feeling bad."

Neither spoke as they watched Myles walk toward them. "I told Mary about Mac. She's calling the boys. They'll all be here within the hour."

It shocked Nathan to hear that everyone would come to the hospital. He never had that kind of support in his life, and he finds he likes it. Minutes ticked by and Nathan grew restless. What would happen if he lost Mac? He never really thought about that, but in their line of work, it's bound to come up. Would he stay with Myles and George and the biggest question is if they want him without Mac?

He decided he would discuss it with George first. But then he said he could find a job some place else, especially with his resume now.

Fifty minutes passed before the rest of Mac's family showed. Mary hugged Nathan, then he shook hands with her brother's. He felt like he belonged here, and that swelled his heart. He'd never had the opportunity to have siblings, and since both parents were gone, he had no true family.

Mary asked Myles about Mac as worry lines etched deeper into her forehead. Myles laid his hand on top of Mary's and spoke softly, soothing her nerves.

A few minutes later, a doctor entered the waiting room and stopped when he saw the number of folks sitting in the corner. "Are you all for Mackenzie Morris?"

Everyone stood, saying, "Yes." There were so many, and no one objected to the group, so he continued. "All tests came back negative. We're monitoring her, but right now, it appears to be a virus. We've taken more blood and are running cultures. She'll remain her until I know for certain her diagnosis."

Nathan was first with the question, "When can we see her?"

"Ah. You must be Nathan. You're her parents." He pointed to Myles and Mary. "Then that makes you two her brothers, and you're George."

Laughter sounded from the room as they realized Mac spoke of them. The doctor looked at the group. "She can have visitors, but I must confirm the illness isn't contagious. Until then, you'll have to wear protective gear. The nurses are putting the clothing outside her door. We'll have our answer in a few hours."

Nathan suggested Myles and Mary visit first, followed by her brothers, then he and George would finish her visits for a while. Everyone agreed, so Nathan stepped to the coffee bar. Just when you dream of a quiet night at home, something spoils it.

George and Nathan spent the time discussing both cases. "Nathan, you and Mac have a great sense about you in your investigations. But it concerns me you're suspecting a detective of crime. While it's not unheard of, I'd tread lightly. You have no idea how violent this guy can be."

Chapter 8

"Of course we will. We've mentioned it only to you and Myles. We know we need more evidence to corroborate our theory. It's just that Chinni is involved with the university way more than necessary. We caught him and Paul in a heated discussion at the school and he stammers when we ask questions about Paul."

George nodded his acknowledgement as Mac's brothers entered the waiting room. Nathan jumped up when he realized he could see Mac. He strode from the room, not willing to wait for George. They entered Mac's room together. It relieved Nathan to see Mac sitting up in bed sipping on a drink.

Mac lifted her arms for a hug and Nathan gladly obliged. Then she hugged George. "Thanks for hanging with me. The reason for this visit remains unknown. But I feel fine now."

"Let's see what the doctor says before you discharge yourself." Nathan said with a snicker. She expressed her displeasure of being in a hospital on multiple occasions, so Nathan expected her to weasel her way out of this one.

Mac lay back on her pillows, knowing she lost the fight. "Did you discuss the cases?"

"Yes, we did. George suggested more evidence on Paul, and any evidence on Chinni must be ironclad. No sense ruining someone's career over nothing." Nathan explained.

Mac agreed. "How's Lizzie?"

"She's safe at the hotel. I'm unsure how long she'll remain there. I need to check on Frederick too," Nathan added.

A nurse entered the room, changing out the IV bags. Nathan asked, "What are those for?"

"Fluids. We've been pushing fluids since the initial tests were negative. It appears it was a virus, but I'll let the doctor explain." The nurse explained as she completed her task and left.

Mac suggested everyone go home, get some sleep, and be ready to offer her a ride home later today. Nathan shook his head. "I'm not going anywhere." Then he looked at George.

"I'll let the others know." He reached over, touching Mac's leg. "See you later, kid."

"Thanks, George." Mac laid her hand on his, then he left.

Nathan sat in the recliner and grunted. "I've slept on worse things, so I'll be fine. You need the sleep." Nathan stood, kissed Mac on the cheek and said, "I love you, Mackenzie Morris."

"I love you too. Thanks for being here."

"There's nowhere else I'd rather be." Nathan sat in the recliner, forcing it back. With his legs in the air, he was asleep in five minutes. Mac envied his sleeping abilities. She takes forever to drift off. She can't turn her mind off.

The doctor arrived shortly after nine, waking up the duo. Mac felt like she had just closed her eyes. "Doctor?" She mumbled with a groggy voice.

"I have good news. Your overnight tests also reveal negative results. We're discharging you with instructions to return to the ER immediately in you feel the least bit of discomfort."

"Sounds good. When can I leave?" Mac asked.

"As soon as we process the paperwork, a nurse will escort you to the main entrance. I'm assuming Nathan will see you get home safely." He looked toward Nathan, who nodded.

He turned, leaving the room. Mac texted everyone before she slid from the bed, heading to the bathroom to change clothes. When she emerged, she grinned.

"What?"

"Can you take me to the office?" Mac asked.

"No, I cannot. You need to shower and rest. Take a nap, then I'll pick you up later." Nathan suggested.

Mac didn't counter because she knew she'd lose this battle. She could use a nap, anyway. While they waited for the nurse, Nathan's text sounded. He moaned when he saw it. "I forgot we had an appointment with Ionna about the genealogy today. Let me reschedule it."

"No, don't do that. Meet her. We need no more delays."

"But Mac, I thought you wanted to see it, too."

"I do, but this case is more important than me watching how they use genealogy. I'll catch the next one, or you can explain it to me," Mac said, grinning. But her insides twisted as she said it. She trusts Nathan, but she questions Ionna's motive.

An hour later, Mac stood underneath a steaming hot water spray, and it felt good. Nathan was right. She needed a shower. She felt like a new person when she emerged.

Nathan's hair was still wet when he walked into the kitchen. "I'm going to the office to meet Ionna. I'll be back in three hours to pick you up if you feel up to it."

"I'll be ready." Mac lifted her heels from the floor, kissing Nathan before he left.

Mac ate a piece of toast, hoping it stayed down. When it did, she wandered to her room, hoping sleep would take over quickly.

It concerned Nathan that Mac wanted him to meet Ionna alone. He knows how she feels about Nathan. While he drove, he tried not to make too much of it, but it still bugged him.

Nathan texted George when he entered the building, letting him know Mac was at home sleeping while he was meeting Ionna.

Ionna met Nathan at the door. "Nathan, why didn't you tell me about Mac? We could have pushed this for a day or two."

"She asked me to meet you so we can get a name." Nathan offered.

Ionna replied, "Well, let's get started." Nathan noticed how businesslike she acted today and wondered why.

His answer sat in a chair in Ionna's office. "George. I didn't know you were coming."

"I wanted to hear about genealogy and since Mac can't be here, I thought I'd take her place."

"Great. Let's get to it."

Ionna sat at her desk and projected her screen to the wall behind her head, which impressed Nathan. She described her technique of tracing the bloods lineage. Until you find the person you're looking for.

She highlighted this blood sample. Then another slide showed multiple legs coming from the drop. These legs, as she called them, are potential relatives. Ionna continued walking through the process until she covered ten slides. On the eleventh slide, she had a word written in big letters: "BINGO."

George and Nathan sat up straighter in their chair in anticipation of the next slide. When Ionna clicked the slide, Frederick's face appeared, but he bore another name. Dunson Dewberry.

Both George and Nathan stared at the slide. Finally, Ionna asked, "Everything okay?"

Nathan cleared his throat and said, "That's the best thing I've seen in a long time. Brilliant."

Ionna beamed as George reiterated Nathan's words. "Now, let's go find out who Dunson Dewberry really is."

The guys couldn't get to Nathan's office fast enough. They wanted to dig into Dunson's background. Something was amiss with this guy changing names from Dunson to Frederick.

Nathan entered the request, and they waited. It seemed to take longer than usual, so they grabbed coffee while the request finished. The computer alert was sounding when they turned the corner. Sharing a glance, they trotted the rest of the way to the office.

With two copies of the background, each man read the report once, then they reviewed it again. Nathan spoke first. "This is a mess. Dunson Dewberry is from Chicago and disappeared from there ten years ago. So he comes here, finding love with Lizzie. But what happened in Chicago that caused him to vanish?"

"Something caused him to leave Chicago and take another identity. Who found him after all these years? He must have made someone angry for them to hold a grudge this long."

"I agree with you, George. Let me call Chicago PD and see if anyone can or will help us." Nathan said. Although, he was unsure what questions to ask or which department handled something like this. Then he shrugged his shoulders and dialed a number.

George sipped coffee, listening to Nathan and rereading the report. He liked Nathan as a person and an investigator. Nathan's people skills were unmatched. Every time the detective on the other end answered a question, Nathan had another one. They spoke for forty-five minutes before Nathan ended the call.

"It seems our guy is a scammer. He's wanted not only in Chicago, but California and Texas. The detective showed he scams older women out of their money, then picks up in another state."

George tilted his head, saying, "We need to share our information with Lizzie. She deserves to know, even though she still loves him."

Nathan and George climbed into Nathan's vehicle and drove to meet Lizzie at a nearby coffee shop. Despite dressing to the nines, she looked tired. Her eyes were red rimmed. They sat across from her and she wiped her eyes with a napkin. "I'm sorry I can't stop the tears. Frederick passed a little while ago with an aneurysm."

George expressed his condolences first, followed by Nathan. That was Nathan's cue to continue with their meeting. Nathan apologized for delivering more disturbing news to her, but when he finished, he noticed the tears had stopped.

"So, Frederick's real name is Dunson Dewberry. That's crazy." Lizzie stammered.

Nathan pulled Ionna's information, proving the news.

"How can that be? Wouldn't I have noticed strange things or was I so in love I was blinded?" She continued. "Wait. Now, that I think back, Frederick or Dunson always refused to have his picture taken. I have a few, but they are only from the side. He was hiding, wasn't he?" Her sad eyes bounced from George to Nathan.

George took her hand. "It's looking that way. I would check your bank accounts and make certain everything is in order." Her eyes went wide.

"Please tell me he didn't siphon money from me. That's all I need. I feel so stupid letting that man into my life." The tears began sliding down her cheeks and there was no stopping these. Lizzie leaned into George and held her until they subsided. Nathan watched the exchange as he had never seen George so compassionate with anyone but Mac. He loves her like his own.

When Lizzie composed herself to speak, Nathan asked, "Did the hospital do an autopsy on Frederick, I mean Dunson?"

"I can't answer that. Why would you ask that question?"

George, still in her hand, said, "Outside events can cause Aneurysms."

"Outside events. What does that mean?" She titled her head as she met his eyes.

George cleared his throat. "Pumping a syringe full of air into an IV has caused aneurysms in some folks."

"Are you saying someone killed him? Because if they did, the police didn't do their job." Now anger flashed in her eyes as she spoke. "That would be your protection detail, right?"

George didn't hide from the obvious. "Yes, it does. We'd like to confirm if the aneurysms occurred naturally."

"Why is everyone always out to protect themselves? No one cares anymore." Lizzie paced back and forth in front of the men as she twisted a tissue in her hands. George's eyes never left her.

"Lizzie, that's not so. We cared enough to move you here, and we cared enough to place a guard at Dunson's door. If someone murdered him on our watch, we want the killer."

Lizzie returned to her chair, taking George's hand. "You'll find out who did it if someone killed him."

This time Nathan spoke, "Absolutely."

Lizzie hugged George, then she smiled for the first time since they arrived. "I'll call the hospital and ask about the autopsy."

"Is there anyone we can call for you?" George asked, clearly concerned for her.

"No, thank you. I'll be fine." Lizzie replied as a tear slid down her face.

George wanted to stay with Lizzie, but Nathan wanted to return to the office. So he finally told Lizzie he had to go to work, but not before passing her his cell phone number.

Then he said, "Call that number when you get the word on the autopsy."

She nodded, and his hand slid from hers. Nathan noticed the connection but refrained from bringing it up. The walk to the car was quiet. Nathan checked his phone for messages and grinned when he saw one from Mac.

He shared it with George. "Mac is awake and ready to work."

"Tell her not so fast. We'll finish today and she can join us tomorrow if she's up to it," George stated as he glanced back at the hotel.

Nathan sent a reply, ending it with a red heart. As he slid into the driver's seat, George said, "I think I'm in love." Nathan dropped the keys on the floorboard because George's statement was such a shock. He recovered quickly.

"Now, George, she just lost a husband. You can't be serious."

"Oh, I'm serious, and you'll keep your mouth shut, too. Not a word to anyone, especially Mac."

"How am I supposed to keep this to myself? I watched your exchange with Lizzie. There's love on both sides. She didn't want you to leave."

George lifted an eyebrow. "I didn't either." Then he laid his head back on the headrest.

Nathan glanced at George and grinned before backing out of their parking space. As they passed a few cars, Nathan caught a glimpse of movement. Two men entered a black Dodge Charger and then jumped in line behind them.

He kept his eye on the rearview mirror for a few blocks, then said, "We have a tail, and they have partners."

"What?" George lowered his mirror, using it to watch the vehicle follow two cars behind them. "And what do you mean, they had partners?"

"I may be wrong on that one, but when I saw movement in the parking lot, four men stood together. Two climbed into the black Charger, and I'm unsure of the other two. Call Lizzie and make sure she stays inside. We're coming back to her."

George grabbed his phone and dialed. He listened to it ring before it clicked over to voice mail. He ended the call, dialing again. "She's not answering."

They were driving along a downtown street, so there was only so much room to maneuver. Nathan quickly turned on a side street, hoping to outrun the tail. George kept dialing while Nathan kept driving. Then he said, "Call the concierge. He said he'd help if we need him."

George dug out the phone number and dialed, waiting for an answer. The guy answered, but he sounded winded. "Hurry. They got her." He shouted.

"Lizzie's been kidnapped."

Nathan floored the car, using his horn to move drivers out of his path. This is another time he could have used his emergency lights. Luckily, they were two minutes from the kidnappers. The concierge gave George a description for the car and the men. George called Atlanta PD to help locate the car.

As they worked to find the car, the black Charger stayed behind them. Three minutes later, an Atlanta PD helicopter flew over the city, searching for the kidnapping victim's car. George's phone sounded. Grabbing it, he listened to the helicopter copilot relay on time information.

"Nathan, go left at the next light. They spotted the car at an abandoned building next to the interstate. Now turn right, then an immediate left." Just as George finished his last direction, the black Charger tried to do a pit maneuver on Nathan.

But he was ready.

Nathan out maneuvered the driver, sending the Charger into a spin. They struck a brick building with a head on impact. Nathan's vehicle skidded to a stop. Both men ran to the occupants as smoke poured from the wrecked car.

George reached the passenger first, pulling him to safety. But the steering wheel pinned the driver down. Nathan pulled at the driver, trying to free him, but it was useless. Instead, he backed away and watched as flames engulfed the car, taking the driver too.

The passenger was unconscious so he would be off with no help to them. So, the guys pilfered through the guy's pockets. They found a cell phone and a driver's license. Illinois issued the license. So, these guys were possibly from Chicago. How did they find Dunson?

Nathan lifted the license for George to see. "Looks like they found him." Then he paused. "Do you want reinforcements, or do you feel comfortable getting Lizzie with just me?"

"You'll do." Nathan said with a grin.

They found the other car parked next to the building's side, out of view. The men walked the perimeter, looking for a way inside. There were two doors on the back side of the building, but without a blueprint, they did not know where the doors led.

George sent a text, then grabbed Nathan's arm. "Wait. I know someone who can help us."

Sixty seconds passed before George received a reply. He pulled up the text, then clicked the attachment. The blueprints appeared. They studied the tiny picture, trying to make sense of the layout.

171

Until it clicked. It appeared that this was a warehouse, but someone had converted the inside into apartments. That made things much worse because they had so much more area to focus.

Nathan saw George text someone, but he didn't ask about it. George explained, "I texted Myles our dilemma. We can't search that many apartments with just the two of us."

Then Myles replied, "On my way."

With the situation being so close to the office, their help arrived within minutes. Myles opened the van, grabbing the heat sensor. This would give them an idea of where they're holding Lizzie. It turns out Lizzie had two captors, just like they were told. They were in the middle of the building on the third floor. Two people were mobile while the other one never moved.

George sucked in his breath when he noticed Lizzie was most likely tied to a chair. "If they hurt her." Then his statement trailed off as anger bubbled to the surface.

Myles heard it and glanced at Nathan, who lifted an eyebrow but said nothing. Three other guys stood around dressed in tactical gear, awaiting instructions. Myles called the group together, explaining Lizzie's location.

One guy, the entry man, asked two clarifying questions, then he snapped his radio on his chest.

He was ready. The entry person gave the team a clear path into the target area. While they would love to have their entry be silent, they know that's not likely. So they carried gear to the chosen entry door.

The guy placed his gear on the ground. He glanced at the lock on the door, checked for explosives, then grinned. As he walked to the door, he plucked a tool from his bag. Kneeling, he took a closer look at the lock, then he reached up, grabbing it in his left hand, while cutting it off with his right.

Myles smiled. There are few entries this silent. As long as they didn't miss a camera, they would make it to the third floor undetected. George opened the door, clearly eager to see Lizzie safe.

They marched two by two. Myles instructed George and Nathan to bring up the rear. They would cover Myles. George wanted to be in the front, but he understood those guys had the proper gear for the operation. How could he help Lizzie if he took a shot in the gut?

The group took the stairs, carefully checking the landings before proceeding past the stairwell doors. When they reached the third-floor stairwell, they stopped, turned to face Myles. He glanced at his phone, reading a text.

"Targets remain in place. The operation is a go."

Another team member turned the knob slowly, bringing the door into the stairwell. Myles walked over and stood with his back to the door, and his foot holding the door open for his team to enter the third floor. Once they cleared the doorway, they heard voices coming from the other side of the elevators.

The team split with George, Nathan and Myles heading one way while the heavy fire power went the other way. Myles hoped the others would create havoc so they could save Lizzie.

Myles counted down from three in a whisper over their radios. When he reached zero, the armed tactical team breached the area where Lizzie was being held. As soon as gunfire erupted, Myles knew it was time to find Lizzie.

When the men turned the corner, they spotted Lizzie inside a room. The kidnappers failed to close the door upon the breach. Myles told George to get Lizzie while he and Nathan would hold off the bad guys.

Then there was silence, except for heavy breathing. "Myles, we're clear. We need an ambulance."

"For one ours?" Myles hated this part.

"No. Both kidnappers."

Myles radioed for an ambulance, then joined Nathan. George hugged Lizzie, who was sobbing.

The kidnappers had tied her to a chair, creating deep cuts on her wrists and ankles. Her eye was swollen shut from the hit.

The EMS workers suggested Lizzie go to the hospital to be checked because of the head blow she endured. They wrapped her injuries in gauze, and George told them he would take her.

George reached his hand out in front of Nathan. After looking at it, he took his keys and placed them in George's hand. "I'll deliver it to you safely." Then they left.

"Nathan, you can ride to the office with me. George's vehicle is in the lot," Myles offered.

One kidnapper muttered to Myles that their instructions were to find any documentation on Frederick because they knew he was Dunson, but they couldn't prove it. Dunson extorted millions from their boss, and he wanted it back.

Myles informed the guy that Frederick or Dunson was dead, and they wouldn't be getting their money back. Nathan leaned over, asking if they killed Frederick. His guys grew large.

"Dunson is dead. We were beating up a woman for nothing." He exclaimed!

"Pretty much." Nathan admitted. Then they watched EMS roll the stretchers to the waiting ambulances.

Myles congratulated the team on a successful mission. "Thanks, guys. Another one on the board."

The team loaded their vehicle and headed out, leaving Myles and Nathan. They took photos from every angle possible before leaving the area. Then he called Atlanta PD and reported the incident. They would send a detective to see Myles and receive a closed case.

Nathan felt odd climbing into the passenger seat, but then an image of Mac floated into his mind. He wanted to see her and tell her what had happened. She'd be sorry she missed it, but she needed the rest.

On the trip to the office, Nathan asked Myles, "Once we get the final autopsy results on Dunson, this case is closed, right?"

"Yes, and my gut tells me he died from the natural aneurysm. Not some killer."

That was Nathan's hope, too. Nathan followed Myles into the office as Myles spoke on the phone. Thoughts swirled in Nathan's mind as he wrapped up Lizzie's case. He and Mac thought the university case would be their first case closed at I^2, but this one was good. The duo learned a lot about investigating Dunson's genealogy.

Nathan worked on his report for a while before growing hungry. As his stomach rumbled, he searched for George's truck keys, finding them in the master key box. The company kept a spare set for each fleet vehicle.

He left the office, knowing he had a lot to share with Mac. Myles called as he pulled into his parking space. "Myles."

"I just got word that Dunson had an aneurysm in his stomach. The doctors are not ruling it a homicide. We're closed."

"Perfect. Thanks, Myles."

Nathan entered his apartment, expecting Mac to be sleeping. Instead, she cooked supper, and set the table for two. She met him at the door and said, "Tell me about your day."

"Well, it's a lot. Do we have time before supper?" He patted his stomach.

"Ok. Then, if it's that much, let's grab our plates and you can share in between bites." She chuckled on the way to the kitchen.

Mac listened intently as Nathan described his day. It disappointed her she missed it. But in the end, she was grateful Lizzie was okay. Then Nathan realized he hadn't heard from George.

He sent George a text asking for an update on Lizzie. George immediately replied that Lizzie was admitted for a concussion and potential damage to her eye. They are monitoring her condition. He also stated that he would remain with Lizzie and that Myles knew of his whereabouts.

"So, George likes this lady, huh?" Mac asked.

"Oh yeah, he does. He admitted it to me, but he swore me to secrecy."

"I've known George to have lady friends, but nothing serious. He always said he was married to his work. It would be nice to see him with someone like Lizzie. She seemed genuine." Mac said as she recalled meeting Lizzie.

The following morning, Mac and Nathan entered the office together. Myles met them at the door. "So, how's my girl feeling?"

"Fine. It's like nothing happened. Congratulations on closing Lizzie's case." Mac said to her dad.

"It wasn't me. I tagged along for the takedown." Myles said, eyeing Nathan. Then he added, "What's your plans with the university case?"

"Oh. We're not finished yet. We'll review the details this morning, then pick up where we left off. I've worked on it while at home and I want to discuss it with Nathan." Mac said with a grin.

"Ok. Let me know if you need anything. Be careful." Then Myles turned to leave but stopped. "Oh Nathan. George is at the hospital with Lizzie. He'll return your truck later today."

Nathan nodded, grinning. It was worth swapping rides to see George and Lizzie. Once the duo poured their coffee, they walked to Mac's office. She sat in her desk chair and turned toward the whiteboard.

"We need to know how much heroin it would take to fill a pallet. Something tells me heroin is not the only item on those pallets. That would be a staggering amount of the drug. I'm unsure if anyone can get their hands on that volume."

Nathan thought for a second before replying. "You're right. I've been assuming the only thing the guys are smuggling is heroin, but that would be an enormous amount. Do you have any idea of the other contents?"

"Not yet, but it must be something that fits into boxes and is easily transportable. Think about it. They used brown cardboard boxes to transport the content, and it required no refrigeration."

"But we're unsure what's inside. Was the brown box a ruse?" Nathan asked with an eyebrow lifted. "If so, it might throw off the police or inspectors if they searched the truck."

Chapter 9

Mac met Nathan's eyes before answering. "It could be a ruse. But are they hiding drugs or something else inside boxes? Besides, we never asked where the destination was for the cargo."

Nathan nodded as he searched a folder for something. "Do we have the FDLE investigator's name we used in Miami?"

"I don't believe so. Dad spoke with them after we got the video from the dock supervisor. I'll ask Dad who we can call for that information. That will help us understand where the shipment is going. Maybe we can have someone on the other end of the trip do a random search for us."

Mac left her office, searching for Myles while Nathan returned to his office. After he completed the report on Lizzie's case, his thoughts turned to George. Wonder if he was in the office?

Nathan strode over to George's office, finding it dark. He grinned, muttering, "That's interesting."

Once he settled into his chair, he laid the papers on his desk for the university case. He started at the beginning of the case so he could refresh his memory. Professor Gregory James was on the rooftop meeting area when a rainstorm moved in. His friends left, but he stayed behind to clean, or at least that's what folks said. Someone pushed him to his death.

Now, Paul, the university president, hired investigators to prove suicide. But the outcome wasn't what Paul wanted. Instead, someone murdered him. But by whom and why?

Nathan reviewed the file about the surveillance on the administration building. The building is troubling. There is no explanation for the workers to be at the building in the overnight hours. It was clear they were not the cleaning crew.

He then turned to the random words James left in his notes. What was James using these words for? Do they make a sentence? Or was James using them as reminders of himself?

As Nathan said the words out loud, it was clear James found something in the financials. Then Nathan realized they hadn't heard from Jackson on the forensic accounting side. He jotted a note as a reminder.

Myles and Mac found Nathan in his office. "Good Morning, Nathan. George is taking a couple of days off, but he will trade vehicles with you. Leave yours in the lot, and drive Mac's today."

"So, is he still with Lizzie?" Nathan asked.

"He is. Lizzie had brain surgery last night for a small bleed. When the guys hit her, it pulled a vein loose, so the surgeons entered her brain about 1:00 am. She should make a full recovery, but she has no one at home to help her. So, George volunteered." Myles said. "I hope he doesn't wind up with a broken heart. He doesn't do well with those."

Mac tilted her head. "I never knew George got that close to anyone."

"That's why you never knew. He doesn't talk about it." Then Myles changed the subject. "Nathan, I called my contact at the FDLE. He'll get the shipping manifest and email it to me."

"Thanks, Myles. I just hope it helps." Nathan said.

As Myles left the pair, he said, "Keep in touch."

Both nodded as Myles rounded the corner. "Once we receive the manifest, what are our next steps? I'm thinking about another trip to the university."

Nathan paused, then added, "I am too, but I'm concerned about your health. What would I do if something happened up there?"

"I'm fine, Nathan. I feel like nothing happened. Food tastes good, no fever, and no aches."

"Let's see what the manifest shows. I also want to call Jackson. Then we'll decide."

Mac nodded, knowing she must fight an uphill battle with her health scare. She'd have to prove that she was fit to work. Her mom and brothers called every day to make certain she was fine. They would eventually stop, just like before, but she wasn't sure how Nathan would react. Maybe time would help ease the worry.

Nathan dialed Jackson. He answered and invited them to his office. Nathan looked at Mac, then suggested, "Might want to grab a pen and paper. Jackson sounded like he had something for us."

Jackson set up his laptop, so the screen showed on the wall behind him. Mac and Nathan grinned because they loved this setup. The presenter sat facing them while they were able to view his slides.

After greetings, Jackson jumped right into his presentation. He gave the duo an executive summary of the reasons for the forensic accounting report. This mainly included their reason for asking for Jackson's help.

Then he covered the background of Professor Gregory and Paul Drummond. There was nothing new there. But when Jackson spoke of the financial aspects, Mac and Nathan were all ears.

"Paul is an outstanding mathematician. I can now explain his enrollment growth at this university, going back to his other university gigs. He enrolls 'fake' students. But not only that, he uses cash to cover the costs of the students. Every quarter, large sums of cash are deposited into the institution's bank. But the sums are never enough for an SARs notice."

Nathan raised his hand, then asked, "SARs is for deposits over $10,000, right?"

"Yes. So, without the SARs' reports, the bank had no reason to question the deposits. Well, I shouldn't say 'no reason' because, as a financial institution, they should've seen the influx of cash and questioned that on an ethical basis. The same bank received the deposits. I'm checking to see if the same person accepted each deposit because if they did, they need to be interviewed for violations."

Mac jotted note after note on her pad. They needed to know if the same person accepted the deposits. That could be crucial. "Wouldn't the faculty know about the 'fake' students?"

"Not necessarily. Their concern is with their students. They probably assumed another professor taught them." Jackson explained.

Mac and Nathan glanced at the other, then Nathan asked, "Where is the money coming from? It seems the university would be 'out' money because of the 'fake' students."

"That's the beauty of this. The university is profiting from the enrollment numbers because the more students that are enrolled, the more money the government provides. The more grants any one university can receive. Paul is a mastermind, but it's of the criminal variety. He's using the university to launder money. The question we need an answer to is where is he getting the cash?"

Nathan explained their surveillance of the administration building and what they found. Jackson asked, "Do you know what was in the boxes?"

"Not yet. Myles was getting the shipping manifest for the truck we saw. The authorities discovered the driver and passenger deceased inside the trailer at the docks in Miami. The CSI team from the FDLE found wood splinters, ink, and heroin residue."

"The heroine explains the cash."

"And they used pallets to transport the boxes. The ink we assumed was from labels for the heroin." Mac shared.

Jackson remained unconvinced by the ink. "That's a lot of ink to leave enough residue for a swab." He pondered that idea. "I think you're looking for something greater that baggie labels."

Mac looked at Nathan, but his eyes never left Jackson's. "Like what?"

With his shoulders in the air, he said, "I've no idea. But I can guarantee Paul and his friends are printing more than labels."

The threesome continued with the report, but Nathan had trouble concentrating because the idea of the ink troubled him. Now, he wanted to return to the university.

Jackson concluded his findings in a simple, no nonsense format that Nathan and Mac had no trouble understanding. Then he gave them exhibits, highlighting the information inside the report. "Here's your paper copy and an email should be in your inbox shortly with the same report."

"Thank you for this. You've opened our eyes." Jackson stood, shaking hands with the pair.

Mac and Nathan had so many ideas running through their minds, they didn't know where to start. Nathan said, "We need to see what's in that building."

"I agree. But how do we do that?"

"I'm unsure yet, but I'll figure it out." Nathan veered off into his office while Mac continued to hers.

Nathan pulled up a satellite view of the university. After he studied it for a few minutes, he noted a few areas that they could use for concealment since it was closer to the building than their other visit.

The university is situated at the base of a small mountain, so there is no construction behind it, but Nathan noticed a road that ran parallel to it. It appeared to be a fire road since it wasn't paved. As Nathan worked out his plan, he wondered if he should ask for additional investigators to tag along.

He didn't want to get caught surveilling the university. All kinds of bad press could come from that.

Mac leaned against the door frame, watching Nathan work. Finally, he glanced up and smiled. "How long have you been there?"

"Long enough to know you have a plan."

Nathan snickered as he realized how much he and Mac had grown together. "You're right, I do."

Mac sat in a chair across from him, waiting to hear the plan. Nathan turned his laptop toward Mac, wishing he had Jackson's setup. "See this road." Nathan pointed to a small dirt road that ran parallel to the university. Then he continued, "If we can find this road, we would be closer than our last visit, and it's from a different angle. Maybe we could get close enough to the loading dock to read the merchandise labels."

She waited for Nathan to continue, but he didn't. "What's the plan when we get there? It sounds like you want to surveil them again."

"I do. This will be the last time we do this before we enter the building. I doubt they will let us walk around the administration building without an escort. With this new location, I'm hoping to spot cameras so I can determine the alarm system. My guess is that they use iris or hand scanners, but then again, they may have thought no one would catch on to their activity and they stayed with the century old keypad entry."

Mac struggled with the plan. She wanted to see inside the building so badly, but she understood the risks, too. It's better to go slow than ruin what you've started just because you're curious. "The only suggestion I have is for us to be there during the day, so we find the road in the daylight. I hope that road is still there."

"Me too." Nathan muttered because if it was not, they would be back at the old location and that one doesn't lend a good vantage of the cameras.

The duo left the office to spend the day at the university. There were a few folks that weren't available to speak with them the last time they visited. So, they would use that as an excuse. But if someone were to look inside the cargo area of their truck, they would realize they have secondary motives for being on campus.

On the drive, they discussed the case, agreeing they needed to know what was inside that building. "How do you think Detective Chinni would react if we asked him what was inside the building?"

"He would turn quiet, then give us a vague answer, like it's an administrative building with unused classrooms. Then he would know that we know something else was happening in that building. Chinni would warn Paul. Paul would leave the university and take his enterprise with him. The case would be closed with that because we have nothing to hold him on." Nathan explained.

The pair grew quiet as the miles clicked past. Wind whipped the tree branches and the remaining leaves struggled to hold on while others floated to the ground. Mac watched Nathan drive for a few minutes before he felt her eyes on him. He asked, "Everything okay?"

"Yes. Just wondering, Paul does what he does when he probably has more money than any one person can spend in a lifetime." Mac shared.

"That's a good point. It could be the thrill of not getting caught. But then I wonder if he's been this close to being caught before."

Mac chuckled, then added, "I bet he's angry at himself for hiring us to prove Professor Gregory jumped. If he hadn't of done that, he would probably be in the clear."

"True. But he probably thinks he's smarter than the average person. He thought he had the perfect murder." Nathan said. Then he added, "But we know there are no perfect murders."

Nathan turned into the university's entrance. Mac admired the landscape and signage. It was welcoming and she could see how kids would want to come here. "What's that?" Mac pointed.

"I've no idea." Once they parked, they walked over to Professor James' building and realized students were protesting. They want justice for the professor. Mac and Nathan grinned. They hit the jackpot.

Nathan walked over to the guy holding the megaphone and whispered in his ear. Immediately, the guy turned back to the crowd and introduced the duo. The crowd grew to about thirty students and a few professors. Mac and Nathan stood apart so they could speak with each student and professor.

Once everyone had their chance to speak, Nathan noted a guy standing off to the side. He acted like he wanted to talk with them, but held back for some reason. So, Nathan walked over to the guy and introduced himself, handing the guy a card.

"What's your name?" Nathan asked.

"I'm Daniel Chinni."

Nathan's eyes met his. "Are you related to Detective Chinni?"

"He's my older brother." Daniel said, clearly uncomfortable speaking with Nathan. His feet never stopped moving.

Mac hung back when she saw the interaction between the guys. Their expressions gave away the seriousness of the conversation. She moved to a bench and began sorting her ideas on what she had just heard. A few students knew of the Professor's struggles with the university, but no one seemed to know the entire story. One of Mac's students admitted the administration made them promise to not disturb activity at the admin building in off hours. She signed a form stating that she would obey. During her orientation, the lady told them they use the admin building for night classes, and they were not to be disrupted.

Night classes. Who had night classes at two in the morning? Just as Mac turned the page in her notebook, Nathan walked over to her with a guy following close behind. "Mac, this is Daniel Chinni. He's Detective Chinni's younger brother."

Mac glanced at Nathan, then back to Daniel. "It's nice to meet you, Daniel." Then Mac waited. She was unsure where this meeting was going, so she waited for Nathan to speak.

"Daniel, had you rather meet somewhere private?"

"We can go to the library. The weather is better inside." He shivered underneath his hoodie.

The duo followed Daniel to the library, then to an upstairs room. Mac noticed how extensive the library was once they got inside. From the outside, it didn't appear too grand.

"I probably shouldn't be doing this, but I have to, and I can't talk to my brother about it."

"Why not?" Nathan asked.

"Because there is a chance that he is tangled up in it. To what degree, I'm unsure. It would destroy my mom if she thought any of her three boys were doing something illegal, but especially her prized detective. David can do no wrong in her eyes." The duo nodded in acknowledgement but offered no words.

Daniel looked at his hands, then said, "David has been acting strange around me ever since I started here last fall. It's like he doesn't want me here. I finally asked him, but he gave no reply. So, I spoke with Professor Gregory about it since I helped in one of his classes. I thought he may shed some light on why my brother wouldn't want me here. But he stammered when I asked. He tried to change the subject. That's when I knew something was going on and it involved my brother. Otherwise, he would've answered me."

"Did he share anything with you at all about the activities here in the overnight hours?" Mac asked.

"Overnight hours?" Daniel paused, then said, "No. He didn't mention that, but I remember one night I was up getting water when I saw lights on at the admin building. I thought nothing of it until you asked me about it." Then he added, "What goes on at that time of night?"

"We don't know. But we think Professor Gregory stumbled onto something before his death."

"So you suspect someone pushed the professor instead of him jumping?" Daniel looked at Mac and Nathan, waiting for confirmation.

Nathan gave it to him. "Yes, we do. The injuries to Professor Gregory posed questionable for someone who jumped. Someone helped him over the edge of the building."

Daniel stood and began pacing. His mind worked fast as memories flooded his mind. He chastised himself for not coming forward sooner, but he couldn't have gone to his brother's police department and ratted him out.

"David carries two cell phones."

"Okay. Do you have the numbers?" Nathan waited for a reply as Daniel struggled with his actions.

"I have his personal number he uses for the police department. But I don't have the number for his small black phone. How can I get that for you?"

Mac shared, "You would have to be able to open the phone and check the contacts for the phone's number. That's too risky. David would know what you're doing. While I don't expect him to hurt you, his friends might."

Nathan asked, "Does anyone know you're speaking with us?"

"No."

"Good. Leave it that way. You escorted us to the library today, then you left." Nathan confirmed the story with Daniel as he nodded his head in understanding.

Mac asked, "Has David said anything about his friendship with Paul Drummond?"

"Not really. But they spend a considerable amount of time together. The Police Chief has all the officers make rounds on the university grounds. So, Paul knows most of the officers by name. It seems David and Paul struck up a friendship which is odd to me, given their age difference." Daniel said as he looked over his shoulder, searching for the noise maker.

When Daniel turned to face the table, the duo was gone. Luckily for him, they had the sense to scatter his books on the table before beginning their meeting.

Mac and Nathan huddled in a closet in the room's corner. Now, if they could hang in there for a few minutes, maybe Daniel would leave. They suspected David had spotted their car in the lot and began searching. It took him this long to find Daniel.

"What's up, bro?" David asked his younger brother.

"Studying. What are you doing here?"

"Just on things. The chief sent a few of us to check on a protest out here. But it was over before we made it. Do you know anything about it?"

"There was a group of students protesting for Professor Gregory. They still don't think he committed suicide, and they want justice." Daniel explained.

Mac's foot was going to sleep because of the way she stood on it. She knew she couldn't move for fear of David hearing. So, she gritted her teeth and prayed for the best.

"Ok. I get it. Let me know if you're coming over this weekend to mom's house. She wants us to grill out."

"I'll text you." David patted Daniel on the back, leaving the room.

Daniel turned his head back to his books and tried to read them. He jotted a few things on his paper, then stood. He walked out of the room, checking for his brother. Then he stood next to the window, watching his brother climb into his unmarked car. Daniel gave two raps on the door, giving the duo a signal to come out.

"That was close. How did you know it would be David?" Daniel asked the pair.

Mac hobbled to the chair, then began massaging her foot. "It's asleep." The others chuckled.

"We parked our vehicle in the lot and David knows it. At least we parked away from this area, so maybe he thinks we're on the other side of campus toward Professor Gregory's building." Nathan explained.

Then Mac handed Daniel a business card. "Keep this secure."

Followed by Nathan, "Mine too. We'll be in touch."

"You can't go out the front door." Daniel said with urgency in his voice.

"We're not. We'll exit the back and walk a few buildings before returning to our car, since David probably has it under surveillance." Nathan said. "He won't know where we came from unless he asked, and I doubt he'll do that."

The pair took the stairs to the bottom floor of the library and exited the rear by the loading dock. No one was visible when they peeked around the door, so they walked to the rear and covered three buildings before emerging onto the campus.

They headed for their car and then they would wait for night to fall. Nathan felt bad for Daniel because he was in a tight spot. He wanted to do the right thing, but that might land his brother in jail, and he knows what happens to officers sentenced to prison. But if David is aiding a criminal enterprise for Paul Drummond, then he needs to spend time in prison.

"Your conflicted emotions are playing out on your face. You feel bad for Daniel, yet David needs to spend time in prison for his criminal activities." Mac shared as she studied Nathan's expression.

Nathan nodded. "But in the end, the only thing that matters is justice for Professor Gregory and Paul behind bars. If David is guilty, then he needs to join Paul. Daniel will be fine."

They climbed into the vehicle when David pulled in behind them, blocking their exit. David raced to Nathan's window. "What are you two doing here?"

"We walked the campus. We're still looking into the professor's death, remember?"

"I thought you finished that."

"Nope. Things just don't add up. Thanks for checking on us." Nathan's window rose slightly when David tapped it.

"I'm not finished." He muttered as his face grew red. "What things are your referencing?" Detective Chinni was nervous. Perspiration broke out across his forehead as he waited for an answer.

"The same ones as before. Professor Gregory's injuries contradict a fall. We've pulled backgrounds on a few folks, so we're going back to review those and see what pops. We'll call if we need anything." Nathan said, clearly enjoying poking David with his explanation.

Nathan raised the window, put the car in reverse, then pointed to David's car. He paused, but eventually moved his car from their path.

Mac chuckled from the passenger seat. "Background checks. That's a good one."

"Well, I couldn't divulge what we know because he'd run to Paul and Paul would vanish. I want to bring his operation to a halt before he disappears." Nathan said.

"I agree. If Paul vanishes, do you think he'd risk starting over someplace else?"

"After his first attempt, I would have thought he'd lie low, but for him, it's the thrill. A little law enforcement questions mean nothing to him. Other departments have investigated him, but not even one has the evidence to convict him. He destroyed all the evidence." Nathan explained as he turned out of the lot with David on his backside. "David is following us. I'm driving out of town, then we'll return once he thinks we're going to Atlanta."

The further they got from the university, Mac's worry meter sounded. "Why is still behind us?"

"He's not. Someone else is. David exited the interstate when his jurisdiction ended, but this guy picked us up at the next entrance ramp. He waited for us. This guy has a muscular build, short cropped hair, and I can't see any tattoos on him.

Mac lowered her visor mirror, using it to view the driver. "He's alone."

"Yes, and that's never good when someone sends one guy to take on two people." Nathan added.

Mac cringed. How far will this guy follow them? What will he do when they stop? "Drive to Atlanta PD. Surely he won't try anything there."

Nathan grinned when his cell phone rang. He tapped the dash button, answering George's call. George explained about Lizzie's surgery and said she was home and doing remarkable. Then George said hello to Mac.

"Hi, George. I'm glad to hear Lizzie is better. She has us worried."

"Thanks, guys. So, what's the latest?" Neither one spoke, so he asked again.

Finally, Nathan rehashed their day with the protest and their meeting with Daniel Chinni. Then Mac added the detail about someone following them.

George's voice changed. "Drive to a police station."

"We're coming home. We'll be introducing this guy to Atlanta PD."

"And me." George ended the call.

The duo shared a glance but said nothing. It felt good having George on their side. Then Mac suggested exiting the interstate for gas since they were low, anyway. She wanted to see if this guy followed them into the lot.

After texting George their location, they exited the interstate and entered the gas station lot. Mac never left the vehicle, but she saw the car pull off to the side and speak on his phone. He was following orders. But who gave them?

When Nathan slammed the door, Mac gave him the update. He nodded as he pulled away from the pumps, entering the interstate again. This time the guy followed from two cars back. He was inching closer.

Nathan snickered when he asked, "Wonder when he realizes we're going to Atlanta PD?"

"I hope when he turns into the lot." Then Mac's cell phone rang. Glancing at the dash, she grinned as she tapped the button for her dad.

"Hi Dad."

"Where are you?"

"We just stopped for gas and are heading south on 75 at Cumberland Parkway."

"Ok. Go around to the back parking lot. We'll be waiting for you."

"On our way. Should be there in fifteen minutes if traffic holds." The call ended. Then Mac asked,

"Wonder what they have planned? I didn't know George was calling in the troops."

When the duo rounded the last turn, they saw no one. But Nathan followed orders by turning into the back lot. When he did, George and Myles stepped out from their hiding places, standing in front of the guy's car while two more people took the rear.

The driver realized his mistake and slammed the car in reverse, nearly running over the people in the rear. As he fled, Myles and George opened fire on his car, sending it into a telephone pole as it burst into flames.

Myles and his team raced to the burning car, hoping the driver had escaped. Upon rounding the car's rear, they discover the driver's upper body outside the car door, while his feet and legs are trapped under the wheel. Myles yells, "He's unconscious. Let's see if we can free him."

George glanced at the guy. "Are you sure? His feet are burned so badly, he may not make it."

Chapter 10

"I have to try." Myles frantically works to reach the driver. Nathan rushed to his side, but as they tugged on the guy, they were afraid of pulling his body from the feet.

"Myles, let him go. The Fire Department is here."

Nathan touched Myles' arm, and he released the driver. He struggled with life every time a death was involved, especially when he caused it.

Mac reached Nathan and her dad. Standing between them, she muttered, "We don't even know his name."

The guys looked at her but refrained from speaking when they noticed the fire was out. Two firefighters worked to free the guy, and they did. The body lay on a white sheet in the roadway, waiting for the ambulance.

George stood next to the Fire Captain, and he shook his head, leading Myles to think the guy was dead. But when George joined their group, he said, "The guy is alive but barely. They're afraid to touch him because of his injuries. The ambulance ETA is two minutes."

Nathan offered, "If I looked like that, don't try to save me. That man will never walk again. I can't imagine the pain he'll endure from surgeries and skin grafts."

Everyone standing with him shuddered at that thought. An officer approached Myles, and after a greeting, he asked Myles to step aside. George followed. They spoke for fifteen minutes as Myles and George pointed out the accident scene. Before Myles left, he asked the officer, "Can we fingerprint the guy, or will you?"

"I'll see that it's done at the hospital. The ambulance is loading him now." The officer glanced at the scene before releasing Myles and George.

"Well, what did they say?" Nathan asked.

"They'll fingerprint the guy at the hospital. But if we don't receive them, then we'll do it." Myles said. He wanted those prints now, not tomorrow. That guy could lead them to Professor Gregory's killer.

Myles and his crew climbed into their vehicles and met at the office. Nathan, Mac and the other investigators on the scene met in the conference room, waiting for Myles and George. Mac grew concerned about the delay, so she stepped out of the room.

The other investigators were quiet, too. No one expected this outcome because no one thought the guy would attempt to escape by running over the two investigators. He was determined to escape capture and anyone's cost. Now, he's lying in a hospital bed with little to no chance of ever walking again, and that's if he survives.

George entered the room first, with Mac and Myles following. The stress of the event was evident on Myles' face. He sat at the table with the others and said, "Go home for the day. That event turned disastrous, but it wasn't our doing that caused it. Come back tomorrow morning. If you can't work, let me know. I'll set your appointment with the doctor."

The attendees nodded, but Nathan didn't understand the need for a doctor, but he tabled the thought. Now wasn't the time or place to inquire about it.

After the meeting, the duo complied with their instructions. They went home to a nice, quiet apartment. Nathan ordered pizza for delivery. The perfect comfort food.

"We are aware that the driver and Detective Chinni know each other. But was the driver associated with Paul's organization? Because if he was and they know what happened, will they know we're close to blowing up their enterprise?"

"I wish I knew the answer to your questions."

The following morning, the duo arrived at the office early. Everyone from yesterday's ordeal was already at their desks. That was a good sign that things were okay. George found the duo walking to their desks.

"Got a minute?" George asked.

"Of course. Join us," Mac said as they entered Nathan's office.

After George sat, he said, "We don't have the fingerprints this morning. What's on your agenda today?"

"Stopping in at the hospital and fingerprinting the guy. Then we're going to the university this afternoon." Mac said nothing about their surveillance plan.

"Let me know if you know need anything. Those prints are critical."

The duo checked email and finished their morning coffee before heading to the hospital. Grady Hospital is always busy and today was the same. People moved in a fluid motion twenty-four hours a day.

Nathan asked the lady behind the desk about the guy, but without a name, she was no help. So they walked to the ER, finding the doctor that treated the guy. He referred them to the burn unit, and he goes by John Doe #9.

When the doctor walked away, Mac stammered, "#9." Then she added, "Does that mean there are nine unidentified people in this hospital?"

"That's what it sounds like." Nathan said as he took Mac by the elbow, ushering her to the elevators.

They had to have a nurse escort them to the burn victim. Then they wished that hadn't. Mac had never seen someone so badly burned before while the scene took Nathan back to his service days. Those days he tries to forget.

Nathan asked about fingerprints when the nurse hesitated. He explained the urgency, and she finally agreed. Mac had her gloves already on her hands when they received the okay. She gently lifted the man's hand and worked each finger into the fingerprint ink and then laid them on the fingerprint card. As Mac progressed, Nathan followed her with the cleaning rag. They worked quickly for fear someone would stop them before finishing.

Luckily, they left the room before the doctor showed. Nathan thanked the nurse for her help and promised to let her know his name.

The pair rushed back to the office, sliding the fingerprints into the scanner in the lab. They waited for the results. When the alert sounded, the duo exchanged a glance. The computer spit out a report on Anthony Chevoski, age 38, single, with a Chicago address.

"Anthony Chevoski. Who were you working for?" Nathan stared at the picture on the paper, knowing he wouldn't receive an answer.

Mac studied the report, then she entered the query for a criminal background. She hoped this would lead them closer to finding out the truth. When Mac pulled into Chevoski's background, she whistled. "Look at this, Nathan."

He pulled himself out of his daydream to join her. "Paul is mixed up with this guy." His movements coincide with Paul's moves. They apparently met in Chicago and have been together since."

"That's not good." Nathan blurted. "Paul will know that something happened to Anthony when he didn't return calls."

"Oh man. I could kick myself."

"What for?" Nathan's eyebrows bunched as he worried about her comment.

"I was right there in his car, and I didn't check for a cell phone."

"Whoa, Mac. Don't blame yourself for that. The flames were too hot and if the phone was in the console or on the passenger seat, there wouldn't have been anything left of it." Nathan grimaced when the sight invaded his memory. "We could give Detective Chinni a scare and let him know we had someone follow us yesterday, but they're now in the Grady Hospital burn unit."

Mac paused, thinking about the ramifications of notifying Chinni. "I like it, but I don't want to scare him or Paul out of town. Let's visit the university tonight, then maybe tomorrow we will contact Chinni, in person, with the news."

Nodding, Nathan agreed. Mac notified Myles and George of Anthony's name while Nathan called Anthony's nurse, giving her his name.

The duo revisited their plan to surveil the university and made no changes. As they wrapped up, Mac asked, "What was Anthony supposed to do to us once we stopped? I would have thought he would make us stop and try to scare us away from the investigation. Instead, he followed us to Atlanta. That is odd to me."

"I've wondered that myself. Was he trying to find out where we live? Or just as an intimidation factor?" Nathan added.

"That part makes no sense to me. Well, let's load and then we can rest before driving north."

Late afternoon, the duo drove in silence toward the university. They would need daylight to find the fire road behind the administration building. Using the satellite view, the road appeared one mile north of the university property. They would hike in from there, as long as there was no one to stop them.

The sun dipped low behind trees as Nathan maneuvered the truck along a rutted dirt road. It was slow going, but Nathan was grateful they chose to do this part in the daylight.

Checking the GPS once again, Nathan slowed. "This might be our spot. Let me stop and take a quick peek."

Mac nodded as Nathan stepped from the truck, grabbing the binoculars as he went. He stood on the edge of the tree line and peered toward the administrative building. Then he went further down the road behind the truck and took another look. His eyebrows bunched together as he walked in the opposite direction. This time, Mac watched him. When he found his target, he relaxed.

After closing the door, he said, "It's just up the road. This road is perfect."

"Yeah, until someone comes along wanting to pass." Mac looked at the tree limbs scraping through her window.

Nathan didn't reply, instead he gently laid his foot on the gas pedal and inched deeper into the woods. Before exiting the truck, he turned off their interior lights. They couldn't take the chance of being spotted over something that simple. He knew the black truck would go undetected.

Mac asked, "Can we get a little closer to the action?"

"We can try. But if we must leave in a hurry, we're doomed." He glanced at the truck as the realization hit him. There were sitting ducks if someone spotted them. He hasn't seen a vehicle turnaround since they turned onto the fire road. He prayed he wouldn't need it for this operation.

"Maybe we should've thought about that before coming out here." Mac said as she lifted her shoulder.

Noise stopped their conversation. Both investigators placed their binoculars to their eyes and watched two transfer trucks enter the lot. The drivers backed their vehicles into a slot, then they exited the cab. They met with a guy before entering the building through a side door.

"Do you think they know what their cargo will be once it's loaded?"

"I can't answer that, Mac. The other truckers were murdered, remember? But eventually word will get around about the university and no driver will agree to a pickup. Then I wonder what Paul will do. He must have drivers to make this work."

Nathan's phone vibrated in his pocket. He read the text to Mac from Raymond saying he would like to see them tomorrow about James' information.

"That's good, I hope. He's had the information for a while. Maybe he found something useful."

"Did Myles give us the shipping manifest for the Miami load?"

"Dad didn't give it to me. We'll ask tomorrow." Mac said as she kept her binoculars in place.

They watched the activity, and the same scenario played out. Once they loaded the trucks, they left in tandem, except this time, there were two. Were they traveling back to Miami?

Nathan called George. "Is there anyone that can track two transfer trucks for us? They just left the university." Nathan waited as George questioned him. "Yes, we have set up camp on a fire road, approximately three-fourths of a mile from the university." Then he waited again.

When he finally ended the call, he glanced at Mac. "I suspect George isn't happy with us."

Mac shrugged her shoulders. Then said, "Here comes another car into the lot. Oh look. It's our neighborhood police detective."

Nathan fumed when he witnessed Detective Chinni climb from his vehicle. Mac snapped photos of Chinni and Paul talking in the lot. It appeared heated, but then things simmered as Chinni and Paul entered the side door.

Mac muttered, "I'd like to know what's behind that door."

"Wouldn't we all." Nathan replied.

The duo stayed in place until they turned the lights off and left the lot. When the duo closed the doors, Nathan stated, "I'm following this road until it ends unless we find a turnaround spot."

He started the truck and continued their trek. After another half mile, they came upon a clearing. In the clearing sat a shiny black and chrome helicopter. "This wasn't on the satellite view."

Both heard motors at the same time. "Floor it. Get away from this clearing." Mac yelled, then she added, "Wait. We need a picture of the numbers."

Nathan muttered, "Hurry" as he pushed the pedal, leaving the clearing behind. When they felt safe, they stopped, let their windows down and listened. The motor noise had ceased, but now something else took its place.

"Is that the helicopter?"

"Yes, and if they fly this way, they'll see us," Nathan said as he glanced at both sides of the dirt road. There was no place to hide a black Suburban. "Hang on."

Nathan slowly pushed the truck's gas pedal, keeping the motor from revving. Then they continued. The further they got, the less they could hear the helicopter. Just as they turned onto a paved road, they heard the copter fly overhead. Neither took the time to search the sky for it. Instead, Nathan drove to the interstate and headed home.

"Do you think they saw us?" Mac asked with a touch of concern in her voice.

"Can't say."

Nathan drove home with one eye on the road and one eye on the rearview mirror. He spotted no one following them, and that was a relief. But he kept wondering if someone saw them from the helicopter. If they did, they would be in Paul's crosshairs shortly.

George called, and Mac tapped the answer button on the dash. "Where are you?"

"On Interstate 75 headed home."

"Good. One truck headed south, while the other truck went north, both on 75. Can you turn around and follow the north bound truck to the state line? I have someone in Tennessee picking it up from there."

Mac glanced at Nathan as he exited the interstate. "We're on it."

"Also, Myles has the manifest information. But it doesn't help us. There's nothing on it for a commercial purpose. It's a personal ship." George stated.

"Personal ship. That's a spin." Mac added.

Nathan said, "We're now headed north on 75. We'll touch base when we reach the Tennessee line."

George ended the call without speaking. Then Nathan added, "I told you he wasn't happy with our idea."

"Oh well. We survived and now we have photos of Chinni with Paul. Now, we know with certainty that we cannot trust Chinni."

Nathan added, "We'll call Daniel and advise him that he must remain vigilant when he sees his brother. I don't want to see him wrapped up in it." Nathan paused as he changed lanes. Then he added, "But since we know about Chinni, we can share information with him that we want Paul to hear."

"Great idea." Mac studied the traffic, searching for the truck. Then she pointed, "There it is."

Nathan slowed, moving to the middle lane as the truck traveled in the right lane. The truck wasn't speeding, which the duo found odd. Then, out of nowhere, he surged ahead.

"What is he doing? Surely, he didn't spot us," Mac offered.

Traffic was getting thicker as they approached the Tennessee line. Brake lights shone in the darkness. Nathan tapped the dash, revealing the road map. "Ugh. It's red. There's a traffic jam ahead.

Mac said nothing as they slowed down for the stopped cars. The truck slowed too, but Nathan's traffic allowed him to pass the truck. As they passed the truck, Mac snapped a photo of the truck's door, giving them the DOT information. After they stopped, Mac tapped her icon for the photos. When she found the picture, she grinned. "It's a touch blurry, but readable."

George called, "I see you're stopped."

Mac and Nathan glanced at the other. "How do you know that?"

"I'm watching you from a satellite link. It's cool. I'll show you one day. We can track your cell phones as long as they're on." George explained. Then he added, "There's a serious crash .4 miles ahead of your current location. It shouldn't be long before the road opens. My guy is waiting just inside the Tennessee line on the entrance ramp. He's driving a black Tahoe."

Nathan stated, "We'll follow until we see him, then we'll head back."

"Be safe. See you both in the morning. Oh wait, it is morning. See you both at 9:00 am." Then the call ended.

After a few quiet moments, Mac rehashed what they'd learned. "A personal ship loaded the cargo, and we have no ownership name for it. Detective Chinni works with Paul. We're following a truck north on 75 while another goes south, maybe to Miami again."

Nathan nodded, acknowledging Mac's comments. "And we still have no idea what kind of organization Paul runs. Whatever it is, it takes transfer trucks to make it run."

"I see no way for one man to handle that much heroin. Two transfer trucks full of the drug would be enough to cover the country. Something else is on those pallets with the heroin. But what could it be? My mind still gravitates to the ink. How could ink from labels leave enough residue on the floor of a transfer truck? That makes no sense to me."

"I'm with you. That isn't logical." Nathan agreed as law enforcement vehicles flew by in the median with their lights flashing.

The pair sat in silence as they contemplated their situation. Nathan kept an eye in the rearview mirror even though the trucker couldn't move. All travel lanes stood still as the first responders worked to clear the interstate. It took longer than expected and George gave them a heads up when it was time to start moving.

The right lane opened first, allowing the truck driver to pass them again. Mac kept her head facing the front because she didn't want the driver to look at her as he passed. Some seconds later, Nathan inched forward until finally the road cleared.

Mac saw the damaged vehicles on the roadside and grimaced. "No wonder it took a while to clear this one. This might be a fatality accident from the looks of the vehicles."

Nathan moaned as he drove through the thick traffic. "Text George that we're on the move and the truck is ahead of us, but visible."

After she texted George, she laid her head back on the headrest and yawned. Nathan never commented, as she looked tired. He was unsure if she was over her illness, whatever it was. That hospital visit still concerned him because they never diagnosed her with anything. That just blamed it on a virus. It's always a virus until it's not.

Fifteen miles flew past, and Nathan woke Mac as they got close to their replacement. He didn't want Mac to be asleep. Just as George described, the first exit into Tennessee there was a black Tahoe on the entrance ramp. When the truck raced past it, the black Tahoe joined the traffic. He jumped in front of the duo and Nathan nodded. Then he exited the interstate, and turned left, crossing the bridge to re-enter the highway.

The trip home was uneventful, and Nathan found himself pacing around the family room because he couldn't sleep while Mac slept peacefully in her bed. Finally, Nathan gave in and laid down, begging for sleep.

Mac woke first, wondering where Nathan was since he was the early riser. She made coffee and was watching TV when Nathan emerged from the shower. With their usual morning greetings, Mac asked, "How are you this morning?"

"Sleepy. Coffee will wake me up. It always does. We need to leave in twenty minutes. We're meeting George at 9:00 am." Mac slid from the sofa and headed to her room.

At the eighteen-minute mark, Mac left her room and met Nathan in the kitchen. "Let's roll."

George met them in the break room. "Raymond is meeting us this morning. Just a heads up."

George and Raymond sat in the conference room when the duo entered. "Raymond, I hope you have good news?"

His eyes met Nathan's and Nathan knew that wasn't the case. "Well, I wish I had better news. The documents you gave me are not coded. They are the writer's own form of shorthand. I've no idea where this shorthand came from, so I'm guessing they created it themselves. But I did find a few things you might use."

Raymond tapped a button on his laptop and a screen popped up. He highlighted several areas on the screen and started at the top of the page. He pointed out the words that Mac and Nathan had on their board. The duo's expression gave all their emotion.

"Why would he go through all this trouble if no one can decipher it?" Mac expressed her disappointment.

Raymond continued, "Then I found this." He pointed to the sum of money, and it matched the sum that Jackson mentioned.

"Hold on, Raymond. I've seen that sum before." Nathan flipped pages in his book. "That's the sum that Jackson gave us. It's the money sitting in an offshore account."

George looked at Raymond. "Go on."

"Is it in a bank in the Cayman Islands?" Raymond asked.

Nathan and Mac nodded. Then Mac said, "How did you know?"

Raymond flipped to the next page, and the top highlighted word was Cayman. "I think your Professor Gregory found Paul's enterprise, and he traced the money. If we knew Paul's shorthand, this would be a treasure trove of information. But that's probably why he used it."

"I wonder if James' wife knows his shorthand." Mac said.

"Call her. It's worth a try," Nathan said.

Mac slipped out of the room, dialing Mrs. Gregory. When she answered, Mac identified herself and explained what they needed. Mrs. Gregory had no idea her husband knew shorthand. Mac felt her shoulders sag with the admission.

She shared her call with the others. Then George said, "We've got this shorthand that no one knows anything about. We have Paul and his group of load trucks who travel north and south of the university. Someone loaded the cargo in Miami onto a personal yacht named 'Easy Money'. We're tracing the owner now."

Nathan added, "The biggest issue is the cargo. What is it?"

No one answered because they asked that very question to themselves daily. This was a frustrating case and one they could leave until James' killer was behind bars or dead.

As the meeting broke, Mac asked, "Has there been any updates on Anthony's condition?"

"Not yet. He's still in a coma. They are treating his burns, but the prognosis is bleak." George replied, clearly bothered by the guy's untimely misfortune.

The duo stopped at Nathan's office. They rehashed what they knew and what they didn't. The biggest obstacle remained the cargo. What is it?

"We haven't heard from Clarence or Joe for a while. Should we check in with them?" Nathan asked.

Mac nodded as Nathan dialed a number. Clarence answered and Mac listened to the one sided conversation. When the call ended, Nathan shared,

"Clarence feels someone follows him around the campus, but nothing else. He invited us to stop by when where up there."

"That might not be the best idea. He doesn't need to be seen associating with us."

Nathan chuckled. "You're probably right." Then Nathan's eyes lit up. "You have pictures of the truck, right?"

"Oh yeah. And the helicopter. Although the helicopter picture may be blurry."

Nathan transferred the photos to their laptops for future use. He enlarged the numbers on the helicopter and jotted them down in his book. Then he repeated the process for the truck. Once they had them, he entered searches into the software database. Then they waited.

The trucker's information returned first. "The trucker is an independent. His name is Jerome Hilson with an Atlanta address. What do you say we take a ride?"

"I'd love to." Mac said as the computer chirped. "Is that for the helicopter?"

"Well, this is interesting. The university registered the helicopter.

"I wonder if the university board of trustees knows they own a helicopter." Mac asked with an eyebrow raised.

"There's only one way to find out." Nathan plucked his cell phone from the desktop and tapped a button. When Joe answered, Nathan asked about the helicopter. Mac grew eager to hear the outcome the longer Nathan remained on the phone. When he finally finished it, he said, "The university never has and never will own a helicopter. Paul approached the subject right after coming onboard, but the board refused to allow him to purchase one through the university."

"So, how did Paul do it without the board's knowledge?"

"That's what Joe wants to know." Nathan printed the report after he saved a copy of his computer. He wanted more information on this helicopter, but he'd have to ask George for help. He dialed George on the company phone and asked if he had time for a question.

The duo ambled down the hall into George's office. This office was the epitome of offices. Mahogany glistened in the light, and there wasn't a speck of dust anywhere. George had files neatly stacked within his arm's length.

"What's up, guys?" George asked in a chipper tone that caused the pair to stop.

Mac was the first to question it. "Why so happy, George? That's a little out of character."

"No reason." But he blushed around his neck.

Mac noticed but refrained from embarrassing him more. So, she looked at Nathan, who shared what they knew about the helicopter.

"The university denies any knowledge of owning a helicopter. That's a pretty intense secret. Let's see the report."

Nathan handed George the report, and they sat in the chairs facing George. They watched him type on the laptop for a few minutes without uttering a word. Finally, he looked up and said, "The report stands. Here are the papers where the university purchased the bird. They've had it for four years. Check the signature page. It appears Paul handled the purchase agreement."

"Amazing he could do this secretly four years ago and still no one seems to know about it. Is he making payments on the helicopter?" Mac asked.

"No. He bought it with cash." George

Chapter 11

"Who buys a helicopter in cash?"

George snickered, "Those that want to keep it a secret."

Then Nathan added, "And no one questions the helicopter landing so close to the university." He shook his head, trying to understand the situation. Then he looked up, "What does he need a helicopter for, anyway?"

"That's just it. The copter landed at a small airport in Virginia. Then it returned to Georgia within two hours. I want to know if he had a business meeting or was it something else?"

Mac opened her phone and searched out the name of the small town. It was on the southern side of the state. What could be there? "Where did the truck stop?"

"It hasn't. They are in Iowa now. My guess is that truck will take his payload to Washington state."

"So, guys, let me see if I have this right. We have a university president who is a drug dealer across the country, but they package the drugs in a used area of the admin building." Nathan said with his eyebrows bunched. "Does that sound right?"

"Based on what we know, yes, that's the jest. But I agree with you that something else is at play here. James knew what it was, and since he was a financial guy, it has to be with the money. If we had someone that knew Professor Gregory's shorthand, we would blow this case up."

The duo stared at George, waiting for instructions. But when none came, Nathan said, "We have Anthony's address here in Atlanta. We're doing a drive-by. Maybe he doesn't live alone, and we can interview a roommate." Nathan shrugged his shoulders. He didn't tell George that they had nothing better to do with their time.

On the walk to the car, Mac shared, "I wish I could ask Margot to look at the shorthand from Professor Gregory. She could figure it out for us."

"I know. My thoughts are the same about Travis. I'd like to run a few things past him."

The pair climbed into the truck, feeling sullen. Their smiles were nonexistent. Nathan drove to Anthony's house, which was closer to the airport than they expected. Then it turned out to be a townhouse, not a home. There were cars on the parking pad outside his place. Before parking, Nathan drove them around the block, just looking at the sights. When they made their way around, Nathan pulled into the drive.

"Did you see that?" Nathan asked Mac. He saw her shake her head. "The curtains moved. Someone is home. We can't break in from the front and we couldn't see the back from the street. He's pretty smart."

Mac walked over to the door and knocked. Nathan stared with his lips apart. An older woman opened the door, but only until the chain held taunt. "May I help you?" She asked.

"Yes, please. We're looking for Anthony. Have you seen him?"

"No, I haven't. Not in a few days. He travels for work a lot, so he isn't here much."

"They asked us to check on him. Do you have a key to his place?" Mac continued.

"I sure do. Let me get it for you. Oh. I hope nothing has happened to him. He's the sweetest boy because he's always willing to help me." She returned, holding the key above her head. Then she unlatched the chain.

"Why don't you stay here, just in case something is wrong? We might need your help," Mac suggested. The lady understood Mac's intentions.

She muttered, "Good idea."

With the key in hand, Mac and Nathan entered Anthony's house. Nathan whispered, "I hope the lady didn't see me use the tissue to turn the knob."

Mac chuckled. "I'm unsure if it would have made sense to her, anyway."

Anthony took pride in his home. Everything had its place, even the dirty clothes were in a hamper. Most of the clothes were out of the closet, presumably in North Georgia somewhere. Nathan rifled through the desk in the closet, finding a calendar. He pocketed it, then he found cash stuffed in a bag in the hamper's bottom. "Look at this."

"Whoa. How much is there?"

"No idea. I'm leaving it but taking pictures. Have you found anything?"

"There was nothing on the nightstand. I'll check the other room. It appears he carries everything of importance with him." Then Mac turned and faced Nathan. "So why didn't he take the money?"

"That's a good question." Nathan said as he placed the bag at the bottom of the hamper.

Then they heard the next-door lady yell, "Are you okay?"

"Yes. We're coming down now. Anthony isn't here and there's nothing on his calendar. Would you have any idea where he might be?" Mac asked in a casual tone.

The lady's eyebrows bunched as she contemplated the question. "I know of no family in Georgia. Actually, I don't recall him ever mentioning family.

But I remember him taking trips to Chicago and Dallas, but that's all."

"Ok. Thank you for your help. Will have Anthony call when we find him?"

"Thank you. You two can stop by, too." The lady closed her door behind her, then slid the chain in place.

Nathan said, "That was brilliant. You handled that woman like a champ."

Mac blushed at the compliment. "Aw. Shucks. Thanks." Mac replied, slamming her truck door.

Before Nathan started the truck, he said, "What do you make of the cash?"

"Well, there's are a couple of ideas. Anthony stole it or he earned it." Pausing, then she asked, "It seems Paul deals in mountains of cash. Do you think Anthony would have skimmed the top and kept some for himself?"

"Possible." But Nathan didn't elaborate. Instead, he glanced in his rearview mirror and moaned. "We have company, and I bet they know we were in Anthony's house."

"Swell. I didn't see anyone tailing us when we left the office. Where were they when we arrived?"

Nathan agreed with Mac that neither spotted a surveillance team on Anthony's house. Then he muttered, "This is getting old."

The car followed the duo halfway back to the office, but they entered the interstate northbound while the duo went southbound. "I didn't recognize the guy, did you?"

"No, I didn't." Then Mac's cell phone rang. "Hi Dad."

Myles greeted the duo, then shared about the boat 'Easy Money'. When he said his team had traced it through multiple layers of shell corporations, it brought him back to Paul Drummond. Paul has owned the yacht for nine years. The yacht is large enough to travel on open seas. He is working to get the last time the yacht traveled, but no one claims to have documented information.

"So, Paul takes his voyages at times and places no one checks." Mac nodded as she looked at Nathan.

"Sounds about right. This guy is doing everything crooked, and we must stop him. Anything else on Anthony?"

Mac updated Myles on what they'd found in his apartment. When she mentioned the money, Myles asked, "Did you count it?"

"No. The next-door neighbor interrupted us, but Nathan took a picture." Mac explained.

"I hope you got a serial number." Myles stated.

Nathan shrugged his shoulders and pointed to his phone. Mac opened his photos icon and enlarged it. "Yes, he did. What will you do with this?"

"I want to make sure it's one of ours. Send it to me," Myles asked, then he said, "I've got to run. Talk soon." Then the call ended.

Mac sent the photo to him. "Good job in the photo."

Nathan shrugged. "That was pure luck. Wonder what Myles meant when he said 'one of ours'? Where else could the money be from?"

"I'm unsure. That was a puzzle." Mac added. She thought about the money as they turned into the office parking lot. Then she realized there were no cars in the lot. "Where is everyone?"

Without an answer, he said, "No idea."

They entered the quiet office and headed to the coffee pot. Both poured their mugs to the brim. Since they planned on using the internet, they felt they needed the jolt to keep them awake.

Nathan's phone blared in the stillness. He answered, then everything went quiet again. Mac knew something wasn't right. She walked next door to check on him.

The phone was to his ear, but the caller wouldn't slow down enough for Nathan to talk. Finally,

Nathan said, "Clarence. Calm down. Just breathe." Nathan gave him a second, then said, "Did they take anything?"

Nathan jotted a few things on this paper, then said. "Teach your classes. You're safer there than at home alone. We'll be there before you finish your last class. You'll have guests tonight in case they didn't like what they found. I'll text you before we get there so you know it's us, since we'll be driving an unfamiliar car."

Mac nodded in understanding as the call ended. "What did the intruders take from Clarence's?"

"A calendar from his desk." Then Nathan pulled Anthony's calendar from his pocket. "I wonder if it's like this one."

"Is there anything noted on that one?"

"There's scribble on a few days of each week, but I can't read it." Nathan explained as he passed it to Mac. She pondered the scribble, but could offer nothing useful.

They gathered their laptops and their backpacks before heading out the door. From the first floor, they stopped in the office, holding the fleet of cars. They chose a four-door Mercedes since they were going to the university, and they needed to blend in with the others.

Nathan slid behind the wheel when he sunk into the soft leather seats. He moaned. "This is sweet."

Mac grinned and laid back in the seat. "I could get used to this." After a pause, she added, "Only until someone started shooting at us. I want the Suburban always surrounding me."

As they drew closer to Clarence's house, Mac texted him, advising him of their ETA. He sent back one word. Hurry!

"He's scared. I hope nothing else has happened."

When the duo pulled into his driveway, Clarence's car wasn't in it. Nathan dialed his number, and when he answered, Clarence called him by another name. The duo exchanged glances. Nathan asked if someone was there, and the answer was yes. Then Nathan asked if classes were over. Clarence said, "Ten minutes". Nathan backed out of the drive, heading to the university. "Clarence, we'll be in the parking lot in a dark gray Mercedes. Don't stare at us, just walk to your car and get in and drive straight home."

The call ended, and the duo raced through town. Mac prayed they wouldn't run into Detective Chinni.

The pair pulled into the lot across from Clarence's vehicle and waited. Two minutes passed before they saw him walking toward them. Then another man followed. Mac snapped photos of the guy as he climbed into a black Tahoe.

Clarence left first, then the Tahoe. The pair took the rear as Mac jotted the tag number on paper for later. Clarence followed instructions well and since Nathan knew Clarence's home address, he didn't want to spook the car, so they turned off before the neighborhood entrance.

The Mercedes passed the house as the Tahoe reversed and drove by it again. This time, he parked across the street. Nathan had an idea, so he called Clarence. "Clarence, we're down the block from you. We see the Tahoe parked across the street. Are there homes behind yours? Any fences?"

"Yes, I have neighbors behind me, but I know them. What are you thinking?"

"I'd like to park in their driveway and come in your back door."

"Ok. Give me a second to call him."

They waited and watched the black Tahoe. He never moved. "I don't see a camera or anything. Why would he just sit there? Is it intimidation?"

The phone rang again. "You have permission. He asked if you could park on the right side of the driveway, in case he needs to leave you wouldn't block him in. His name is Randy, if you see him."

Clarence rattled off his address and Nathan drove to Randy's house.

"This is brilliant, Nathan."

"Not sure it's brilliant, but we now have the element of surprise. The bad guys think Clarence is home alone." Nathan grinned as he said it.

As they climbed from the car, Randy walked out of his front door. He wanted to meet the duo because he was concerned about Clarence's safety. After introducing each other, Randy made it clear they could use his house anytime, but Mac and Nathan had to promise to keep Clarence safe.

Randy showed them the easiest way to Clarence's backyard. They installed a gate many years ago, but a vine had covered it over the years. It didn't take long for Nathan to rid it of the vine. Once they opened the gate, Randy wished them well.

Clarence stood at the back door, watching them traverse the yard. Both homes had a downward slope, so to get to Clarence's, the duo had to walk sideways up a hill. Then Nathan understood why the vine was there. The men were older and walking up the hill would be troublesome for them.

The door flew open and their feet landed on the deck. "Thank goodness you're here."

"Hi Clarence. Tell us what happened."

Clarence produced cookies and coffee before he started on his story. The pair sat in wingback chairs while Clarence sat in the middle of the sofa, facing them. "This guy shows up in my class right after I returned from lunch. He said nothing. Just sat and stared. He left after class. But after supper, he showed up in my night classes. I asked him if I could help him, and he shook his head. So, I never spoke to him again. A few of the students felt uncomfortable with him watching class, so they left. I called the police department, and Detective Chinni showed up. Why a detective, I'll never know. Anyway, he took the guy to the hall. They spoke for a minute, then Detective Chinni waved at me. When I go outside, he says the guy is observing my class for his daughter. I didn't buy that story for a minute, but Detective Chinni left him alone. That's when I called you."

Nathan pulled Anthony's calendar from his pocket. "Does this look familiar?"

"How did you get my calendar?" Clarence asked with a head tilt.

"This isn't yours. We found it in Anthony Chevoski's residence. He followed us to Atlanta and died trying to escape."

"Oh my. Another death. How many more will there be? This is a disaster." Clarence stood and began pacing in front of the sofa.

Mac was grateful this room was on the back side of the house instead of the front. With the guy out front, she was afraid he would shoot them through the window.

Clarence muttered, "I don't understand. None of this seems real."

Nathan shared about the helicopter, and a few other tidbits that they'd found. He didn't elaborate about the truck drivers yet. He would in time, but now wasn't the right time. As Nathan sipped his coffee, Mac noticed a black smudge on his index finger toward the middle finger.

"Nathan, you've got something on your finger."

Grabbing a napkin, Nathan wiped it from his finger. "What could that have been?" He asked himself.

No one answered, but the residue bothered him, like he was supposed to know what it was.

Clarence's cell phone ringing brought everyone back to their dilemma. Clarence spoke with Randy and confirmed he was okay. Then Clarence cleared the room of coffee cups and dishes. While he was away, Mac and Nathan discussed sleeping arrangements. They needed to cover the front and rear of the home, so one would take the rear and one would sleep in the living room.

Clarence provided blankets and pillows. He went to his room at the end of the hallway, leaving the duo alone. They wanted the guy to think Clarence was alone, so they turned on no lights and no TV.

Instead, they lay on their sofas, waiting for the intruder. At 3:00 am, Mac saw headlights traveling down the street. They stopped in front of the house. Was someone else taking over surveillance, or were they planning something?

Mac texted Nathan from under her blanket, so no one saw her screen light. Thirty seconds and no reply, so she resent the text. Nathan replied with a thumbs up.

Lying on the sofa, wondering when the assault would take place, Mac became agitated. She hated being a sitting duck in any altercation. Mac knew she couldn't look outside, so she rolled off the sofa and belly crawled to another room. She had to know what was happening out there.

When she lifted her head, she peeked through the plantation shutter in the lower right corner of the window. Just in time to see two men climb from their vehicles and begin walking toward the house. Both carried handguns down on their thighs.

Mac texted Clarence to get into his closet and stay there until one of them comes to get him. She heard footsteps hurrying to safety. Nathan whispered, "Are you ready?"

"Yes."

Minutes ticked by as the men worked on a plan to enter the home. Nathan had the rear covered, while Mac covered the front. Then the front doorknob rattled. When they couldn't open it, someone knocked it from its hinges. The door landed with a thud. Luckily, nothing stood in its way. Both men entered the door.

They looked both ways, then headed for the hallway. Before they reached it, Mac and Nathan stood behind them with their guns raised, as Nathan yelled, "Stop! Drop your weapons." The men spun around, facing the duo. Each wearing menacing scowls.

The intruder on the left fired a shot at Mac. In her leap over the chair, Nathan fired at the man, hitting him in the right shoulder. Then the second intruder raced to his partner, firing a shot at Nathan.

Nathan winced as the bullet tore through his upper arm. Then a shot sounded, and Nathan instinctively ducked for cover. When he turned his head, he saw Mac lying on the ground with her gun in the air.

Both intruders were down, but they had access to their weapons. And with Nathan wounded, they were in a standoff. Mac pulled her phone from her pocket and dialed 911. She spoke loud enough for the men to hear her. When they heard sirens, they fled the scene.

Nathan sat on the floor, leaning against the wall, with a towel against his left arm. "I think it's just a graze."

"It's bleeding like it's not." Mac replied. Clarence paced behind the pair, rubbing his neck and mumbling.

Clarence pouted. "I'm leaving. I can't stay here with this." Then he trotted down the hallway to his bedroom. Just as the police arrived, Clarence returned carrying a suitcase.

Mac's insides twisted when she saw Detective Chinni pull alongside the curb. "I should have known it would be you two. Who wants to tell me what happened?"

"I do." Clarence said, standing next to Mac and Nathan with his shoulders squared.

"These two folks saved my life tonight." Pausing, then he finished with the story, explaining the guy in the school for which Chinni was aware, then how the guy followed him home, and then the shootout.

Chinni asked, "You still have no idea what these guys are looking for, right?"

"At this point, if I did, I would gladly hand it over." Clarence said. Then he said, "I'll be leaving this house to stay with a friend. My cell phone will be on if you two need me for anything. Find out who's doing this."

Mac and Nathan nodded. As Clarence left, the EMS guys showed up with a bag and a stretcher. "I don't need the stretcher. Just patch this up and I'll be fine."

The medics shared a glance as they inspected the wound. "It's going to take more than a patch. You need stitches."

"Ok. Can you do it, or can I do it?" Again, another glance.

One medic asked, "When did you serve?"

Nathan looked at the man, then answered him. Memories flooded his mind, and most of them were not so grand. He had to stitch himself multiple times in the field and a few friends. As it turned out, he was adept at using a sewing needle.

Mac had no idea Nathan had endured anything like that. He had never shared his military stories with her. Same as her dad. What makes service men hold in their stories? It seems talking about it would help them come to terms with it.

"Ok. I'll go to the hospital, but she'll drive me."

"Nope. You ride with them, and I'll follow. The doctors will see you faster if you show up in an ambulance." Mac stated in a tone that Nathan knew all too well. He didn't test it.

The medics knew not to question Mac, too. So, they wrapped the arm with gauze to staunch the bleeding and Nathan walked to the waiting ambulance. On the drive to the hospital, Mac called George, giving him the update. He said he would be on his way, but Mac stopped him. Once they stitched up Nathan, they would come home.

Mac sat in the freezing cold ER waiting room alone until a group of students rushed to the registration desk. The young nurse behind the counter was taken aback by the number of people. He tried to register the kids one at a time, but the ones in the back of the pack started falling to the floor.

Seeing the commotion, Mac raced to the kids on the floor. Then she yelled, "Who knows what she took?"

When no one answered, she asked again, adding, "She will die if someone doesn't tell me what she took."

A petite blond poked her head out from behind a tall guy. "Heroin. We all did, and we started feeling sick right away. We've used it before, but this time was different."

Mac yelled, "Narcan. We need Narcan and lots of it.'

The nurse flew from the chair, happy to have instructions. When he returned, he brought a red bucket with dozens of Narcan shots and several nurses.

Mac grabbed one Narcan pen and delivered a dose to the girl. It took a few seconds for the drug to reverse the effects of the heroin, but it eventually did. Another nurse loaded the girl onto the stretcher and wheeled her into the emergency room. Once the kids lying on the floor had been treated and removed from the floor, the others followed.

The nurse that sat behind the desk thanked Mac for her quick action. "I've seen this stuff work enough times, so I understand your shock."

"I've never seen it in action. Drugs are a horrible thing and the damage they cause to a body is unimaginable."

Nathan exited through the double doors. "What happened out here?"

Mac chuckled and said, "I'll explain it on the way home." Then she looked at the nurse. "Take care of yourself."

They surveyed the area, ensuring that they were not in someone's crosshairs. Once they felt safe, they walked to the car. "I forgot we were in the Mercedes."

"Yeah, with your arm in a sling, I get to drive it again." Mac said, grinning.

She pulled from the lot and headed to the highway. On the way home, she described the ordeal in the ER. "Are you thinking what I'm thinking?"

"Paul's drugs are tainted."

"Exactly. Either he's getting nervous, or someone did it on purpose to generate police attention."

Nathan nodded in acknowledgment as he thought through the information. Who would taint heroin for pure publicity? Someone that is involved with the dealers but is scared to tell the police. But they take a substantial risk doing that. If those kids hadn't gone to the ER, several would be dead.

A thought popped into Nathan's head. "Did Detective Chinni act different tonight?"

Mac paused as she changed lanes on the interstate, then said, "I believe he did. Almost tired."

When Nathan didn't respond, Mac glanced over at him. His attention was on the road in front. "What are you thinking?" She asked.

"I'm unsure yet. Things are still not making sense. We have to get into the administrative building. That's the only way to solve this problem unless someone calls us and tells us what's going on."

"I don't see that happening. Unless Daniel knows something."

Nathan nodded. "Too early to call. I'll call him later."

Mac parked in the lot as the sun broke the horizon. "I've notified George that we wouldn't be at the office until noon."

"Sounds good. Thanks, Mac." He leaned over, peeking at her on the cheek.

When they entered the apartment, Mac shrieked when she saw the damage. Someone had been in their apartment and had turned everything upside down. Every drawer stood open with pillows slit from top to bottom.

"The bright side is they didn't slice the sofa. We still have a place to sit."

When Mac turned to face him, he couldn't believe the anger behind her eyes. "I'm over this, Nathan. They have violated our home. The next time I get the chance to kill one, I am. I refuse to aim for the shoulder."

Nathan said nothing because Mac's response caught him off guard. He had seen her angry before, but this was something deeper. Something more personal. Maybe he would ask once this case was over because if he asked now, she would explode.

After clearing the house of unwanted visitors, they got busy taking photos and inspecting the apartment. The only damage they found was on the pillows. They had strewn everything else about. So, whatever they searched for was small enough that a throw pillow could conceal it.

"Did the intruders come here searching for a calendar? Clarence had the same calendar that we found at Anthony's. What is so important about it?" Nathan asked.

"Where is Anthony's calendar?" Mac asked, concerned they lost it.

"In here." Nathan lifted his backpack from the floor. He unzipped a side pocket and gave it to Mac.

Mac studied the front cover. Then page by page, she scanned them. When she made it to the end of the last quarter of the year, notations were on several days a week, but they appeared as scribbles. "I need Margot, again." Mac muttered. She showed Nathan the calendar. "These are important enough to write on a calendar, so they mean something to someone. How can we find out what they say?"

Chapter 12

"I'm with you. It would be nice to have Margot run our tests for us. She never failed us."

Mac spent a restless night in bed because she couldn't stop her mind from running through possibilities. She always came back to the subject of drugs. But then, that didn't feel right. It's like something is missing. Then her mind would return to her FBI days. Did she make a mistake by joining her dad's private investigation company? Her heart says no, but her mind is another story. While they didn't have certain protocols to follow, like the FBI, getting information was more difficult. When she had no answers, she finally gave in to sleep, but it wasn't nearly enough to start her day.

"Trouble sleeping?" Nathan asked.

Mac looked at him. "Is it that noticeable?" Mac asked while her hands flew to her eyes.

"It is to me. Is everything okay?"

"The case and our decision to join dad. I'm struggling."

"I can answer the second question and say yes. We made the right decision. We're not comfortable with processes yet. It will come. The case is a puzzle for sure, but in time, we'll solve it too. We always do." Nathan said as he rubbed Mac's arms.

Mac walked closer and laid her head on his shoulder. "Thanks for being here. You always know what to say."

"That's why I'm here."

When the duo arrived at the office, George called for them as soon as the elevator sounded. Mac and Nathan chuckled. George asked for an update before the pair could sit. Nathan started with Clarence leaving town, but they know how to contact him. Then they explained about their apartment being trashed when they arrived home last night.

George went ballistic at them for not calling him, even though there was nothing he could do. Then he circled back to the pillows. "Before we discuss the pillows, how's your arm?"

"Sore, but fine. Stitches dissolve, which is nice."

George took the pause and asked, "Why only the pillows? Have you found anything small that you were unsure what it was?"

"The only small item is this calendar. Clarence has one too. Apparently, the university uses them. This one was found at Anthony's. The notations start toward the year's end. If I remember, it's the third quarter. The handwriting is illegible, so we have no clue what it says."

"Take it to Ionna. She can help with that. Let me know what she finds."

The duo stood, leaving George with his thoughts. He pulled his file from his desk, adding the pillows. Now, why pillows?

Mac stopped at the copy machine and made copies of the dates with writing on them. She didn't want to give up the calendar completely. This would allow them to continue working on it while Ionna did her thing.

After dropping the calendar off with Ionna, they returned to their desks. Nathan wanted to check on Daniel Chinni and Clarence. Then he realized he hadn't heard from Joe.

Mac, on the other hand, wanted to dig a little deeper into the university. How did they find Paul? Was he a referral? Plus, she wanted to see how Anthony and Paul knew each other.

The whiteboard greeted her as she pondered where to start. She stared at it and immediately knew it needed updating. So, Mac added things to the board. Pillows were at the top of the list because they had no idea how they played a role in the scheme.

During Mac's research, she traced Anthony's path right along with Paul's. They have known each other for a decade. Every time Paul moved, Anthony followed. Along with some of Anthony's jail mates. Were the jail mates the men at the loading docks?

When Nathan entered Mac's office, he found her comparing their photos from the loading docks to the pictures of Anthony's jail mates. "What is this?"

After Mac explained Paul and Anthony's commonalities, Nathan said, "Impressive" as his head bobbed.

"I might have found a match, but our photo is so dark, it will take an IT tech to match it for sure."

"We can handle that." Nathan said as he inspected the photos. He pointed to a photo on Mac's desk. "This one matches this guy."

Mac nodded as she jotted names and printed more pictures. The duo went through every photo they had, matching 80% of them. "The unmatched photos could be recent hires from around here. We need clearer photos of these guys so we can run them through facial recognition. If they have a record, we will get a name."

"Can Ionna, or someone from IT, lighten up the photos like Margot did for us?"

"No idea." Mac replied, clearly sad about Margot not being around to help. "Let's ask."

The duo left her office and headed for the elevator when Nathan shared that Clarence was safe. But he left messages for Daniel and Joe.

Mac looked up at Nathan. "Should we meet with Daniel again?"

"I'll see what he says before offering it. He'll be safer without us hanging around him." They chuckled at the comment, knowing it to be gospel.

Ionna had her head down as she inspected the calendar. When she saw them standing at the door, she waved for them to enter. "Hey, you two."

Mac and Nathan greeted her, then Nathan asked what they needed. Ionna tilted her head, then said, "I see no reason. We can't do that."

"Great. I'll forward the photos to you through email so you can manipulate the digital prints. Anything on the calendar?"

"Not yet, I'm afraid. I thought bringing the writing closer would help me see the words, but it doesn't. It's not over yet. I have a few other things I can do on this. I'll call soon." Ionna said.

Nathan and Mac retraced their steps so they could get the photos emailed to Ionna. They needed this handled pronto, just like everything else on their list. While Nathan handled Ionna, Mac returned to the calendar.

She noted there were no times listed, so she assumed whatever was written didn't coincide with a meeting or anything requiring a specific time.

That means that something was to happen in those days. But what? Shipments? Pickups? Deliveries?

Mac couldn't stand it any longer. She had to talk with Margot. So she drafted an email and sent it to her personal email. Mac didn't want the FBI reading her email to Margot.

Her finger hovered over the send button for a few minutes, contemplating if she should do this or not. She hadn't spoken to Margot since leaving the FBI, but in her defense, they had been busy. She emailed Margot before she could second guess herself again. Mac had no idea how often Margot checks her personal email. But she hoped she would check it often.

As the duo circled back to the beginning of the case, Mac constantly checked her email for a reply from Margot. After the first hour, when nothing came, Mac lost hope. She knew Margot was mad at her and that bothered Mac more than she thought it would.

Nathan watched Mac check her email but didn't question her. He knew she was up to something, and that she'd shared when she was ready.

They sat in front of the whiteboard brainstorming ideas. It all circled back to the administrative building at the university. A thought crossed Nathan's mind, so he pulled his cell phone from his pocket, dialing Clarence. When Clarence answered,

Nathan asked, "Have you ever been in the unused rooms in the administration building?"

"There are no unused rooms in the administration building as of last year. Some Professors used those rooms as offices. The math building had a roof leak, so a few professors were moved to the admin building. They stayed there once the roof was fixed, claiming it was too much trouble to move."

"That's interesting. Did James have another office over there?" Nathan asked.

"He did for a while, as did I. But we returned to the math building. Even though the admin building is next door, it made it difficult for the kids to meet with us."

"What are the room numbers where your offices were?" Nathan asked, grabbing a pen and paper. When Clarence gave him the requested information, he ended the call.

Mac blurted out, "Did I hear that right? James had another office in the admin building."

"Yes, you did. But that brings another question. If all the classrooms are being used as offices, where are the guys working overnight?"

Mac's eyebrows bunched. "There's no way they could use the teacher's offices without their knowledge."

"Agree. So, is there a concert hall or maybe an auditorium in that building? Wait. We see no light when we surveil them at night. So how can that be?"

Something was niggling at Mac, but she couldn't bring it forward. Then her email alert sounded.

While Mac clicked her email open, Nathan offered, "If the hallway lights stayed off, the lights inside the auditorium or meeting hall could remain lit with no one from the outside seeing it."

"True." Then Mac read her email from Margot. It elated her to hear from Mac, then she added that she'd slip on the calendar work sometime soon. Mac said, "I need to confess."

Nathan raised an eyebrow and said, "Um, okay." He braced for whatever news Mac shared. "I emailed the calendar pages to Margot. I wanted her to take on them. She'll slip them into her workflow sometime soon."

"That's it. I thought it was something awful when you used the word confess. It's surprising you haven't done it sooner." Nathan said with a grin.

"I don't want her to get in trouble and lose her job with the FBI, especially with Travis there. Have you spoken to Travis?"

"Not in any great length. We text each other, but it's really a way to check-in. We've discussed no cases since we left." Nathan explained. Then added, "It's actually kind of strange at how quiet he's been. He used to turn quiet when he had a secret because everyone teased him because he couldn't keep a secret." Nathan's eyes glazed over as those memories rushed in.

Mac kept her thoughts to herself because Travis' actions were alarming. Travis and Nathan discussed everything before they left the FBI. Now, Mac felt responsible for busting up a friendship.

Nathan asked, "When should we look at the administrative building offices?"

"Now. We have a reason to walk around it, and no one can question us," Mac replied, grinning.

Before leaving, they gave George their itinerary. The last time they were there, things went sideways when a bullet grazed Nathan's arm, resulting in forty stitches. Mac glanced over her shoulder at Nathan. "Grab your sling."

He moaned, but he grabbed it, stuffing it under his arm so he could carry his computer bag with the good arm.

They opted for the Suburban this time, since it made them feel safer. The drive to the North Georgia Mountains was picturesque. The seasons had changed, and the trees were showing off. Dots of color shown through at intervals on the mountainsides and Mac couldn't get enough of it. Even though she was a beach girl, the mountain had its special allure, too.

When they arrived, it appeared classes were just let out. Tons of cars were exiting the campus as they tried to enter. Once they cleared the entrance, things simmered. People walked along the sidewalks, staring at their phones or putting earphones into their ears. It's crazy how attached everyone is to their electronics.

Nathan parked in front of the administrative building. He wondered how long it would take before Detective Chinni showed. Mac asked, "Is it a good idea to park in the front?"

"I hope so. I wanted everyone to see us."

Mac shrugged, hoping Nathan was right. They entered the building shoulder to shoulder and went to the wall map and building directory. Mac snapped a picture of it right before Paul walked up behind them.

"Can I help you two?" He asked in a terse tone.

"I hope you can. We came across information that some of the math professors had an office in this building. We'd like to search James' office." Nathan stated.

"Unfortunately, they cleaned out those when they moved back to the math building. So, there's nothing to see here." Paul reached up to pat Nathan on the shoulder when Nathan shifted.

"Injured arm." Nathan spat.

Then Mac stated, "We'd still like to look at it. You never know when something could help us. We're so close now, it shouldn't take us long to put the last puzzle pieces in place."

Nathan stared at Mac, wondering what caused her to poke Paul. He wished he could take back her words, but that was impossible. They officially put Paul on alert. What was his next move?

"If you feel you need to see it, then let me get you an escort. The offices were in unused classrooms, and they were a little out of the way." Paul said as he tapped a speed dial number.

He mumbled something on the phone, then he returned to the duo. "Detective Chinni should be here momentarily."

"Does he work here because he's here an awful lot?" Mac asked.

"No, he works for the county, but the Sheriff allows me to have him on standby for university safety." Paul said in a practiced statement. Mac nodded while Nathan stared at Paul.

Paul was right. Chinni showed up within ten minutes of the call.

"What's up?" Chinni asked.

Paul instructed Chinni to take Mac and Nathan to James' office. When Paul walked off, Chinni said, "Boy, guys, you two are rubbing the big man in the wrong way. He wants you off the property."

"Why is so eager to see us gone? He hired us to start with," Mac asked.

"I think he realizes his mistake now. But when the board questioned James' death, he thought he would appease them by hiring an outside private investigation firm. Little did he know this would happen."

Nathan looked at Mac. "You're saying that Paul thought the crime scene was perfect and everyone would say James died of suicide."

"That's it in a nutshell."

"Do you know who pushed James to his death?" Mac asked.

"No, I don't. I wasn't on that rooftop. I was working an overnight shift. If I had of been on that rooftop, James would still be alive. James was a good guy," Chinni admitted.

Now, Mac and Nathan bunched their eyebrows as Chinni's demeanor had changed since the last time they were together. What caused the change?

Chinni stepped aside and said, "This is it. This was James' office."

Before entering, Nathan looked down the hall in both directions. Then they entered. It still held a desk, but nothing else. Mac took the desk with Nathan, opening each metal filing cabinet. He found a few pieces of scrap paper when Chinni's phone rang. Nathan assumed it was Paul, but Nathan thought he heard Chinni say Daniel.

Chinni popped his head into the office and said, "Would you mind if I stepped away for a second? My brother is outside."

"Not at all. We shouldn't be long." Nathan said.

Mac pulled open drawer after drawer until she reached the middle drawer. Then it acted like it was stuck. She worked to free it, only to realize that the drawer sticks if it's shoved too far inside the desk. That was another letdown, because she thought she was onto something, hoping James hid information inside the desk.

Nathan saw Mac's face. "Did you find anything?"

"Nothing. You?"

"Just a few bits of paper. I thought James would use this place to hide something, since few folks knew about it. It would have been the perfect place."

Mac repeated, "The perfect place."

Nathan said nothing as he watched Mac walk around the office. She tapped the wall in several places, then her eyes landed on the half-filled bookcase. "You don't think he would hide anything important in there, do you?" Mac asked, pointing.

With his head tilted, he said, "Those books look untouched for years. But maybe."

So, one started at the top, the other at the bottom. They removed each book, shook them out, then replaced them. By the time they finished, they were sneezing uncontrollably, and dust flew throughout the room.

Chinni returned to a dust cloud. "What on earth did you do?"

"We checked the books, but it seems no one has touched them in decades," Mac said between sneezes. As she stood from the floor, her foot hit the bottom of the bookcase, causing a board to shift. She refrained from saying anything because she didn't want Chinni to hear it.

But how or when could they return without Paul or Chinni knowing? And then again, it maybe nothing. In time, she would have to satisfy her curiosity.

Chinni escorted them to Clarence's office next, and it was in the same shape as James, except he had no bookshelf or filing cabinets. This one held a desk and a chair, requiring little effort.

When they stepped outside, they inhaled the mountain air deeply. Then the sneezing subsided. The duo thanked Chinni for the escort, then he said, "Call me before you come back. It would save everyone a headache." He gave them a half wave as he turned toward his car.

The pair nodded, but they both knew that wouldn't happen because if they did, Chinni would give them a reason not to show up. But Chinni seemed different this time, and neither could explain it.

On the way home, Nathan said, "No one followed us. That's weird."

"Do you think Paul is planning on skipping town?"

"That's the most logical explanation. But why would Chinni be nice to us if he saw his payday leaving town?

Mac said, "Oh, I found something in James' office, but with Chinni there, I didn't want to tell you."

Nathan looked at Mac, "Well?"

"My toe hit the bottom of the bookcase, jarring a board to come lose. I'm unsure if it means anything, but it was odd, and Chinni didn't seem to notice." Mac explained.

Nathan pondered the information. "How can we get back into the office without Chinni or Paul?"

"If we had a reason to get Paul away from the building, we could slip inside, then find our way back to the offices without someone catching us," Mac offered. "Like a protest would do it."

"Daniel." Nathan muttered. "I haven't heard from him. That's concerning. But Chinni supposedly stepped away from us to speak with his brother.

Neither spoke for a few minutes until Nathan tapped Daniel's contact card. He answered, "Nathan, are you okay?"

"Yes. Why wouldn't I be?"

"I just haven't heard from you, and it concerned me. The last time I spoke with David, he said he would leave town for a few days, but he didn't say where he was going." Daniel shared. "Have you found out anything else?"

"Yes, we have, but we can't share yet. We need to get back into the administration building without Paul or your brother knowing. Can you help us do that?"

Daniel thought for a second, then said, "Sure, I can. When do you want to do it?"

"Paul was still in his office when we left a few minutes ago, so we'll have to do it later."

"Oh. You were with my brother today when I called him. I wondered why he walked outside to talk. He actually sounded more like himself today than he has in a while."

"You know, Daniel, we said those same words. Any idea what's happened?" Nathan asked.

"No idea. But I can tell you the students are having a memorial for Professor Gregory in two days. Paul has been scheduled to speak at the memorial for Professor Gregory. That might be your opening to the admin building." Daniel offered.

"Sounds perfect. Keep in touch." Then the call ended.

Mac turned to face Nathan. "At least we're not the only ones thinking Chinni acted differently this visit."

Nathan drove with one eye on the rearview mirror, and when they entered the lot, he let out a breath he didn't realize he held. They surveyed the lot before entering their apartment. Seeing no unfamiliar cars, they let themselves into the apartment. Another relief when everything was in its place.

When Mac's alarm sounded, she grabbed her phone, turning off the hideous sound quickly. Then she checked text messages and emails, finding nothing from Margot. Mac's day started in a foul mood. She just knew Margot would come through for her.

Nathan noticed the quiet mood but refrained from asking questions. He found out early on in their relationship that Mac would share when she was ready. So he handed her a steaming cup of coffee.

She took two sips, then said, "Margot never replied about the calendar entries."

Nathan grinned, knowing the reason for her mood. "She's busy, but she'll get back to you." Then he turned around, holding a plate with a perfect omelet.

"Wow. That's pretty. Why haven't you served these before?" Mac asked as she accepted the plate, then took a bite. "Oh my. This is incredible. What's in it?"

"I can't share my secret." Nathan said, as he ate his omelet. He watched Mac look at each piece, trying to figure out what ingredients he used to make it.

Once they finished, they headed downtown to the office. Nathan knew that Mac was still feeling down about Margot, but she seemed to accept the situation. On the way to the office, Ionna called Nathan.

"Hi Nathan, I have your photos ready. Can you stop by on the way to your office?"

"Sure can. Fifteen minutes away." Then he ended the call.

"Did she run them through facial recognition?" Mac asked as her gut twisted. There's something that bothers her about Ionna, but she can't figure it out.

"No idea."

They made good time reaching the lab with the morning traffic. Ionna waited at the door and greeted the duo. "It worked. I have your photos ready, but I haven't added them to facial recognition yet. The system was undergoing maintenance overnight."

"Ok. Email them to me and I'll handle that part. Thanks." Nathan turned to leave when Ionna placed her hand on his arm. "Is there anything else you need?"

Mac stepped forward and said, "No, we're good."

Then the duo left. "She's acting strange." Nathan stammered. "I need to talk with George."

When they made it upstairs, Nathan headed for George's office when another investigator said, "He's not in yet. Might be lunchtime."

"Do you know where he is?" Nathan asked.

"I'm not supposed to say, but yeah, I know. He's with Lizzie at the doctor's office. They're hoping she gets released today." The investigator grinned. Then Nathan did too.

Nathan shared George's whereabouts and Mac chuckled. "This is a first for me, seeing George with a lady friend. I like it. It will be good for him."

Then Mac's email alert sounded. Her eyes grew wide as she opened her laptop. "It's from Margot." She exclaimed.

She read it twice before sharing with Nathan. "We've stumbled onto something massive. Margot wants to get the FBI involved, as does Travis. Travis will call you shortly. It appears the calendar is a shipping itinerary. They ship cargo to Argentina, Brazil, Venezuela, Peru, Colombia and Panama."

"Wait. You're telling me Paul's group ships drugs to those places when some of them have their own drug cartels? That makes little sense. What makes Paul's drugs better than their own?" Nathan asked, clearly confused by Margot's information. "Why spend money shipping drugs to countries that have their own drug trade?"

"Now that you put it that way, it makes no sense. Something else is in play here." Mac wrote the information on the board that Margot provided. Then Nathan's phone rang. It was Travis.

Nathan stepped out of Mac's office. He wanted to discuss some things with Travis privately. It was time to find out what was going on with him.

As Nathan and Travis discussed the case, Travis suggested involving the FBI. But then Nathan admitted to Travis, they had no proof of anything yet. They only had the calendar of a dead guy. It proved nothing. Nathan promised that as soon as they had usable evidence, they would notify the FBI. Travis spoke of Margot and his plans to marry her soon. When Nathan asked about the FBI office, Travis turned quiet. Then he admitted it wasn't the same without him.

Travis promised to see Nathan soon. Then they ended the call. By the time they finished, Mac had the board updated with the new information. She had her notecards sorted into piles around her desk. She looked at Nathan as he entered her office.

He rehashed the conversation, even telling her that Travis promised to see them soon. Mac grinned. "I hope so."

While Mac worked with her cards, Nathan ran the facial recognition from the enhanced photos. They garnered no new information from that. Either the photos weren't good enough or the guys weren't in the system. He shared it with Mac. Then they were at a loss, again.

They stood ready to grab lunch when George popped his head in the door. "Nathan, I hear you wanted to see me."

"Just whenever you have a minute."

"Come on."

Then Mac asked, "How's Lizzie?"

George couldn't contain the grin. "The doctor released her today. So, we're on cloud nine."

"That's great, George."

Nathan followed George to his office, then Nathan explained the situation with Ionna. George's eyebrows drew together, then when Nathan finished, he said, "I'm to blame for Ionna. I should never have hired her, and I'm working to remedy that situation now. It might be a few more weeks, but she'll be gone. Can Mac speak with her instead of you?"

"I'll handle it. Just knowing something is in the works makes it tolerable." Nathan stated. He left feeling better about the issue, but wondering what the remedy might be.

Mac stood at the elevators waiting for Nathan when her dad stepped off. "Mac. How are you?"

"Good, Dad. Waiting for Nathan. We're heading to lunch."

"Mind if I join you? I need an update on your case, and we can catch up."

"Sure. Come on."

"Give me a second to drop this." Myles lifted his bag in the air as he walked to his office. Myles and

Nathan walked to meet Mac. They spoke briefly about the case before the elevator doors opened to a group of folks standing inside.

Scenes like these caused Myles to flinch. Too many folks in an elevator can be dangerous. He knows because he's survived several incidents on elevators, but he joined them for the ride down, anyway.

Chapter 13

On the walk to the food truck, Mac asked Myles where he's been, but his response was vague, and his eyes never met hers. Nathan observed the exchange and understood that something was going on that he wasn't ready to reveal. Mac was subdued after that exchange, letting Myles lead the conversation.

As the trio ate their food, they discussed the case. Nathan shared the information about the calendar entries but left out the fact Margot helped them since Ionna couldn't. Mac hit Nathan on the knee with hers when he mentioned the calendar, so he knew he had better keep a secret.

Myles pondered the information on the calendar. "Why would someone send drugs into places that already have a drug business? Is Paul the mastermind behind the drug cartels across South America?" He shook his head. That wasn't logical.

So, when Myles couldn't think of anything further to ask about Paul, Mac started in on James. She shared about their second office search and the bookcase. Myles' eyes grew wide.

"Now, that's promising. When are you planning to return to the university?"

"Tomorrow. Detective Chinni's brother, Daniel, told us about a memorial for James. It's happening tomorrow and we'll be there since Paul and his staff are reportedly speaking at it."

"Nice. What about Chinni?" Myles asked as he swallowed a gulp of iced tea.

"We hope he's at the memorial. But if not, we'll deal with him. He hasn't hurt us yet, and he's had plenty of opportunities, so I'm assuming he'll listen to reason."

"Ok. Nathan. Sounds like you have a plan. Run with it. But if you want backup, take it from the office, not Chinni or his department. We don't know who's involved with Paul." Myles gave them a dire warning, and he hoped they would take it.

George stood next to Nathan's office when the trio returned from lunch. Nathan's eyes flew to Myles when he saw George. George caught on to the action and said, "Hey, guys. Any updates on the case?"

Nathan exhaled a sigh of relief because he didn't want to share his issue with Myles. He didn't want to come across as petty. But George needed to know. After Myles greeted George, he said, "George, come see me when you're finished with Nathan and Mac."

George followed Nathan into his office, and he shut the door. "I saw the look you gave Myles. What's going on?"

Nathan started from their first day on the job and how Ionna acted toward him versus Mac. Then he explained how it's only gotten worse and now it's to the point Ionna is placing her hand on his arm.

The entire time Nathan spoke, George's face turned red, starting at his neck and working its way to the top. By the time Nathan finished, it concerned him that George might explode. But once Nathan finished, and George took a few seconds to calm, he seemed okay.

Nathan added, "I don't want to sound petty, but I think there is something wrong with her."

"I've wondered. Our top analyst left after working with Ionna for two months. That makes me wonder if something happened between them. He never explained why he left. Just said he had another opportunity."

George turned his chair around and unlocked a door in credenza. He pulled Ionna's file from the drawer. Nathan gave him time to peruse it. George said, "Nothing in here seems suspicious. All her references checked out, too. I'll work on getting her replaced. Thanks for letting me know and I understand why you didn't want to share with Myles. Besides, this is my screw up. I hired her. Now, I wish I had Brady back. He was fantastic."

"Call him. Now that you've heard my story, he may share his," Nathan suggested.

Mac was knee deep in cards when Nathan stopped by her office. "How did it go?" She asked him.

"Better than I expected. Brady, their top analyst, left after working with Ionna for two months. George wants to know if she's the reason he left."

"If she treats all males like she does you, then I say he left because of her. How is George handling it?" Mac while shifting cards to new piles.

"He'll replace her when he has someone to fill her spot."

Mac nodded, then said, "Since everyone has issues with Paul shipping drugs, there must be something else on those pallets."

"We've said that before. But we don't know what it is." Nathan clarified.

"Is there anything the US has that these places don't have or can't get?" Mac asked.

"I'm unfamiliar with some of the areas, but a few could use ammo and guns." Nathan stated. "That's just from my time in the service." Then he stopped. "Come on, you don't think Paul is shipping illegal firearms to these places, do you?"

"Pallets. Ink. Heroin. Guns. Ammo." Mac smiled. "What better combination is there?"

"Where do they keep these weapons? Chinni escorted us through the building to the offices. I saw no rooms large enough to store the weapons."

"I'm still working on that."

Jackson raced up to Mac's door. "Thank goodness you're here."

"Jackson, are you okay?"

"Your Paul Drummond just received an enormous deposit in his offshore account. I haven't tracked the original sender because it's bounced around the world for two days. But I thought you should know. The sender should show itself later today. I'll text you when I find it."

"How enormous is the deposit?" Nathan asked.

"2.25 million."

"I agree. That's enormous." Nathan said as Mac nodded her head.

When Jackson left, the duo pondered the latest development. Mac muttered as she doodled, "If Paul received payment today, when would the goods ship?"

"Good question. Open the calendar on your computer. Let's look."

When she did, their mouths fell open. "Venezuela is printed on tomorrow's date. So, after the memorial, Paul and his crew will be working." Mac's mind worked in overdrive. "You're going to say no to this, but what if we hid until the workers showed, then we could follow them to their hideout?"

"You're right. No way are we doing that. We're asking for trouble. That's way too dangerous. Besides, we'll already be there. We can watch and follow again. We'll have George give us a few agents because the truck will head to Miami for Venezuela."

"George can speak with Dad about the docks in Miami. Maybe Dad can find that same guy we spoke with earlier. He was a tremendous help." Mac recalled. Then she asked, "Can you obtain a shipping manifest before they ship the cargo?"

Nathan lifted his shoulders because he had no answer. Then the duo shifted gears and began laying out their plan. Once they felt comfortable with it, they sat back in their chairs.

The duo left for home early as tomorrow promised to be active. They advised George of their plan and he agreed to it. He made several calls, rounding up four investigators for their backup. Tracy, Everett, Jose, and Nicholai will join them tomorrow at the University. Everyone is dressing down for this operation since it's on the university grounds, but they are to remain armed and wear ear comms.

Since they had three teams of two, Nathan and Mac would drive a Suburban while the others would drive a fleet car. Nathan didn't want three black Suburbans entering the University simultaneously. Paul and Chinni would be on them so fast, and that's what they hoped to avoid.

The two teams agreed to meet at a predetermined area near the university, then each car would enter at ten-minute intervals. Tracy and Everett were both younger looking than the others. So, they would attend the memorial. No one would question them.

While Jose and Nicholai would serve as backup for Mac and Nathan when they entered the administration building. Mac wanted to check out the loose board in the bookcase. Then they'd have time to spare before the night's activities began.

Mac and Nathan rehashed the plan over supper but decided on no changes. With the impeding activity, Mac struggled to fall asleep. And when she did, it was restless. When she awoke to her alarm, she couldn't explain the dreams she endured. So, she dressed and headed out to meet Nathan.

He stood ready in jeans and a flannel shirt, which he left untucked. Mac noticed how good he looked in flannel but kept her thoughts to herself. As she sipped coffee, the events of the day returned to her mind. "Is everything a go?"

"Nothing has changed, so I say yes."

Then Mac's cell phone beeped for a text, as did Nathan's. Both texts were from Jackson, and he sent one word. Venezuela. After reading it, their eyes met, and they nodded.

"Call Myles. Alert them to the shipment. Let's see if we can find out when the cargo is leaving."

Mac wasted no time calling her dad. She explained the latest development, and he agreed to help find out about the shipment.

They traveled north on I75 then went east. Their backup arrived behind them at different intervals. "OK. Everyone is ready. They are in a silver sedan and a small white SUV. "

Mac nodded as she entered the information into her phone. If something happens, she doesn't want to be without that. She noticed the sun breaking through the morning clouds as their plan ran through her mind.

Upon entering, Nathan turned toward the memorial, as did Tracy. While Nathan and Mac would park in the lot near the memorial, they had no intention of attending. Tracy and Everett would attend the memorial standing in the back of the crowd. They would wear ear comms and let Nathan and Mac know of Paul's whereabouts.

Jose and Nicholai were backup. They will park in front of a nearby building and find a spot to hide. Nicholai was the sniper for this operation, although Jose could shoot, too. Nathan was glad they were available. He'd heard stories of both guys taking ridiculously difficult shots and succeeding.

When everyone gives the 'all clear' signal to Mac and Nathan, they slip into the administrative building. They give each other a nod, since there are no discernible noises. As they walk around a corner toward the hallway, they hear voices and they're getting closer.

The duo ducked into the closest room and held their breath. Once the threat passed, they continued to James' office. But this time someone had locked the door. Nathan whispered, "Why is it locked? It wasn't the last time we were here."

Mac shrugged as Nathan pulled his picks from his side pants pocket. He worked the picks inside the doorknob for a few seconds before it clicked. Then he opened the door, and the duo slipped inside, gently closing the door behind them.

They immediately knew someone had been in the office because they left dust prints where objects once sat. Wearing gloves saved them from worrying about fingerprints. So Mac went about trying to undo the board from the bookcase bottom.

After several attempts to move the board again, Mac became frustrated. Sweat beaded on her forehead, eventually running down her face. She'd swipe it with her shirt sleeve and continue.

"Something's not right." She whispered to Nathan, but everyone heard her.

"Need help?" Jose asked in a clipped tone.

"Negative. We're having difficulty with the board." Nathan replied.

"10-4."

Mac stood from the floor, looking around. Then Nathan said, "Try from over here. Maybe it's the angle."

So Mac did. And nothing. The next time she tried a little to the left, and they heard the click. When they looked down, the board shifted slightly, revealing a hiding space. Mac glides the board inside the case, then with gloved hands, she put her flashlight to the hole first before slipping her hand inside.

The hole is barely large enough for her hand to fit, so she knows it's up to her to find whatever is in there, if anything. She started with the left side first, since it was the easiest to reach. After running her hand around the bottom, she gave up and moved to the right side.

Nathan never uttered a word as she worked to clear the area. He noticed Mac getting more frustrated by the minute. It worried her they were taking up so much time. But Tracy and Everett had remained quiet on the comms, which helped calm the nerves.

"I'm finding nothing in here." Mac whispered. Then she added, "Wait. I touched something small and hard. It moved, now I can't find it."

"Take some deep breaths, Mac. Return to the area you felt it and work out from there. You'll find it." Nathan suggested in a calm voice, even though he knew their time was running out. How long do memorials last? It had been half an hour, and they still hadn't completed it.

Mac tried again several times before she said, "I have it." Then she slowly slid her hand from the hole. She lifted it in the air, so Nathan could see it.

"A thumb drive."

They nod their heads when Tracy warned them that Paul was on the move. He's trotting toward the administrative building. Mac quickly slides the panel back in place, turned off the flashlight, and slipped the thumb drive into her side pocket. She wanted to put it into her backpack, but Tracy's voice halted that step.

Jose spoke next. "Paul is twenty-five steps from the front door."

"Copy. We'll exit the side door on the west."

"Copy."

Nathan took the lead and Mac followed. They walked toward the side exit when Everett gave another update. "Chinni pulled up to the front of the building and is running inside. Something is up."

"10-4." Nathan replied. Since he scoped out the side entrance on their last visit, he knew the route.

When Nathan opened the door and stepped aside for Mac to exit, they heard someone yell, "Halt!"

But they didn't. Instead, they bolted for the woods behind the building. Neither looked over their shoulders as they sprinted through the woods, going deep enough that everything turned dark. When Nathan realized no one followed them, he stopped running.

"Someone tell me what's going on," Nathan begged.

Seconds passed before Tracy gave them the update. "Chinni has a girl in handcuffs and he's escorting her to his car."

Mac and Nathan exhaled as that explained what had happened when they were inside the building. Chinni was yelling at the girl, not at them. Nathan spoke to the team, telling them what happened too. That gave everyone a chuckle.

So, they walked around the building, joining the others. After they met, they left separately, knowing the next meeting place. With a few hours to spare before their surveillance, they would take advantage of a little downtime.

Later that day, as dusk arrived, the teams found their spots. With the addition of the teams, Mac and Nathan felt more relaxed than they had on previous stakeouts. Each team held cameras with telephoto lenses. They asked for close-up photos of people and merchandise.

Mac nor Nathan had been fortunate enough to capture a decent photo of the merchandise. Paul's group wraps each pallet with enough plastic wrap. No one can read the outside of the boxes. The duo knew the contents were different from the outside of the boxes, but it might help them track the shipment.

Nicholai was the first to report the activity. "Two cars parked near the loading docks with three entering the University grounds."

All replied with a "10-4."

Mac and Nathan readied themselves for the night. They leaned across the hood of the Suburban, giving them a steady surface for placing their elbows. Mac couldn't hold the camera up to her eye for long stretches of time without the hood. This way, she could take pictures all night, if needed.

Nathan paced, changing positions so he could watch the workers from multiple angles. He whispered, "Nothing new here."

Nicholai replied, "Transfer trucks entering." He stopped, then added, "Helo approaching from Southeast. Take cover."

No one replied. They stayed off the comms until the bird sat down in the field behind Mac and Nathan. They swore under their breaths because that wasn't expected. Every time they had been here, the helicopter never flew until after the operation. So, what changed? Mac wondered to herself.

Mac and Nathan watched the helicopter fly overhead, but they felt relief as it failed to fly directly over them. They hoped the lights didn't reflect from their vehicle. Time would tell if it did.

Activity picked up at the building once the trucks were in place. The team knew the last trucks went to Washington State and Miami. They would travel with it until replacements could take over.

Mac snapped photos of the merchandise. She thought it was a picture of schoolbooks. Are they printing labels for their boxes? Her heart rate inched up as the thought worked out Paul's plan.

No one spoke until the trucks left the scene. Tracy and Everett followed the guy toward Miami while Jose and Nicholai headed west.

Mac and Nathan packed up their gear, wondering how long it would be before they had the last bit of information on Paul's enterprise. It was time to end this. If every box on the pallets contained heroin, he was killing people at an alarming rate.

As they loaded into the truck, they heard a vehicle close by. Nathan pointed to the dirt road behind them. They squatted down as the noise drew louder because they couldn't chance entering their vehicle. Even with the interior light disabled, there could still be a reflection.

Everett called over the comms, "Nathan, are you and Mac en route to the rendezvous point?"

"Negative. We're still in a lookout position. Sounds like someone is driving to the helicopter. Stand by."

After the vehicle passed, Mac muttered, "They seem to be in a hurry."

Nathan didn't offer a response right away. Instead of climbing into the vehicle, he motioned for Mac to follow. He grabbed his backpack, slinging it over his shoulders. "Let's go see what's going on."

Mac's head tilted, but she agreed. They hiked toward the chopper. When they heard car doors slamming shut, they stopped. Nathan extracted his binoculars from the bag and lay in the leaves, searching for the activity. Mac did the same.

They spotted two men climb into the chopper. The rotors began spinning, and that's when things turned. Mac whispered, "Nathan, is that Chinni?"

"Yeah. He's the one with the gun pointed at his head."

Then silence as the duo witnessed Chinni's kidnapping, and there was nothing they could do to prevent it.

When the copter took off, the duo felt certain that would be the last time they would see Chinni alive. But when Chinni looked out of the window, Nathan could have sworn he looked right at him.

"Why would they take Chinni?" Mac questioned.

Nathan didn't answer her, instead he spoke in his ear comm giving the group the update. When they asked the same thing, Nathan had no answer for them either. It made no sense. Unless Chinni backstabbed Paul.

"We need to talk with George now." Nathan plucked his phone from his pocket and hit George's speed dial.

He spoke rapidly to George, describing Chinni's issue. When George asked Nathan for his gut feeling, his response was, "I think Chinni is undercover. That was the change Mac, and I noticed the last time we met him. He let his guard down and Paul noticed it."

George said to meet the others and await word from him. So Mac and Nathan packed their gear and drove to town. The others had already arrived in the parking lot and stowed their gear.

Tracy was the first to ask, "What happened back there?"

Nathan explained it, but when he told them about Chinni, their mouths formed the letter O. No one likes to hear of another law enforcement member in trouble.

Everett advised he would stay with them if they went after Chinni. "No matter who Chinni works for, he's still law enforcement."

Everyone else agreed. The team stepped into their vehicles to wait on George, which didn't take long. George's phone number popped up on the dash, and Mac tapped it first.

"George."

"OK. I've got someone at the airport tracking the helicopter. It looks like it's headed to a small airport north of Macon. I'm still digging into Chinni. I'll call you back. You might as well head south."

Nathan spoke to the others and in a convoy, they drove south with no known destination. When they reached Atlanta, they stopped for gas and a break. Since they hadn't heard from George, they didn't know how long they'd be driving.

"Mac, what's north of Macon?"

"Forsyth is the closest that I'm familiar with. That's where law officers go for training." She paused, then asked, "Why would Paul go there? The last time I was there, there wasn't much happening."

"See if Paul's corporation owns any buildings in Forsyth? Although just because he lands there doesn't mean that's his last stop." Nathan said with a head tilt.

Mac typed several searches into her phone before she finally found it. "He owns warehouses in Macon. Or I should say, the warehouses have a Macon address, but it's on the edge of Forsyth."

"Send the addresses to the team. That's our first stop."

Mac followed the instructions, then she muttered, "I hope Chinni is okay."

"Me too, Mac. Me too."

George called, "They set the chopper down in a field outside Forsyth."

Mac blurted out, "Paul owns warehouses in that area. We're headed there now."

"Wait, you can't go alone. I'll send backup."

"George, the others are with us. We're just going to see if we can rescue Chinni. If not, then we'll be home." Nathan shared.

"I didn't realize they stayed. Ok. That works, but you must give me updates."

"Understood." Nathan said and Mac agreed verbally.

Every time Nathan changed lanes, the others followed. Mac wondered what folks thought when they saw the choreographed movement. Then her mind shifted to Chinni. Is he an undercover officer?

Why didn't he share that with us? We're on the same team.

Unless he's DEA. Then they keep their undercover close to their chest for fear of detection. But if they'd have known, they might could have prevented the kidnapping.

The phone rang and Mac tapped Myles' number. "Dad."

"Hi Mac. George filled me in on your escapade. I hope you find Chinni. It doesn't sound good for him. I have messages out to several folks trying to find out about Chinni. Maybe they could lend a hand to help him." Then silence.

"Dad, are you still there?"

"Sorry. I have another call. Hold the line." Then emptiness. Mac stared at Nathan as the miles flew past.

Myles returned to the line, "Still nothing on Chinni. We'll stay in touch."

When the team got close to Forsyth, they exited the interstate. They didn't want to show up in a convoy when they're aiming to be unnoticeable. After pulling into an all-night fast-food joint, the team entered, finding hot coffee and food.

Just as they were wadding up their paper remnants, Nathan's cell phone rang. "George. Yes, we are all here. OK. Send it to me."

"George is sending me the address of where the helicopter landed. He thinks it's close to the warehouses." When Nathan's phone beeped, he glanced at it, then forwarded it to the others.

Everyone studied the map. If they intended on helping with this rescue, they needed to know the area intimately. Everett and Nicholai offered options for surveillance that Nathan adopted. Mac noticed how the men acted after Nathan agreed with their ideas. Another bond had formed.

Then her gut twisted when she thought of Travis and Margot. She wanted Travis here for Nathan, but she didn't know how to make it happen. When Nathan called her name, she studied his face and nodded. Hoping she caught everything he said.

They loaded up into their vehicles and headed in different directions, but with the same destination in mind.

Tracy and Everett would verify that the tracked helicopter was indeed Paul's, while Jose and Nicholai would take the North side of the warehouse park while Mac and Nathan took south. After visiting the helicopter, Tracy and Everett would come in from the west. Roadway covered the East side.

Mac and Nathan found a suitable location for their surveillance. As they unloaded from the truck, their comms confirmed their teammate's location. Tracy and Everette spotted the helicopter before they noticed they were in plain sight of it. Luckily, when they turned into the woods, they realized the area was void of human life. The only living things they found were squirrels. And they were everywhere.

As Nathan lifted his binoculars to his eyes, his cell phone rang. He answered it and listened. "The helicopter is parked in the field, not at an airport," he said.

"Did I hear you right?" Mac asked.

"Yes. That means Paul didn't file a flight plan. Wonder why?" Nathan said as he resumed his position.

Mac noted a dim light on the rear of the warehouse, but there was no other activity. Nathan agreed.

"How many warehouses are out here?" Mac asked. "If Chinni is in another one, may be the others can spot him."

"I hope so."

They waited for word from the others before commencing their plan. Each team would work their way to the warehouse and get a visual inside. Everyone knew their prime target was Chinni. Now that they knew about the warehouses, they could return for the contents anytime.

Minutes passed before everyone had a chance to surveil their warehouse. No one claimed to see movement. Each building had a dim light in the back, next to the loading docks.

When the time came, Mac and Nathan crept forward toward their building. They knew time was of the essence because the sun would pop over the horizon within the hour. The cover of darkness was their friend.

Mac spotted a window in the building which would give them partial access to the interior. The only issue was the window was high on the wall above the air conditioning unit. Mac stood in Nathan's hands, and he hoisted her to the top of the unit. She grabbed the top and lifted herself the rest of the way.

She walked on the unit's edge for fear of falling into the spinning fan. When she made it to the window, she rubbed dirt off it and peered inside. With her phone in her hand, she snapped photos of the interior showing full pallets of cargo. But no Chinni. There was also no movement, and she heard no sounds.

Chapter 14

Mac turned to face Nathan but lost her balance. In the process of trying to catch herself, her phone went airborne. Nathan was unsure whether he should catch Mac or the phone until Mac yelled, "Phone!"

Nathan sprinted to the other side of the air conditioning unit just in time to catch the phone before it smashed into the asphalt. He stood up, grinning, holding the phone high in the air. "Just like the good old days."

Mac steadied herself as she shimmied down the side of the enormous unit. She studied the palm of her left hand when Nathan rounded the corner. Blood dripped onto the ground as she grimaced.

"Let me look at it." Nathan reached for her hand as he unzipped his backpack. "This might sting, but it will stop the bleeding." He laid a gauze pad on top of the laceration and pulled the self-adhesive wrapping tight.

Mac groaned. "I got it good, didn't I?"

"I've seen worse. At least it's still attached." Nathan smiled, then he continued, "You will need medical attention to avoid infection." Nathan explained.

"Call the others. Let's hear their findings." Mac suggested as they returned to their truck.

Jose and Nicholas were the first to respond. "We have a transfer truck parked at our building, but we find no driver."

"OK. We're coming to you," Nathan said. "Tracy, Everett. Respond."

Nathan glanced at Mac, and she saw the worry creep into his eyes. He was just about to call again when Everett answered. "We just concluded our search. There are five guys in the warehouse near the front door. We did not spot Chinni. I repeat. We did not spot Chinni."

Mac said, "Where could he be?"

Nathan replied, "Do you have eyes on Paul?"

"Negative."

"That's where Chinni is. He's with Paul wherever that is," Nathan said. He rubbed his neck as he conjured up places Chinni might be, but nothing stuck. Why would Paul put a gun to Chinni's head and force him into a helicopter? Was Chinni's cover blown if there was one to blow?

Nathan dialed Daniel with the premise of checking on him. But in reality, he hoped he would shed some light on Chinni's whereabouts. He left another message for Daniel. Now he had another worry.

As the duo drove to meet Jose and Nicholai, Mac studied her hand, even though she couldn't see the wound. Nathan wrapped it so tight that she couldn't even peek at it. At least there was no blood on the outside of the gauze.

Jose explained their location and Nathan pulled in behind their car. Once they left the car, Jose and Nicholai pointed to the window they used for their surveillance. It had the exact design as the one Mac used. Somehow, the guys came away unscathed.

Nicholai drew a diagram of the building's interior in the dirt. He pointed out the truck's location. Then he confirmed there was no movement inside the warehouse.

Nathan offered, "Did you find a way inside?"

Nicholai and Jose exchanged a glance. "We were told this was a surveillance mission."

"I realize that, but the last truck we found in Miami, the driver, was inside dead. We need to check if we can get in with no one noticing."

Everett interrupted the conversation with the news. "Nathan, Mac. The guys are leaving and will pass your location. I repeat. The guys will pass your location."

Nicholai and Nathan jumped into action. They hid deeper into the woods, but there was nothing they could do for their vehicles. Since Nathan drove a black truck, they prayed the gray sedan would stay hidden.

No one spoke, not because they were afraid of someone hearing it, but because they held their breath until the guys passed their location. The guys drove a van with an electric company logo on it. That was something new.

As soon as the threat passed, the guys went to work in the warehouse. The back door proved entry was unattainable. Someone rigged the warehouse with a security alarm. Nathan wanted to bust a window and shimmy inside, but he knew he couldn't do that. So, he let the notion go. He knew if the driver was dead, there was nothing he could do for him, anyway.

The foursome loaded up and drove to the last warehouse. Tracy and Everett stood outside, holding their weapons ready. Tracy said, "Close call. Glad it worked out."

Mac sighed, "Me too."

Tracy said, "The five guys sat around a square table toward the front of the building. The back is so dark we couldn't see inside."

"Did you notice any pallets full of cargo?" Mac asked.

"Not at the front. But who knows what's in back?" Tracy offered.

Nathan took the guys with him. While someone peeked inside, the others stood guard. When the guys made it to the rear of the building, the darkness encompassed everything. There was no way to know what it held. And because of where the warehouse sat, it would be impossible to sneak a view in the daytime.

When they finished, Nathan suggested, "Let's go back to town. We need to update George and Myles. My guess is we'll be driving back to Atlanta."

Nathan led the convoy again to another fast-food location. This time they met in the parking lot since folks were stopping for breakfast and they couldn't speak of their night in front of others.

George and Myles spoke to the group, gathering all the facts they could. In the end, the team received instructions to return to Atlanta with a promise that Nathan could search for Chinni.

Everyone climbed into their vehicles and returned to Atlanta, but with a day to recoup. Nathan looked at Mac. "I noticed you tell your dad or George about your hand."

"There is nothing they can do about it. It's done. I'll go to urgent care. They can stitch it if it needs any," Mac said.

"Now that the bleeding has stopped, it will be easier to treat. Hands bleed a lot because of the veins running through the fingers. You might get lucky and need a few butterfly sutures. They are like tiny miracles."

Mac chuckled. "How many have you used in your lifetime?"

"Too many to count." Nathan said as he turned into an urgent care parking lot.

Mac grimaced. "I thought we could sleep before I had to do this."

"No way are you waiting ten hours for that to be cleaned. Come on. I'll hold your hand," Nathan said, then he corrected himself, "Actually, I'll just hold your elbow." Then he snickered.

Mac never uttered a word, and she didn't need to, because her eyes said it all. The idea of someone poking around her sore hand didn't thrill her. But Nathan gave her no choice.

When the nurse saw Mac, she took her straight into an exam room. The nurse asked Mac who wrapped it, and Nathan raised his hand. "You can join my staff anytime."

Nathan smiled but didn't reply because his cell phone rang. He winked at Mac and stepped outside the door, eventually walking out the front door, when he heard Daniel's voice.

Mac's insides fumed as Nathan left her sitting there alone. But the nurse was chatty and that kept her mind busy even when she gave Mac a shot inside the laceration. There was debris inside the cut and infection worried the nurse. Because of that, there were no stitches. Mac had never been happy to hear the infection until now.

The nurse applied medicine after the shot and closed it with butterfly strips, saying, "The laceration will need to heal from the inside out." Then she wrapped it again in a similar fashion to Nathan's.

On the way out, the nurse suggested, "Get your husband to wrap it for you after your change your dressings." Mac stared and nodded. Then she felt Nathan standing behind her.

When she turned, Nathan asked, "Did she call me your husband?"

Mac nodded, unsure how he would react.

"Sounds good to me." Then Nathan took a stunned Mac by the elbow and ushered her to the car. Once they were inside, Nathan said, "Daniel called. He's fine, but he's worried about his brother. I didn't have the heart to tell him what we knew about Chinni."

"Someone will have to tell him." Mac said, concerned.

"Agree. But I want something definitive to tell him. Not that Paul had a gun to Chinni's head and forced him into a helicopter, and now he's missing."

Nathan said, adding, "Paul could have shot him and thrown him from the helicopter. If he did that, we'll never find him."

Mac laid her head back, thinking about the situation. Would Paul kill Chinni and toss him from a helicopter? Is he that cruel? Then she nodded, "You're right. We'll never know."

Nathan drove Mac home after a stop at the pharmacy for antibiotics. Mac decided she couldn't think about the case now. She needed a break. So, she slept for six hours straight until the pain meds wore off.

The sun was far from going down, but Mac sat at the dining table working through scenarios with her notecards. She added information about Chinni's abduction, the warehouses, and the thumb drive. Mac's thoughts circled back to Margot and how she'd like to give her thumb a drive instead of Ionna. Margot was always willing to discuss ideas where Mac didn't feel that way about Ionna.

"What are doing awake at this hour? Remember, we worked all night." Nathan asked through a yawn.

"I couldn't fall back to sleep once I woke, so I moved in here."

"Is your hand okay?"

"I suppose." Mac said without making eye contact with Nathan.

Nathan walked to Mac and rubbed her neck. "What's really going on in that pretty little head of yours?"

Mac shrugged but finally gave in by sharing with Nathan that she thinks she made the wrong decision about joining her dad's firm. She added about losing Travis and Margot and how they could use friends right now.

"Look at me, Mac." Nathan placed his hand under Mac's chin and tilted her head until she met his eyes.

"People change careers all the time. We did not make the wrong decision. We're in a learning curve, that's all. It's an expected phase. Once we finish with this case, we'll feel better. You'll see."

Mac nodded, trying to believe Nathan. Between her hand and losing Chinni, depression took over. She didn't know if she should cry or scream. Or maybe both.

Nathan calmed her enough that she agreed to fall asleep. She needed sleep and rest to help heal the hand. Working twenty-four hours straight does something to a person's body, and not in a good way.

When Mac woke the second time, she smelled food and her stomach rumbled. She walked into the kitchen just in time to witness Nathan flip pancakes in the skillet. "I saw that." Mac chuckled. "You'd make a talented chef."

"No thanks. But I enjoy showing off. We're having breakfast for supper since we missed it."

Mac nodded as she poured two cups of coffee. "Let's eat. Then we can work on the case. I have an idea I'd like to discuss."

"So do I." Nathan added.

They ate with gusto, as they were eager to work on the case. Once they cleaned the kitchen and refilled their coffee cups, they sat at the table. Nathan pointed at Mac. "You first."

Without waiting, Mac suggested, "I'd like to trace Chinni's cell phone. If it's on, we could get a ping."

Nathan said, "I like it. We should have thought about that yesterday, or was that the day before?" Nathan shook his head because he couldn't remember. "I want a blueprint of the administration building. The workers intrigue me. I can't figure out where they work without lights shining from the building."

"Brilliant." Mac said, smiling. "First thing in the morning, we'll get started. Tonight, we're resting."

The following day, the duo met with George and Myles. When Myles saw Mac's hand, his face turned red. "Why didn't you call me?"

"What could you do? Nathan took me to urgent care. They gave me a shot of antibiotics and a prescription. But hold on to Nathan because the nurse tried to recruit him for his bandage tying abilities." Mac said as Nathan cringed.

Myles reached over and shook Nathan's hand. "Thank you again for taking care of Mac. I am thankful for your tying abilities. Now, tell me what's on your mind."

Over the next hour, the foursome discussed ideas, and George agreed to show the duo how to trace cell phones and get blueprints. While Mac and Nathan knew it would be different, it wasn't difficult. Mac then realized she needed to stop comparing I^2 to the FBI. Nothing compares to the FBI, but that doesn't mean I^2 wasn't the right decision for them.

Mac's demeanor changed as they worked alongside George on the blueprint. They had the means to get blueprints on any building. However, the question was if they were correct. If someone made unauthorized changes, the prints would never show it.

Chinni's phone wasn't on when they set up the tracking, but they were hopeful he would need it shortly, and they'd be waiting.

The blueprint took longer to find, and George printed it out and sent a digital copy to Nathan's email. The print was so small, Nathan would need a magnifying glass to study it.

"Both of you have gone above and beyond on this case. I like the way you think. Keep this up and you'll be in line to train the next set of investigators," George said, winking on his way out the door.

Mac and Nathan sat speechless as the printer groaned in the background. "What did he mean by that?"

"I do not know." Mac muttered, still trying to decipher the meaning too.

Once the printer finished its job, the duo left for the conference room. Mac wanted to check on the tracking for Chinni's phone and Nathan wanted a closer look at the blueprints.

He spread them out on the table and leaned as close as he could. There was no way he could read that fine print. So, he slipped out to find a magnifying glass. Mac stood over the blueprint, squinting. "This is impossible."

"I know." Then he showed her the glass. "I'm trying with this." As he put the glass to his eye, he still squinted. "This isn't working."

"George sent it to your email, right? Then put it on the screen." Mac grinned.

"There you go, being all smart again." Nathan grabbed his laptop and had it connected to the screen in seconds. He opened the email, and the blueprint flashed onto the screen.

"It's still small, but we can work it on a grid. Just like a crime scene." Mac suggested.

Nathan nodded when he understood her idea. He started in the upper left and went across the top, but it felt off. So, he backtracked and instead of going across, he went down. He got to the middle of the building before he noticed something odd.

"Look at this. What is this area?" He used a laser to showcase the empty area in the middle of the building.

Mac surveyed the area, then she moved the picture around. "I don't recall that area when we sent to Professor Gregory's office. There were no empty spaces on that floor." Mac looked at Nathan just to make sure he agreed.

"So, where is it?" Nathan asked. Then he had a thought. He pulled his phone from his pocket and called Clarence. "Clarence, it's Nathan. We're studying the blueprints for the administration building. We've found an unexplained area in the middle of the building. Do you know if the building has a basement?"

Mac waited while Clarences spoke to Nathan. She held her breath, as this could answer a major question for them.

Nathan nodded as the call ended. "Clarence isn't positive, but when they first constructed those older buildings, they had basements. Later, as the buildings were renovated, they sealed them off." Nathan paused, then added, "I think Paul unsealed the basement. This might be the key to Paul's past jobs, too. We could find out if those university buildings had basements too."

"Oh my. This is a major. We need to share." Mac said and she hit a speed dial button for George.

When she explained, George and Myles rushed into the room. "I thought you were leaving for a meeting, Dad. Anyway, I'm glad you're here. Nathan, tell them."

Nathan jumped into his tale about the space which led them to the basement. George and Myles grinned. "Nice work. Now, let's figure out a way to look inside that basement."

This time, Nathan and Mac grinned. Mac admitted to herself, she felt better about her place at I^2, now that she stopped comparing this job to her job as an FBI agent, because really, there was no comparison.

George asked, clarifying questions about the building and what the duo had witnessed on their surveillance. Then Myles jumped in with a few of his own. The men asked the pair for a little time to work on a plan. They wanted to glimpse inside the basement but not scare Paul away. So somehow, they had to gain entry without being seen during daylight hours or find a night where no one worked. Then they had to arrest Paul and his team with the proper evidence so they could see them behind bars.

When George and Myles left, Mac asked Nathan, "If we break inside the basement, we can't use the evidence to arrest Paul. Surely, Dad and George will think of a way to make it all happen."

"I agree. Even though I'm eager to see inside the basement, we've come too far to mess up now. What do you suppose is in there? Drugs, weapons?"

"Probably both."

The duo split, heading for their offices. They would develop suitable scenarios for the team by sketching a layout of the university grounds, including the helipad. Their knowledge would be beneficial on their next visit.

Mac wandered over to Nathan's office to check on his status. "How are you coming long with your ideas?"

"I have the rendering of the property, and only one thing seems to get in the way. We don't know how the workers enter the basement."

Nathan saw the question float through Mac's mind. "I never thought about that. Most basements have exterior doors, but since this basement is an interior room, the door would be inside."

"That makes things a little more difficult since we don't know where the door is or another access point."

Mac's mouth opened into an O. "We know that loading docks have access. Maybe we could enter through the docks.

"Based on the blueprint, there isn't a door."

"Unless they made one," Mac added.

Nathan stared at the blueprint while thoughts bounced around his head. "I see two possible places where they could have added a door without causing too much damage to the building." He pointed to both areas.

Then Myles tapped on the doorframe. "We have a question. Do you know the location of the exterior door?"

The duo smiled. Then Mac said, "That's what we're discussing. Nathan has two possibilities for the door that would connect to the loading docks."

Myles looked at the blueprint, then asked, "But no exterior door?"

Nathan shrugged, saying, "Not that I can find. Unless we take a trip to the university and look for ourselves."

"Grand idea. Let's do it tonight if you're up for it." Myles glanced at Mac's hand. But asked nothing.

The foursome made a trip to the university after stopping for a meal at Mac's parents' house. Mary had supper ready for the group when they arrived. After attending to Mac's hand, she felt gleefully satisfied with the wound. Mary made Mac and Nathan promise to visit more regularly.

Mac grew sleepy riding in the backseat while holding Nathan's hand. She always eats too much when her mom cooks. But she can't walk away from the table.

Nathan woke her before they entered the town. On cue, Nathan gave George directions to their parking place or their hiding place. They parked away from the helipad this time, hoping to remain undetected again. From their location, they couldn't see the helicopter, so they had no way of knowing if it was there.

When they pulled into the wooded area, they met at the back of the truck. The group pulled out their night vision googles, ballistic vests, binoculars, weapons, and a camera. Mac oversaw the photos. She would stay with the truck. It would provide concealment for her and give her some place to rest her arm while taking photos.

The men formed a line with Nathan leading, followed by Myles, and then George. It impressed Mac how well the men worked together. They had similar training, and it showed. The men were out of sight within seconds, so Mac relied on her binoculars to track their progression.

When the men reached the woods' edge, they stopped and watched for movement before running to the building's rear. There was twenty-five yards of grass that the guys must clear to make it to the building.

Mac counted down with them. Then she watched the guys sprint across the open area, reaching the building without interference. One step down.

Now, onto the next. Mac readied her camera, lifting it to her eye. She used the lens to scope out the area. Finding nothing of interest, she placed her elbow on the hood of the truck and began her mission.

She checked on the men often to see if they found the door. When they didn't, she watched them backtrack to the loading docks. All three entered, and she lost visual. That caused her pulse to rachet up a bit. She could only do so much outside alone.

Mac kept her surveillance up, checking for guests, and finding none. But she heard nothing from the ear comm. Were they working or were the men not speaking?

She didn't want to startle them by asking questions, so she left it alone. Finally, Myles whispered, "Let's reconvene outside."

Mac's head tilted as she wondered if they found the door, but by Myles' comment, she couldn't tell. So, she waited until she the men turned the corner, heading in the opposite direction. She couldn't hold it in any longer. "Where are you going?"

"There appeared to a be a door inside, but it's bolted shut and it's inside a closet. So, we're thinking they have a way outside, we just have to find it. There are so many workers, I can't imagine them using the interior door." Nathan replied.

The men separated themselves by six feet and began walking the rear yard of the building since they found no doorway in the exterior. Once they reached the middle of the building, George stepped on something that sounded hollow. He stopped, then backed up, looking at the ground.

"Guys, did you hear that?" George asked.

Since he was the furthest from the building, Myles asked him to retrace his steps. When George did, they heard the distinction. Mac saw them stop walking, and she asked, "What's wrong?"

Nathan replied. "Nothing yet. We're searching for a door."

"In the grass?"

"Yes. A perfect hiding spot for a door." Nathan said as he reached down and lifted the door. "They built the entrance like a storm door."

"Close the door and hide now. A car pulled into the parking lot," Mac whispered. She snapped a photo of the car and then the driver. "It's Chinni."

"What? Are you sure?" Nathan asked excitedly.

"I have a photo of him. He appears to be fine." Mac shared. Then she added, "He seems to make rounds in the lots. He's leaving the lot now, turning right. Now, he's pulling into the next lot."

"Tell us when he leaves that lot. Then he'd be far enough away he couldn't see us," Nathan suggested.

"10-4," Mac replied as she turned her camera to the next lot. "Hold tight. Chinni is out of his car, walking to the rear of the building." Mac watched Chinni throw something in the dumpster. Then she relayed that information to the group.

Myles replied, "I want his trash."

Everyone chuckled because Myles has solved many crimes from someone's trash. Mac advised Chinni left the lot, and the guys resumed their position at the door. Nathan opened it and lights turned on, showcasing the stairway.

"Interested?" Nathan asked.

"Absolutely. We'll take it as far as it allows." Myles replied.

Cautiously, the men walked down the staircase, heading into the unknown. Someone took great care to open the basement. They reinforced the walls with metal inserts and ceiling. The light wasn't too bright, giving enough to see the way.

At the bottom of the stairs, they could go left or right. They chose right. It led to another door that was bolted shut, so they tried the left and the same thing.

Nathan stood away from the doors and snapped photos. They could use the pictures to help them when they made plans to breach the doors. Nathan wanted to see the other side of those doorways in the worst way, but he knew he couldn't force it.

Before leaving, the men scoured the outer room, looking for evidence of activity. They already knew about the drugs, but if the organization sold weapons, they needed proof.

Nathan ran his fingers across a tabletop. Residue formed on his fingertips. He sniffed it, then said, "This looks like more ink." He said as he placed his fingertips onto a white evidence collection envelope and scrapped the residue into it. Then he found a piece of something stuck in the corner between the table and the wall. He held it up. "What do you make of this?"

George and Myles joined Nathan. "Is it paper?"

"It appears to be paper, but a strange texture and color." Myles answered. Then he looked around the room. "They count money in here."

The others looked around the room. Then Nathan said, "So they sell drugs and count money here. Interesting. There are no chairs or counters. Do they move them in case someone finds the door?"

"I would assume so. Are the landscapers on the payroll too? Surely, they know when they ride the mowers across the door." George asked.

"Who knows how deep this organization goes?"

Then Mac interrupted. "Guys, the helicopter is landing."

The men quickly left the basement, trotting up the stairway, and closing the door behind them.

"Paul is alone. He just entered the lot, heading to the back. Hide NOW." Mac exclaimed.

The men sprinted to the woods, hoping Paul didn't spot them. "He's exiting his car and walking to the grassy area behind the building."

The only reply was, "Copy." She wasn't even sure who said it. Then they went radio silent.

Chapter 15

When he walked to the rear, he stopped at the door, looking around before lifting it. Then he kneeled so he could study the ground before lifting the door. Mac wondered if Paul noticed the footprints. Then she chuckled and thought, *how could he not see them?*

Paul stayed inside for over an hour. He finally came out carrying a folder. Mac zoomed in on the folder, hoping to capture the label, but the label was blank. He held something that he didn't want to lose.

Once Paul left the area, the men rejoined Mac. "Thanks for the notice. We almost didn't make it. It was obvious he found our footprints."

"Yeah. He studied the ground, but he didn't follow the trail. So, either he isn't worried about intruders, or he knows who we are." Mac explained. "When Paul left, he carried a folder, but there was no label on it."

"Interesting. Well, now that we know how to enter the building, we'll meet tomorrow and devise a plan. No law enforcement agency will be able to convict Paul without entering the building, or a trucker turning on Paul. And I don't see that happening," Myles said.

Nathan looked at the others. "Should we try that avenue before we break into Paul's basement?" He paused before adding, "It might be safer."

Mac agreed with Nathan. "As long as there isn't an escort for the truckers, I'd say we try that first. While the driver might refuse cooperation, we'd still have access to his cargo."

Myles nodded, "I understand, but let me play devil's advocate here. What do you suppose we do if the trucker calls Paul and tells him of our search?"

No one had a reply. So they pondered the question. Finally, George said, "So far, all the truckers that Paul has used to transport his goods are dead. That should be an incentive to keep quiet."

Mac muttered, "We didn't do a full background on the truckers. I'd like to know how Paul picks his truckers. What makes them special?"

"When we get back to the office, work on the truckers. Now, let's get out of here. Don't forget to grab Chinni's trash from the dumpster." Myles reminded the group.

George pulled up beside the dumpster, facing the lot. He didn't want someone surprising him. Nathan climbed from the truck and lifted his body onto the dumpster's edge. It was too far to reach, so he let himself into the dumpster. He landed with a thud.

The others waited and watched for activity while Nathan retrieved the trash. Then they heard Nathan ask, "What type of trash was it? The bottom of this dumpster is full."

Mac described a brown bag, but she couldn't recall seeing a logo. Myles suggested throwing Nathan a trash bag, so she did. Once he'd recovered the trash closet to the top, he climbed back out. Then he slid into the backseat, and everyone made gagging sounds.

"Sorry." Nathan muttered.

Then George said, "You don't stink, Nathan. We rehearsed the gagging." He felt bad for Nathan and couldn't resist sharing.

Nathan grinned, asking, "What are we looking for in the trash?"

"Anything usable from food places to purchase receipts. It might give us a hint of where Chinni has been." Myles explained.

Mac and Nathan nodded, then they stared out their windows. Both ran through scenarios for Chinni, and neither could explain what they witnessed. It made no sense for Paul to hold a gun to Chinni's head, then have Chinni walk around the building unescorted. Was Paul testing Chinni?

After the night's escapade, everyone went home to bed with the promise to be in early. There were still things to do before they could arrest Paul.

The following morning, Mac and Nathan arrived early at the office, thinking they would beat George and Myles. But that wasn't the case.

Myles stood at the coffee bar with this phone to his ear. When he heard movement, he turned and hung up the phone. Mac thought that was strange, but she didn't question it. "Dad. Good Morning."

"Good Morning, Mac." He said as he pecked her on the cheek. "After you get coffee, meet us in the conference room."

The duo followed instructions, and when they entered, they stopped. Paper covered every inch of the massive table. "What is all this?"

George greeted them, then explained the papers. He pointed as he spoke. "This is the stack on the basement. Here is the storm door in the yard. And this stack is yours. It's the information on the truckers."

"Fantastic. We don't have to run the backgrounds. Thanks." Mac said as plucked their stack from the table.

Mac and Nathan took their paperwork to Nathan's office, so they had space. Otherwise, they would destroy George's system. Mac noticed right off that the truck drivers were single. When she shared that information with Nathan, he asked, "So, how did Paul know that?"

With her head tilted and her shoulders in the air, Mac replied, "No idea."

Nathan answered, his phone ringing. Then he glanced at Mac, writing Daniel on a piece of paper. Mac listened to the one side conversation while sorting through the stack of papers.

"Daniel said that Chinni stopped by his dorm room last night. Said he was away for a day. When he asked if everything was okay, he never answered Daniel."

"That can't be good. Maybe we should check in with Chinni." Mac suggested.

"We'd need a reason to call him, and we don't have one."

Mac paced, "What is it Mac?"

"I want to confront Chinni. Is he an undercover cop? That makes more sense than anything."

"But what if he isn't?"

"Then we would've tipped our hand. That wouldn't be good either. Everywhere I turn, I feel like I hit a roadblock." Mac paced again, but this time she rubbed her neck. That was her sign of stress.

Nathan jotted notes about the truckers. The most noticeable was their marital status. All of them were single, just like Mac said. And they all had mountains of debt. Most were gamblers.

"Here's the commonality. Besides their being single, they had mountains of debt, and most of that was from gambling."

"Paul continues to show his intelligence. But how does he locate these guys?" Mac asked.

"I'm still digging into that." Nathan flipped over a few pages, then returned to the beginning. "They were all associated with the same union."

"Same union. So, Paul has someone on the inside there, too." Mac stated as she jotted notes. Then she looked at Nathan as he entered something into the search box on his internet homepage.

He read for a few minutes, then shared, "This union is across the country. So, Paul could conceivably use his person for the country. Unbelievable."

"Is there any way to track down this person? Other than asking Chinni?" Mac asked.

"Let me dig a little deeper. This would be something Margot could sink her teeth into." Nathan said, as his eyes met Mac's. "I shouldn't have said that."

"Yes, you should. I feel the same way, but I'm trying to get over not having them with us," Mac shared.

Myles stuck his head into the office, "Found anything?"

The duo invited him inside so they could share. Once it was over, Myles asked, "So, what's your next step?"

Mac suggested meeting with Chinni away from the university campus. If he denied being an undercover cop, then that's that, but if he is, then we can use him to get the information we need to make Paul's arrest ironclad.

Myles pondered it, then said he'd run it by George before committing to it because that was an enormous step that they couldn't take back once they took it. The duo watched Myles leave, then Nathan said, "He'll go with your idea."

"I don't see another one. Since the union is countrywide, we have no way of knowing who or where the inside person is. So, that leaves us nowhere to go."

Then Nathan said, "Paul killed the drivers. That proves he wants no loose ends."

"Unless we join his workforce, there is no way to get enough evidence of Paul for a conviction. This guy is smart, I'll give him that. But every criminal makes a mistake, right?"

Nathan grinned because he'd heard that before from Mac. She loved that saying. "If Myles and George agree, how do we want to handle Chinni?" He waited for Mac to share.

"We'll meet him at a coffee shop where we can talk freely. Then just be truthful. He knows why we're at the university, now it's his turn to tell us why he's there. If he's working with the police department, why does he spend so much time at the university?"

Nathan nodded as he understood her thoughts. "You think he, if he wasn't undercover, the police department wouldn't let him spend so much time at the university when other calls are going unanswered?"

"It only makes sense. Unless the Police Chief is in cahoots with Paul." Mac said with an eyebrow lifted.

"And then there's that." Nathan said, clearly frustrated with the case. They still had too many variables that could destroy the case, and they desperately wanted justice for Professor Gregory. This was their first case with Mac's dad, and they wanted a successful close.

Nathan watched as Mac moved her thumb back and forth and something niggled the back of his neck, but he couldn't bring it forward. "Is your thumb hurting?"

"No. It's tight. I'm unsure if I injured the tendon, but the more I work on it, the better it feels. I'm taking the bandages off tomorrow. So, we'll see how it reacts."

"Why are you fixated on my thumb?" Mac asked with her eyebrows bunched.

"I feel like we're forgetting something and when you mentioned thumb, I had a niggle." Nathan said.

Mac pondered his comment for a few seconds. "Oh my. I still have the thumb drive."

"That's it. We need to get that to Ionna. So much has happened. It never crossed my mind." Mac stopped, looked at Nathan's expression, and added, "I'll take it to her."

"Are you sure?"

"Without a doubt. I'd love to." Mac said with a smirk.

Mac slipped out, leaving Nathan to continue digging for usable information on the people involved with Paul's operation.

Thirty minutes later, Mac returned. "Ionna wasn't in the lab, so I left it with a guy named Luke."

"Did George fire Ionna? I hope not." Nathan said.

Mac's face turned red. "Are you taking her side in all this?"

"Absolutely not. She's the reason I went to George. But I feel bad when people lose their jobs. The world is hard enough as it is."

"You're too nice. She has a problem, and she needs to see a doctor. I want nothing to happen to her either, but I also want her to work somewhere else," Mac explained.

Nathan nodded because he agreed with Mac. Myles returned, asking, "Is everything okay here?"

"Yes, it is. We're waiting for your decision."

"You have our blessing. Do you want backup, or are you comfortable meeting Chinni alone?" Myles asked, trying to get a feel for the meeting.

"We're good without backup this time." Mac stated.

"OK. Make it happen." Myles nodded at the pair on his way out.

Mac and Nathan didn't know what to do first. Then Mac suggested Nathan call Chinni and set the appointment. They could make their plans around the meeting.

Nathan dialed Chinni, but the phone went to voicemail, so he left a message. He didn't expect that, so he questioned the meeting. "What if he doesn't call me back?"

"Why wouldn't he? He may be with Paul, and he wants to talk with you in private." Mac offered, trying to ease Nathan's mind.

While they waited, Nathan scanned the internet for anything pertaining to Paul. He started with Paul's last place of employment. Once he had that information, he pulled blueprints for the administration building but found no basement. *So, how could Paul conduct his business?* Nathan kept searching for answers by reading the university's website. It went into detail about the rich history of the university, including the description of the first building built on campus. That was all Nathan needed. He found the blueprints for the first building, which is now an annex used for the billing department and extra offices. He called for Mac when he found what he was after.

"Nathan. What did you find?"

He explained how he traced the building and then he said, "Here's the blueprint for the annex."

Mac scanned it. "It has a basement, too. Wow, Nathan. Do you know what that means?"

"This will become a federal case when they find out how many states this involves. Wonder if dad will let us work with Travis and Margot?"

"Our work will be over once we help arrest Paul and his friends." Then Nathan added, "I'll finish with Paul's other workplaces, and hopefully Chinni calls back today."

Mac nodded, returning to her notecards with added information. She added the basement information to the board, confirming Paul has been at this business for decades. So, there's no way of knowing the amount of money he's made or the volume of drugs he's moved around the world. Mac shuddered at the thought of the number of lives he's destroyed over the years.

The duo opted for a food truck for lunch. Tacos would hit the spot today, and while the sun was bright, there was a definite chill in the air.

While standing in line, Nathan's phone rang. He answered it, mouthing Chinni to Mac. She ordered for them, but she wanted to hear the conversation. As she walked to Nathan, the call ended.

"Well, what did he say?"

"He said he's been waiting for our call. We're meeting at 4:00pm in a coffee shop halfway between the office and the university. He said he'd be in a hat and driving a different car."

"Interesting. Suppose he thinks Paul is having him followed?"

"I'm positive he does."

They ate in silence as their minds raced with thoughts about the upcoming meeting. Mac asked,

"Did Chinni elaborate on why he expected our call?"

"Not at all. But he already had the meeting place in mind because he never hesitated when I asked. It rolled off his tongue like he'd been holding it inside." Nathan explained between bites.

"Maybe Chinni wanted to ask us for help but couldn't for some reason, and this is a way of getting it without instigating the contact." Mac suggested.

As they threw their wrappers in the trash, two men walked up behind the duo, pushing guns into their backs. Nathan wanted to spin around and take down his assailant, but he knew that would jeopardize Mac. So, his eyes turned to hers. She nodded that she was okay.

The man holding Nathan pushed him forward, but Nathan held firm. "What do you want?"

"Come with us." Mac glanced at the street and saw a black van. She shivered. There was no way she was getting inside that van. Her dad always said that your chances of survival diminish when your attackers force you into a vehicle.

"Yeah. I don't think so. You can tell us what you want right here," Mac said, trying to hold her voice steady as her insides twisted. As the attackers stared at one another because Mac's actions were unexpected, she pushed her dad's speed dial button, hoping he'd answer and come to their rescue.

The men continued pushing the duo, but Mac reached out, grabbing a metal bench. "I refuse to get in your van, so you might as well shoot me." She said, glaring at the men.

Nathan hadn't budged. He wanted separation between himself and Mac. Once he had it, he would take out his attacker, but he had to do it quickly. He didn't want Mac in the crossfire or any innocent person.

The foursome was at a standstill. The attackers still used their guns to show force, but it failed. Mac and Nathan held their ground, refusing to get inside the van. Nathan acted like he tripped on the sidewalk, but when he raised himself up, he reached for his attacker's gun, forcing it away from him and Mac.

While Mac and her attacker watched Nathan's fight, Myles and George appeared from behind. They made fast work of Mac's attacker, and then George finished Nathan's fight. Atlanta PD arrived at the scene seconds after the fight ended. After the officers handcuffed the men, they showed Myles and George the attacker's IDs. George snapped photos of them. Then, the officers escorted the two attackers to jail.

"Good job you too. You knew better than getting into a van. Did the men say anything about why they wanted you to get in the van?"

"Nothing. They poked guns in our backs, hoping we'd follow their instructions, but neither of us did. Instead, we held our ground, but I was forced to the bench. It gave me something to hold on to." Mac described her ordeal.

"We'll run backgrounds on these guys. I imagine they will tie back to Paul. Have you heard from Chinni?" Myles questioned.

"We have scheduled the meeting for 4:00 pm today at a coffee shop halfway between here and the university. Chinni said he'd be driving a different car and wearing a hat. So, something has definitely happened. He's never acted that way before."

George nodded. "If Chinni is feeling the heat, I'd feel better with backup. I'll handle it. We don't want to spook him or potential followers. I'll drive a fleet car too. Text me the address and I'll be there."

Nathan texted George the address, then when he was gone, Mac and Nathan discussed their meeting with Chinni. Mac's idea of simple won out. They'd share what they knew, hoping to follow by sharing his knowledge of Paul's operation.

When the pair arrived at the coffee shop, Nathan circled the block before parking at the end of the lot. He backed into his space. Then they surveyed the cars in the lot. Once they were satisfied, Nathan sent a text to George, asking if he was in place. George replied with a thumbs up. Nathan chuckled.

"Since when does George answer text messages with an emoji?"

"Since he met Lizzie." Mac said with a grin.

The duo entered the coffee shop, finding Chinni already sitting at a table in the far corner with his back to the wall. After grabbing coffee, Mac and Nathan sat with Chinni, waiting for him to begin the conversation.

Chinni greeted the pair, then thanked them for calling him. That's when Mac jumped into her spiel. She wanted Chinni to understand their place.

No one spoke for several minutes. Chinni hesitated on speaking, clearly concerned for his life and his family. But, even with the concern, he needed help.

"What I'm about to say must stay between us. My family doesn't even know yet. I am a DEA undercover agent. Paul Drummond has been my assignment since he arrived here. The agent before died when Paul found out their identity. I'm using my real name because my family lives here. It was easy to fit in with the police department. You know, in FBI school, they teach us to go undercover with the fewest lies possible. It's easier to remember. Well, this assignment has been a breeze. I haven't told any childhood memories that weren't real."

Mac faced Nathan, then Nathan said, "You were right, again, Mac." He faced Chinni, "She pegged you for an undercover but never specified DEA as the agency."

Nathan asked, "Is this a good place to talk?"

"Yes. I left home last night, headed to the university, but instead, I came here. I've been driving around for hours, making sure I had no tail." Chinni offered.

"We must confess, we have one of ours somewhere around here, in case this went sour. He's our boss, George." Mac said because she wanted to keep no secrets.

He nodded, "I get it. No one can blame you for that. Well, are we ready to get started?"

Mac and Nathan nodded.

"I can't tell you how happy I was to see you two investigate Professor Gregory's death. It was not suicide. But I've been unable to pin his death on Paul. I have a recording where Paul said that the Professor got in his way, but he never confessed to the murder." Chinni paused, sipping his coffee. "It took me months to get Paul to let me see the operation. Once he accepted me as a divorced detective with a gambling problem and tons of debt, he started talking. I know you found the door to the basement. That was brilliant. It's what on the other side of the door that's important."

Chinni waited for a customer to find a seat before he spoke again. "The outer room is for counting money. Paul removes the counters when they're not in use. The interior room is the basement. One side is for packaging the Heroin, while the other side is used for making it."

"Whoa, wait a minute. You said he makes his own heroin. How's that possible? Wouldn't that be an extensive manufacturing gig?" Nathan asked.

"Oh, it is. But Paul has connections all over the world. His poppy plants come in shipments for the university. Customs never check that. So, when the plants get here, the process begins. The section of the basement for manufacturing is so clean you could eat off the floor." Then he chuckled, "Or maybe not. As the workers make the Heroin, the other side packages it for shipping all over the world. People know Paul for producing the purest of the pure. Some of the students here are not really students. Instead, they are drug dealers. They deliver drugs across state lines. Paul has been at this game for so long, he thinks he's untouchable."

Mac nodded. Then clarified, "The fake students are his dealers. Paul gets two for one. One for enrollment numbers and the other for the drug business. Sounds like he has thought of everything."

"Not exactly." Chinni said. "He didn't bargain for your involvement. And the beauty is that he hired your company." He chuckled. "The Board of

Trustees forced him into doing it. He bucked the idea for a few days, but he finally caved, knowing he must keep them happy."

"So, what evidence do you have linking Paul to this operation?" Nathan asked.

"I've got photos of Paul inspecting a pallet of drugs, standing over the money counters, and a video of him walking through the manufacturing side. My boss has those. We're waiting to see how you want to play this. If I bust him for drugs, he'll go through the courts first, but if you want him for murder, I'd rather see that happen. James deserves nothing less."

Nathan's phone chirped for a text. "It's George. He wants a status."

"Invite him inside."

Before Chinni could change his mind, Nathan sent a text to George and within ninety seconds, the bell hanging over the door rang. George picked up a cup of coffee and joined the meeting.

Once George was brought up to date, they continued discussing Paul. Mac admitted with no evidence against Paul, they couldn't arrest him for murder. But deep down they know he pushed James from the rooftop.

Chinni looked at his coffee, then back up at the group. "I have nothing substantial, but I have an email from James' personal email account stating if anything happened to him, to investigate Paul Drummond."

"Wow. James knew Paul might kill him, but he never quit." Mac looked at Nathan, then said, "We found a thumb drive hidden beneath the bookcase in James' office in the admin building."

"You found it? That's fantastic. James said it holds incriminating evidence of Paul's operation and the laundering of drug money through the university's books." Chinni said.

Then George raised his hand. "Let me clarify. Paul manufactures the drugs, packages the drugs, then launders the money through the university."

"That sums it up beside killing James. We can't forget that." Chinni added, as sadness shone in his eyes. That's when Mac knew that Chinni and James had become friends.

"You and James were friends?" Mac asked.

"Yes, we had become friends when I noticed James poking around. I didn't want to see him get caught in anything, but I failed him." Chinni couldn't keep his voice from cracking as the emotions welled up inside of him. He cleared his throat, then added, "Where is the thumb drive?"

George answered, "We have it. It's with an analyst."

"You'll never break the encryption. James once told me he developed his own way of writing and encryption."

Mac turned to George. "I know someone who could break it." George grinned. But offered no words. Mac was unsure how to take that grin. Was it to placate her, or did he already know about Margot's ability?

The group continued talking about Paul with Chinni, telling the group Paul's enterprise was enormous, spanning the globe. "If we can bring this one down, we'll put a massive dent in the drug trade across the US. Now we know it will never end illicit drugs, but I'll take a win where I can get one."

"Chinni, it was great meeting you and thank you for the work you do. Give us a few days to work on a plan. Then we'll be in touch. Don't let it surprise you if you hear we've sent a report to the university saying we feel James' death was not suicide, but we have no proof of the offender."

Chinni nodded. "That way, Paul thinks the case is closed and he can continue. Smart move."

The group stood, shook hands as they then split, going separate ways. Mac's mind raced with the new information. With the doors closed, Mac settled into her seat, then asked, "Did you suspect Paul making the drugs?"

"No. It never crossed my mind. But things still bother me. We have no explanation for the ink residue. They must print something, but what?"

As Mac considered Nathan's question, her phone rang. George called. "Great job on handling Chinni. We'll take Paul for the drug operation, since we can't pin him on the murder. He'll spend decades in prison for his involvement. Send the report to the university tomorrow morning. Let's wrap this investigation up."

"Do you want me to ask Margot for her help with the thumb drive?" Mac asked George while looking at Nathan with a hopeful gleam in her eyes.

Chapter 16

"We may not have to." George replied. "Talk soon."

Mac processed George's comment and was left speechless for a few seconds. When it didn't resonate, she asked, "What does George's answer mean?"

"I was hoping you could explain it to me," Nathan replied as he drove the car south toward home.

The ride home was quiet other than the car noise. Mac pondered George's reply but couldn't figure out the meaning. Finally, she turned to Nathan. "Does George think the thumb drive isn't needed since we have Chinni?"

"That could be, but George has always acted on more evidence is better than less. If something were to happen to Chinni, then the thumb drive would play a major role, so why not have someone decipher it?"

"That's my thoughts too." Mac said, grateful that they were on the same page. "Oh, no, Nathan. We forgot to ask Chinni about the ordeal, with Paul holding a gun to his head."

"You're right. We did. Well, we'll speak with him soon and find out why it happened."

The following morning, the duo arrived at the office to find it empty. "This is so strange. Some days this place is full of folks and activity abounds, then some days it's like this."

"At the FBI, there's always someone at the office." Nathan said.

After grabbing coffee, Myles called Mac's cell phone. "Hi Dad."

"Mac, are you and Nathan on your way to the office?"

"We're here. Where are you?"

"Come to the conference room when you get a chance." Myles ended the call without saying goodbye.

"Come on Nathan. Dad wants us in the conference room."

George and Myles sat at the table with laptops open and paper in stacks. "Good morning. Great job with Chinni. We have our case with what you've found. Now we need a plan to capture Paul. I know you just arrived, but have sent your report to the university yet?"

"No, but it's ready."

Myles nodded. "Send it this morning. We want Paul to think our part of the investigation is over. Then in a few days, we'll arrest him. But we'll have help do that since there's so many folks involved. I've spoken to Chinni's handler and boss, and they want to take part in the operation to arrest Paul. So, we'll share the duties."

Mac nodded. "I wanted to get Paul on murder." She muttered under her breath.

"We do too." That's when Myles smiled. "And we have just what we need to do that."

Mac looked up. "What does that mean? You're talking cryptic, just like George."

A knock sounded on the door, and Myles invited the caller inside. When the door opened, Margot stood there with Travis peering over her shoulder.

It took Mac a second to realize what was happening. She jumped up from her chair and raced to the door. "Are you really here?"

"Yes, we're really here." Margot said.

Then Travis shook hands with Nathan. "I couldn't talk to you very often or I'd spill the beans. We've been working on this since you two left."

"I'm glad it happened. Now, it's perfect." Nathan grinned.

"Everyone, take a seat for a minute. Mac and Nathan meet your new investigators. You can show them around and you four can work out the office arrangements any way you want. You'll have the four next to George and me. Margot, your first assignment comes quick." Myles removed the thumb drive from Mac's evidence bag and handed it to her. "This is prime evidence in a murder and drug operation. Supposedly, it's encrypted with the dead man's own form of encryption."

"I got it, sir."

"Please just call me Myles." Then he explained Mac and Nathan's first case and why the thumb drive is so important. Margot and Travis were in awe of what the duo had done and congratulated them. "George and I have a meeting with a new client. We'll leave you at it. Margot and Travis, your new laptops are in my office. Follow me and I'll hand them over."

Mac and Nathan beamed with pleasure as they waited for their partners to return. Then, they spent a few minutes catching up with each other, then things turned to business and it felt right.

The basement aspect of the university intrigued Travis. Nathan sketched the layout of the basement based on what they saw and Chinni's description. Then Travis asked, "How can Paul manufacture heroin inside a concrete vault? Wouldn't there need to be a ventilation outlet somewhere? If not, it's amazing that the building hadn't blown up."

Nathan tilted his head. "We didn't find one. The only door we found was in the grass area behind the building. They designed it like a storm door with steps and motion lights." Moaning, Nathan said, "I never went back to Paul's previous employer for information on basements."

"Good. Let's work on that now," Travis suggested, mentioning that Margot is tied up with the thumb drive and expressing confidence that the three of them should be able to knock it out quickly.

"Let me get Paul's folder from my office. Back in a second." Then he bolted. When he returned, Tavis had his laptop powered on and had set up a log in.

"I'm ready to go." Tavis beamed.

Nathan read off the universities where Paul worked prior. He worked at six universities in six different states across the southeast with a two-year tenure in New Jersey. Mac jotted the information on a pad, then they split the duties.

The threesome worked in the conference room as they worked their way through the lists. All of Paul's past universities had a basement, except one. He worked for a short while at a university in north Florida, then he moved on to improve things.

Travis asked, "So, if this Paul guy manufactured drugs at these other universities, are they in danger of blowing up too?"

"We don't know. We'll notify the proper authorities once Paul is in custody. I don't see Paul working in an enclosed place, knowing it could blow up with one misstep." Nathan explained.

"But do they manufacture heroin different from meth, right?" Mac added. "I know meth is extremely volatile." Mac added.

"That's my understanding too."

When lunch time came, the foursome enjoyed each other's company. While it had only been a few weeks, it felt like forever to Mac. She was grateful her dad sought Travis and Margot.

Margot gave the team hope that she was close to cracking the encryption and she didn't foresee a huge delay. Then she said, "With the information on this thumb drive, you may not need Chinni to testify."

"That would be wonderful. He has family in the area, and he's concerned with their safety as well as his own." Mac replied.

After lunch, Margot returned to her office, locking herself inside. She needed total concentration to complete this task. Professor James Gregory was topnotch when it came to encryption.

At 3:00 pm, she got her breakthrough, and she sat back in her chair, reading the contents. When she realized what she had, she jumped up and ran down the hall to the conference room.

"I have the contents of the thumb drive. You need to read this." Margot clicked a single document labeled ring.

The others read it and Mac's lips separated. "We retrieve that camera. James felt threatened enough to place a ring camera on the roof. It's amazing we didn't find it."

"Did someone else find it?"

"Oh, Nathan, I hope not. This will prove who killed James," Mac stated with emotion in her voice. She lay awake at night trying to pin murder on Paul. They knew he did it, but without proof, he would avoid a murder charge.

"We need to get back to the university. First, share the information with Myles and George, then I'll call Chinni and let him know what we're doing, so he isn't caught off guard."

Mac and Margot headed off to find Myles or George, while Nathan dialed Chinni. Chinni was just as surprised as they were about the camera. He had only been up there one time, and that was when James died, and James had never mentioned the camera to him.

Myles couldn't believe Margot cracked the encryption so quickly. He praised her and she blushed. George suggested retrieving the camera tonight, then they could make their final plans tomorrow, and he hoped that included arresting Paul for murder.

George agreed to review the information on the thumb drive while Mac, Nathan, Travis, and Margot headed to the university for the camera. Myles had an appointment to meet a client.

The foursome loaded up into Nathan's vehicle and he turned the vehicle north. Then everyone started talking at once. That brought laughter. Once everyone calmed, Travis started the conversation about how Myles and George approached them by meeting them in their apartment parking lot. The meeting was strange at first until Travis verified their identities. He had only met them once and while they looked familiar, he didn't want to mistake them for friends if they weren't.

"Wonder why they met you there?" Mac asked.

"Their response was they didn't want to ask Nathan or you for our phone numbers because you would beat them until they told you why they wanted to see us." He chuckled, knowing it for the truth.

"I'm glad Dad found you two. So, what happened at the FBI?"

"After you and Nathan left, it wasn't the same. We finished a case we had and we're going into the office for a new assignment when your dad and George showed. It was perfect timing." Travis explained.

Then Margot asked, "I know this is your dad's business, but how do you like it? It must be weird being on the other side."

This time Nathan replied, "It was at first. We had a lot of talks, but now that we've been here a while, we like it. The man's difference is information gathering. We had to come up with ways to get the information we needed since we couldn't throw warrants at the folks."

Travis swallowed. "We don't have warrants."

"Nope. Not as a private investigator. But the cell phone information, background information, and CSI tests remain the same. We just get our information a little different from the FBI."

This trip seemed shorter than the others, but Mac decided it was because they talked the entire way to the university. When they arrived, classes were still in the session which they wanted. Nathan pulled into the lot and backed the Suburban in between two other trucks. He didn't want it to stick out.

The foursome exited the truck, then walked to the side of the administrative building. Nathan didn't want to risk walking in the front door. They found the door unlocked, so Nathan held it open for the others to enter.

The stairwell was void of people and sounds, so the group walked up the steps quickly, keeping noise to a minimum. When they reached the top, they stayed in the middle of the roof. No one was supposed to know they were there except Chinni.

Margot whispered instructions on the location of the camera. Nathan and Travis did the honor of locating and removing the camera. It was exactly where James said and there's no way anyone would have found it. He hid it amongst the foliage. Someone had a green thumb and had placed potted plants and vines around the meeting area.

When Nathan opened the door to head back downstairs, voices radiated upward. He quickly closed the door. "People are in the stairwell. We must be between classes. Stay here."

He walked to the edge of the roof and peered around a trellis. Students raced across the campus while others climbed into their vehicles. When he joined the group, he said, "It shouldn't be much longer."

Mac added, "I should have remembered they were using a few of these classrooms in this building."

Then Travis made them feel better when he said, "It helps to obscure our visit, too. So, it's all good."

Nathan cracked the door, then smiled. "All clear."

No one spoke on the way downstairs. Once they were safely inside the truck, Margot said, "When we return to the office, I'll plug in the camera, and we'll watch the show."

"Do you need passwords or anything for that?" Nathan asked as he turned left from the lot.

"No. Just the plug. And I have that." Margot grinned.

They talked about the case on the way home. Agreeing with Mac and Nathan that Paul Drummond needs to stop.

Nathan and Mac met Travis and Margot in the parking lot the next day. George and Myles waited for them in the conference room. After greetings, Margot left with the camera. There was no way to know how many hours of video she'd have to watch before she found the footage of that fateful night.

George announced, "We will not need to involve Chinni in the arrest. The thumb drive had enough incriminating evidence against Paul to arrest him. It also included the list of workers that Paul used to transport his drugs and his connections inside and outside the country. This will probably be the largest drug bust in US history. Thanks to your persistence."

"You're kidding, right?" Mac asked.

"I'm not kidding." George looked at Myles, who agreed.

"He's not kidding. I've been on the phone with every three letter agency most of the night. Everyone wants a piece of Paul Drummond. Some of these agencies have been tracking the drugs for a decade but could never ID the owner. Once we have confirmation of James' murder, we'll arrest Paul for murder, then the DEA will get him on behalf of Chinni. He did his part, so he gets the credit for the drug bust."

"That's fantastic. I know Chinni is relieved."

"He is, Nathan. I spoke with him a few minutes ago. He also told me he watched you at the university last night in case you needed back up."

Nathan and the others nodded their acknowledgement. They would have time to thank Chinni in person.

Minutes later, Margot rushed into the room, holding her laptop. "Sorry to intrude, but I have what you wanted."

"Show us," Myles said, as his face turned dark.

Margot connected the laptop to the big screen, then started the video. "I snipped the portion of the video we needed. Otherwise, we would watch birds and other critters do their thing."

Thirty seconds into the video, people arrive on the rooftop. Things seem tense amongst those in attendance. Then the rain began and everyone escaped down the stairs. They watched as James cleaned up the area as rain drops pelted him. Then, Paul stepped out from behind the walled staircase.

James took a step back, and Paul stepped forward. Their voices could be heard, but it was hard to understand. This part played on for a few minutes, until finally, Paul walked over to James and forced him to the edge. James faced Paul when Paul gave him the final shove over the edge. The last image of Paul was his fingers grabbing the roof's edge.

Everyone sat back in their chairs. Then George broke the silence. "That should help in the murder trial."

Murmurs sounded from everyone as they agreed. The mood remained somber because they witnessed the terror in James' eyes as he endured his last moments on earth.

Myles cleared his throat and said, "Give us a few minutes to make some calls. This puts a kink in our plans. I never expected to have video footage that showed the murder. Stay close by and we'll reconvene in a bit. Mac and Nathan, show your new investigators around the office."

Mac stood as she knew when she'd been dismissed. The group left the office in silence. Each was afraid to break it. No one had ever witnessed a murder like that, even though Nathan had witnessed death in the service. That was different.

Margot stammered, "I'll never forgot those eyes. Poor James."

"Me neither." Replied Travis. "But James had the forethought to install a camera on the rooftop. That says something about the man."

All heads bobbed as they agreed with Travis.

Mac walked them to the lab to start the rounds. "Margot, I'm sure you've seen this, but I wanted Travis to see it, too."

"Actually, I haven't. There was no time. I've worked from an office." Margot said sheepishly.

"You accepted the job without visiting the lab. That's amazing." Mac said. Then she lifted her arm, showing the way. She opened the door for them and Nathan hesitated.

"Come on, Nathan. I've got your six," Mac said with a chuckle. The other two stared at Mac and Nathan with their eyebrows bunched because they didn't understand Mac's comment.

"We'll explain later." Nathan covered for them.

But when they entered the lab, Ionna's desk was clean. Nathan and Mac stared at each other for a moment, then Mac asked, "Is she really gone?"

"I hope so."

"Who's gone?" Margot asked.

"Ionna was the lead lab tech, and she had her eyes set on Nathan, but in an odd way. Apparently, George handled the situation perfectly." Mac beamed. "So, Margot, if Ionna no longer works here, then you'll be sitting here."

Margot smiled as she glanced around the lab. "This is more than I expected, but I recall you two speaking of the labs, both in the office and at Myles' home."

"Dad has always prided himself on the latest and greatest technology. That will never change." Mac glowed as she spoke about her dad.

From the lab, they made their way around the office building, pointing out different areas. Then Nathan took over, describing the software programs on their new laptops. Once they finished with that, Mac called her dad.

"Come on back to the conference room. We're ready."

"I hope you two got the grand tour."

"We did. Thanks." Travis replied.

"Where's Ionna?" Mac asked.

"She took another offer." George answered without expression. Mac knew not to ask further questions until George was ready to discuss it.

Myles gathered his thoughts and papers and began the conversation. "With the video of the murder, we get Paul first on murder, then the DEA gets him on drug charges. All charges will happen at once. The

DEA agreed to keep Chinni out of the trial since you found the thumb drive laying out the operation. There's no need for him to testify and blow his cover."

"Fantastic. We can arrest Paul." Mac asked, ready for the task. She'd been waiting for this day.

After deliberation, the group agreed to arrest Paul overnight after he left the admin building. They would have local police stop the transfer trucks from leaving town, too. That way, the drugs and weapons wouldn't pollute other areas. Once everyone was on board with the takedown, Myles and George left because their workload was just beginning.

An operation of this magnitude will take a considerable number of trained individuals to make it happen. There were two major objectives for the team. Arresting Paul was the number one on the list, and the second was to secure the drugs and weapons. While there would be several workers in the building, those arrests could come later. The thumb drive provided names and addresses of the workers because they were listed in the university student enrollment.

George popped back into the room. "I have one ask. Review your notes. We must be certain about the plan. Paul cannot slip through our fingers."

Mac replied, "Will do."

Nathan pulled their file, and they meticulously covered everything they had on the case. The only item they failed to discuss was the helicopter. "Mac, Myles nor George mentioned the helicopter. Are they planning to guard it? Paul would definitely seek refuge in the helicopter, hoping to fly away."

"You're right. I see nothing in my notes about it. George needs to know." Mac dialed George, and he agreed to meet them in the conference room.

"What did you find?" George asked before he sat.

"The helicopter."

George's eyebrows bunched together. "We never discussed that. OK. Thanks for that, guys. We'll change our plans, ensuring we have folks covering the helicopter. Talk soon."

Once George left, Nathan said, "I guess we're good until we head north."

So the foursome left the office, discussing plans with I^2. Mac couldn't wrap her head around Travis and Margot joining the company. But she was happy they did. After lunch, Margot spent time in the lab while the others joined Myles and George for the final run-through.

Myles called for Margot during the meeting. When she joined them, she had a look of disbelief. Her insides twisted at the thought of participating in an arrest. She told Myles when he hired her that she was nothing more than a CSI analyst.

"Margot. You will not battle. We had a question and thought you might like to join us."

The tension in her shoulders subsided as she settled in next to Travis. She gave the group a weak smile.

George asked her, "Can you operate a drone or a satellite feed?"

"I can do both. What's the aim?" She sounded confident, but her insides refused to settle.

While George spoke, Margot listened intently, then when George stopped, Margot suggested, "Give me a minute." She tapped the keys on her laptop in rapid motion.

Then she showed the group her laptop by connecting it to the big screen. "This is the satellite from over the university. This feed updates every ninety seconds for thirty minutes, then it will take two minutes to start again for its rotation."

The guys watched the satellite, then Nathan said, "I can't see through the trees, can you?"

Everyone answered a resounding 'no.' "Can you operate both simultaneously?"

"Sure, I can, Myles. That would be the most ideal way of tracking the operation. It takes more concentration for the drone, of course, but the satellite would give us another layer."

Then George, "How close to the operation do you need to be?"

Margot tilted her head, "That depends on the drone."

Myles suggested showing the group the drones and letting Margot decide for herself. While that transpired, Myles handled phone calls. When the group returned, Myles spoke to someone in a clipped tone. Mac knew that tone from when she did something bad as a kid.

When the call ended, Myles apologized to the group, then explained that their London office had lost someone they had under surveillance.

Margot chose her drone, and she understood she would need to be within a mile of the university to operate it. But with the screen of an iPad, she saw no reason it wouldn't work.

With the plan in place, the group would meet at 11:00 tonight. There would be twelve folks involved in the arrest plus the Georgia State Patrol and Department of Transportation. They would help stop the transfer trucks before they entered the interstate.

Traveling to the university under the cover of darkness, Mac prayed for the operation to be successful. While she wanted Paul arrested, she knows how vicious he can be and he wouldn't hesitate to kill again.

The back lot was active when the group arrived. There were more cars in the lot than Mac or Nathan had ever seen. "I think he's packing to make a run for it. This is too much activity."

Nathan scanned the area with his binoculars, then said, "Agree. There are four transfer trucks instead of two."

"Oh no." Mac immediately dialed her dad. When he answered, she explained.

"Sounds like they're going somewhere. I'll handle it." Myles replied.

Over the next few minutes, Mac, Nathan, and Travis watched men walk back and forth from the building to the trucks. They rolled huge pallets of cargo into the trucks.

Travis was in awe. "Do they have enough cargo to fill four transfer trucks?"

"We've never seen this number. Typically, there's only two," Nathan explained.

Myles and George arrived and set up at their predetermined spot, then the other investigators did the same. The comms were active for a few minutes as everyone checked in, then they turned silent.

When the trucks pulled away from the loading docks, the operation began. Myles alerted the State Patrol and the Department of Transportation to be on the lookout for the trucks.

Then everyone stood their ground until they saw Paul exit the building. He was with another man than no one knew. Myles stated, "3, 2, 1 go."

Mac, Nathan and Travis were the first three to race to Paul. He heard the commotion and sprinted into the woods. Travis veered off from the two and captured the man that was with Paul. Once he was placed in the back seat of a patrol car, he raced to join the others.

Mac and Nathan ran together, trying to force Paul back into the open. Instead, a bullet whizzed between the two. It was so close, Mac reached up and touched her hair. "Too close." She muttered.

Then Paul cut left and ran again, but someone else was chasing him. It was Everett. There is no one else that can run like him. Everett chased him back into the woods. Travis was gaining on Paul until a barrage of bullets were sent in Travis' way.

Margot spoke calmly and quietly into the comms. "Paul is running toward the helicopter."

"Copy that." George said.

Then the sound of metal-on-metal scraping, then the explosion. Everyone stopped because they couldn't figure out what. George requested, "Team. Check in."

Everyone did except Jose. George said, "Jose, check in." Silence. "Check in, Jose. I repeat. Check in, Jose." Then silence.

Mac and Nathan kept following Paul. They heard twigs snapping as Paul was closer than ever before. Mac and Nathan split, hoping to corner Paul.

George returned, "Jose is OK. He was thrown from the explosion and lost his ear comm. Where is Paul?"

"Fifty yards from the helicopter. We have him covered on three sides." Nathan explained.

Then someone fired a gun, sending the bullet into an unknown location. Everyone dropped to the ground, expecting it to race past their heads. But no one knew where it went. When the group stood, they couldn't spot Paul.

"Paul is no longer visible." Mac fumed as she said it. How could she let that man slip away? She trudged through the woods, finding Nathan leaning against a tree scouring the area.

"There he is. He's at the top of the rise." Nathan barked into his ear comm.

Chapter 17

Mac raced forward, not caring if Paul heard her. She was not about to let him get away because if he did, he'd never face the murder charge or the drug charges. But then he heard her approaching.

He turned, dropped to one knee, and raised his gun. Then Margot ordered Mac to drop as the gun barrel lit up the night.

Mac followed instructions just in time for the bullet to travel over her body. "Thanks, Margot." Mac grunted out as she lay face down in the leaves. Nathan and Travis raced to find Mac.

"I'm okay. Let's finish this," Mac barked.

The threesome raced through the woods, staying close to the trees. Just as they crested the top of the hill, they heard grunting. Then George shouted, "Stop Paul!" He was angry at Paul for shooting at his friends.

Mac sprinted the last few yards until she found Myles and George standing over Paul. Myles handed Mac a pair of handcuffs. "You get the honor."

Grinning, she took the cuffs and placed them on Paul's wrists. They the men lifted him from the ground. Paul shook his head. "I can't believe this. A two-bit private investigation company put me out of business. Who would've thought?"

Myles grinned. "Priceless." As Nathan and Travis escorted Paul to a waiting patrol car, Paul asked, "How did you know?"

"We're good at our job." Nathan said.

Paul climbed into the back seat and never uttered another word. While Paul raced his way up to the helicopter, other investigators made plenty of arrests, too. Of course, a few of Paul's workers managed to escape capture tonight, but their names and faces would be shared throughout the country, and they would remain on the most wanted list until they were caught.

Myles and team joined Everett, Tracy, Nicholai, and Jose in the parking lot. Jose had a few scraps on his face with a laceration on his arm. Jose described the ordeal. "The State Patrol tried to stop a truck, but they refused. So the Department of Transportation laid stop sticks on the entrance ramp. When the truck hit those, he ran off the road striking trees. The gas tank exploded before we reached the driver."

"Wow. Jose. You're lucky. It could have been you." Nicholai stated.

Jose nodded. Then George suggested he visit the waiting ambulance for treatment. So Nicholai and Jose walked to the ambulance.

Myles and George spoke on the phone and with other departments that were there for the arrest. The DEA worked to apprehend the workers while Myles and his crew captured Paul.

Our operation was a tremendous success and one that spanned the country. The DEA has already begun arresting folks involved in Paul's corporation. There was no way that his company would exist after tonight.

By the time the crew made it to Atlanta, the sun was peeking over the horizon. Myles thanked everyone for a great job and gave them the day off, but he expected everyone's completed report by 8:00 am the following day.

Mac hadn't slept so good in nights as she did after arresting Paul. But her phone blared her awake at noon. She moaned as she rolled over to answer it. "Mrs. Gregory." Mac answered.

"Yes, Mac. I hope I'm not disturbing you, but I just heard that Paul got arrested for James's murder. You'll never know how much I appreciate you and your team." Then sniffles.

"Mrs. Gregory, there's no need. It's what we do." Mac ended the call quickly because she didn't want to join Mrs. Gregory's crying.

The rest of the day flew by. Mac and Nathan caught up on household chores and then they visited Travis and Margot. It felt like a lifetime ago since they'd cooked out. As Mac and Nathan were leaving, Mac's cell phone rang.

"Hi Dad."

"Your next case awaits. All four of you need to be in the conference room at 8:00 am."

Books by Series

MacKenzie 'Mac' Morris

MOA Book 1
Flames of Murder Book 2
Wage of Murder Book 3
Murder Front Book 4

Digger Collins

Pieces of Murder Book 1
Murder for Justice Book 2
Murder by Testimony Book 3
Murder Cell Book 4

Sheriff Jada Steele

Promises of Murder Book 1
Murder Cove Book 2
Murder Moon Book 3
Murder You, Murder You Not Book 4

Detective Ryker Bartley

Mission: Murder Book 1
Minds on Murder Book 2

Detective Clint Rugbee

Murder at Beachside Book 1
Waves of Murder Book 2
Murder Post Death Book 3
Murder Dunes Book 4

Other Novels

Eyes that Bind
Chasing Murder

About the author:

A.M. Holloway is an author of clean murder mysteries
where crime and suspense take hold. Her catalog spans
five series. A.M., who is married, relies on her husband's
expertise in the CSI field to ensure accuracy in her
books. She was born and raised in Georgia but now lives
in Central Florida. When not writing, you will find her
with her family, enjoying the outdoors, or sitting in her
favorite chair, daydreaming about her next book.

Visit www.amholloway.com for new releases and
to sign up for my reader's list or simply scan the
code.

Also follow me on:
Facebook @amhollowaybooks
Instagram @amhollowaybooks

www.ingramcontent.com/pod-product-compliance
Lightning Source LLC
Chambersburg PA
CBHW070636180626
46817CB00006B/2138